The *Fair Wind's* engines roared . . .

. . . and the ship swung about in the water in a desperate attempt to evade her pursuers. Lieutenant Tom Paris couldn't see any way out of the ambush. They were surrounded by superior firepower and more maneuverable craft.

"I think we should surrender," Ensign Harry Kim Said.

The shelling increased.

"I don't think they're interested in our surrender," Paris replied grimly. "Harry, can you swim?"

Look for STAR TREK Fiction from Pocket Books

Star Trek: The Original Series

The Ashes of Eden
Federation
Sarek
Best Destiny
Shadows on the Sun
Probe
Prime Directive
The Lost Years
Star Trek VI: The Undiscovered Country
Star Trek V: The Final Frontier
Star Trek IV: The Voyage Home
Spock's World
Enterprise
Strangers from the Sky
Final Frontier

#1 Star Trek: The Motion Picture
#2 The Entropy Effect
#3 The Klingon Gambit
#4 The Covenant of the Crown
#5 The Prometheus Design
#6 The Abode of Life
#7 Star Trek II: The Wrath of Khan
#8 Black Fire
#9 Triangle
#10 Web of the Romulans
#11 Yesterday's Son
#12 Mutiny on the Enterprise
#13 The Wounded Sky
#14 The Trellisane Confrontation
#15 Corona
#16 The Final Reflection
#17 The Search for Spock
#18 My Enemy, My Ally
#19 The Tears of the Singers
#20 The Vulcan Academy Murders
#21 Uhura's Song
#22 Shadow Lord
#23 Ishmael
#24 Killing Time
#25 Dwellers in the Crucible
#26 Pawns and Symbols
#27 Mindshadow
#28 Crisis on Centaurus
#29 Dreadnought!
#30 Demons
#31 Battlestations!
#32 Chain of Attack

#33 Deep Domain
#34 Dreams of the Raven
#35 The Romulan Way
#36 How Much for Just the Planet?
#37 Bloodthirst
#38 The IDIC Epidemic
#39 Time for Yesterday
#40 Timetrap
#41 The Three-Minute Universe
#42 Memory Prime
#43 The Final Nexus
#44 Vulcan's Glory
#45 Double, Double
#46 The Cry of the Onlies
#47 The Kobayashi Maru
#48 Rules of Engagement
#49 The Pandora Principle
#50 Doctor's Orders
#51 Enemy Unseen
#52 Home Is the Hunter
#53 Ghost Walker
#54 A Flag Full of Stars
#55 Renegade
#56 Legacy
#57 The Rift
#58 Face of Fire
#59 The Disinherited
#60 Ice Trap
#61 Sanctuary
#62 Death Count
#63 Shell Game
#64 The Starship Trap
#65 Windows on a Lost World
#66 From the Depths
#67 The Great Starship Race
#68 Firestorm
#69 The Patrian Transgression
#70 Traitor Winds
#71 Crossroad
#72 The Better Man
#73 Recovery
#74 The Fearful Summons
#75 First Frontier
#76 The Captain's Daughter
#77 Twilight's End
#78 The Rings of Tautee
#79 Invasion 1: First Strike
#80 The Joy Machine

Star Trek: The Next Generation

Kahless
Star Trek Generations
All Good Things
Q-Squared
Dark Mirror
Descent
The Devil's Heart
Imzadi
Relics
Reunion
Unification
Metamorphosis
Vendetta
Encounter at Farpoint

#1 Ghost Ship
#2 The Peacekeepers
#3 The Children of Hamlin
#4 Survivors
#5 Strike Zone
#6 Power Hungry
#7 Masks
#8 The Captains' Honor
#9 A Call to Darkness
#10 A Rock and a Hard Place
#11 Gulliver's Fugitives
#12 Doomsday World
#13 The Eyes of the Beholders
#14 Exiles

#15 Fortune's Light
#16 Contamination
#17 Boogeymen
#18 Q-in-Law
#19 Perchance to Dream
#20 Spartacus
#21 Chains of Command
#22 Imbalance
#23 War Drums
#24 Nightshade
#25 Grounded
#26 The Romulan Prize
#27 Guises of the Mind
#28 Here There Be Dragons
#29 Sins of Commission
#30 Debtors' Planet
#31 Foreign Foes
#32 Requiem
#33 Balance of Power
#34 Blaze of Glory
#35 Romulan Stratagem
#36 Into the Nebula
#37 The Last Stand
#38 Dragon's Honor
#39 Rogue Saucer
#40 Possession
#41 Invasion 2: The Soldiers of Fear
#42 Infiltrator
#43 A Fury Scorned

Star Trek: Deep Space Nine

Warped
The Search
#1 Emissary
#2 The Siege
#3 Bloodletter
#4 The Big Game
#5 Fallen Heroes
#6 Betrayal
#7 Warchild
#8 Antimatter

#9 Proud Helios
#10 Valhalla
#11 Devil in the Sky
#12 The Laertian Gamble
#13 Station Rage
#14 The Long Night
#15 Objective: Bajor
#16 Invasion 3: Time's Enemy
#17 The Heart of the Warrior

Star Trek: Voyager

#1 Caretaker
#2 The Escape
#3 Ragnarok
#4 Violations
#5 Incident at Arbuk
#6 The Murdered Sun
#7 Ghost of a Chance
#8 Cybersong
#9 Invasion 4: The Final Fury
#10 Bless the Beasts

STAR TREK VOYAGER

BLESS THE BEASTS

Karen Haber

POCKET BOOKS
New York   London   Toronto   Sydney   Tokyo   Singapore

An *Original* Publication of POCKET BOOKS

POCKET BOOKS, a division of Simon & Schuster Inc.
1230 Avenue of the Americas, New York, NY 10020

A VIACOM COMPANY

This book is published by Pocket Books, a division of Simon & Schuster Inc., under exclusive license from Paramount Pictures.

ISBN: 0-671-56780-2

First Pocket Books printing December 1996

10 9 8 7 6 5 4 3 2 1

Printed in the U.S.A.

For me, thirty years ago,
and my father, a little bit too late

BLESS THE BEASTS

CHAPTER
1

THE *U.S.S. VOYAGER* SWEPT THROUGH THE LONG NIGHT of the Delta Quadrant and all around it the unknown stars were white diamonds strewn across the black velvet of space.

Captain Kathryn Janeway gazed at the vast starlit field on the bridge's main screen and pondered the distance between *Voyager* and home. Seventy-thousand light-years. It was a figure that haunted her dreams.

"Captain?" The voice belonged to Lieutenant B'Elanna Torres, chief engineer.

Janeway swung her command chair to face her. "What is it, B'Elanna?"

Torres peered at the diagnostic screen of her engineering console. A frown wrinkled her already corrugated brow. "Our power levels are much lower than they should be. I've detected a problem with the theta-matrix compositing system. It's not recrystallizing the dilithium fast enough."

"Can you fix it?"

"Unknown," Torres responded. "I suggest we supplement with additional dilithium stores while I run a level-one diagnostic on the system."

Janeway might have paused to wonder where in this vast quadrant she would find a fresh source of dilithium. But her expression was one of complete confidence and self-possession: the armor of command "How much time do we have before this problem becomes critical?"

"Perhaps twenty-six hours before we experience serious power fluctuations. After that I won't be able to guarantee our warp capability."

"We'll initiate a priority search for dilithium immediately," Janeway said.

The crew moved to do her bidding as smoothly as well-maintained microrelays. The sound of the captain's voice—the confidence and certainty within it—kept morale high, an important consideration for a crew traveling through an unknown quadrant.

"Initialing short-range scans," announced Ensign Harry Kim. *Voyager* was his first deep-space mission and he was obviously determined not to disappoint Janeway.

"Bearing zero-three-five, mark-two-five," he said. "Negative results."

"Mr. Tuvok, assist Mr. Kim."

Tuvok, with that deep, steady Vulcan composure which had seen him and the ship through so many crises, moved swiftly to respond. Only his expressive eyes occasionally betrayed him, and they now revealed that although the head of *Voyager*'s security was controlled he was not at ease, not at all. "Long-range sensors reveal no trace of dilithium, Captain," Tuvok said.

Janeway's nod was barely perceptible. "Increase sensor range."

Harry Kim bent over his scanner. As he reconfigured his scan parameters the young ensign forced himself to look unperturbed, but his hands gripped the console and his heart began to pound. The fate of the ship might depend upon his search.

Then he saw it. There. Quickly double-checking to be sure, he smiled with relief as the scanner reconfirmed his findings. "Raw dilithium crystal deposits," he reported. "Class-N planet bearing three-two-nine, mark one-seven-five."

"Excellent," Janeway said, smiling briefly. "Good work, Mr. Kim. Mr. Paris, divert to the planet on half-impulse power."

"Full impulse would be faster," Torres said.

"And use up our resources more quickly, too." Janeway let that sink in for a moment before turning back to the helmsman. "As soon as you're ready, Mr. Paris."

"Ready now, Captain."

"Engage."

The ship shot forward through the cold night, hurtling toward its goal.

This is not a diversion, Captain Janeway told herself. This is a necessary step on the long path home. And we *are* going home, even if it takes us years to get there.

A sudden arcing light, the sparking of electrical components, and a startled cry brought Janeway to her feet.

Tom Paris was sprawled motionless at the base of the helm controls. The explosion had left his console a fused and blackened mass.

Commander Chakotay, the Native-American first

officer, was already on his knees beside the fallen pilot, searching quietly for a pulse.

Janeway was again grateful for Chakotay's rock-steady dependability in a crisis. He had been a formidable antagonist for both Starfleet and the Cardassians in his days as captain of a Maquis ship, but fate—and the Caretaker—had led him to the Delta Quadrant and bound him to *Voyager*.

She tapped her communicator. "Sickbay, medical emergency on the bridge. Initiate emergency medical holograph on screen."

A moment later the image of a sour-faced, balding man in medical uniform appeared on the viewscreen, "Please state the nature of the medical emergency."

"Explosion. Crewman unconscious."

On screen, the doctor read the ship's internal sensors. "Hmm. Second degree burns on the left hand and arm. Shock. Blood pressure dropping. I'll transfer him to sickbay. Please ask Kes to meet me there. I'll need her assistance to treat him properly."

Commander Chakotay looked at Janeway, who nodded. "Transporter," Chakotay said. "Prepare for intership beaming, on my signal." The bearlike first officer tapped in coordinates and Tom Paris disappeared in a shimmer of light.

The holodoctor smiled thinly. "Now if you'll excuse me, I'll attend to my patient."

"Of course, Janeway said.

The doctor's image rippled and was gone.

"B'Elanna," said Janeway. "I want some answers. To begin with, I want to know why that panel went up."

The engineering chief was already examining the damaged comm with obvious chagrin. "I wish we could fix machinery as quickly and easily as that doctor does flesh," Torres said. "Sometimes I envy him." Crawling beneath the console, she pulled at a protruding wire and half a panel came loose, narrowly missing her head. "Captain? I could use some help."

"Mr. Kim," Janeway said.

Ensign Kim covered the space between his station and the helm in two long steps, taking his place at Torres's side. Already deep into her diagnostics, she gave him the barest nod of acknowledgment.

Janeway watched quietly, musing on the strange fate that had brought a rebel half-human, half-Klingon engineer into *Voyager's* life and engine room. Thank goodness, she thought, for the woman's quicksilver brilliance and for her surprising friendship with Harry Kim. Their joint victimization on the Ocampa planet as subjects of the Caretaker's biological experiments had welded a solid rapport between them. Janeway had to acknowledge that Harry's interest in physics didn't hurt the bond.

The two crew members worked smoothly together, probing, quietly commenting. Soon Torres stood up, brushed herself off, and nodded with studied control.

Janeway steeled herself. "How bad?"

Dark eyes met hers. "Not good. Backup flight controls can be temporarily improvised from engineering, but it'll make an unwieldly system worse, and even that won't last very long."

"We need to replace the parts and rebuild the helm," Janeway said. Her heart sank at the thought of yet one more obstacle blocking their path back home, but she banished the notion that *Voyager* was an accursed vessel. She'd had her share of bad luck, yes, but most ships did. "Any thoughts as to what caused the damage and how likely it is to happen again?"

Torres shrugged. "My guess is that a power surge

caused it, but I won't know for certain until I've run more tests. As to its source, and whether it will recur, unknown."

Janeway felt that word grating upon her. *Unknown.* It just wasn't acceptable. An unknown power had brought her ship and crew halfway across the galaxy. But she fought back her irritation. "Get started, B'Elanna. Mr. Tuvok, how far off course did that power surge send us?"

"Approximately fifteen degrees off course," the Vulcan replied. "Might I suggest . . ."

Harry Kim burst in, garnering a frown from the protocol-conscious Tuvok. "Captain, there's a class-M planet in the next system, fifth planet from a type-B binary sun. We might find dilithium mineral deposits there—or metals that we could refine and use."

"Well," Janeway said. "We don't have much choice, do we, Mr. Kim. Chakotay, you'll work helm temporarily from engineering. Let's get into a wide orbit. Mr. Kim, once we're in range, scan that planet within an inch of its life. And get Mr. Neelix up here in case he can identify it."

"Aye, Captain."

Under the first officer's steady guidance, *Voyager* limped into orbit.

The lift doors flew open and the short, stocky figure of Neelix, a Delta-Quadrant native and volunteer member of *Voyager*'s crew, entered the bridge. His coxcomb of stiff orange hair straggled above his heavily freckled scalp, looking even more unkempt than usual.

"Captain," Neelix said. "I was just popping a meeg truffle soufflé into the oven. If it falls I don't know what the crew will have for dessert."

"Somehow we'll manage, Mr. Neelix," Janeway

said dryly. "Take a look and tell me if that planet ahead seems familiar."

Neelix squinted at the viewscreen and muttered, "Could be the Donyx System—that has a binary sun. In which case that's Donyx Five. But its landmasses are the wrong color. Maybe the Giddis System? No, the suns are too small and far apart." He ran a hand through his sparse hair. "Now, don't rush me."

"Captain," Ensign Kim said. "I've finished my scan and I have good news and bad news."

"Report, Mr. Kim."

"The planet is inhabited, and its civilization is advanced enough to provide at least rudimentary engineering. They seem to have some mass transportation and communications systems and there are signs of developing air travel."

"And the bad?"

"The system's binary suns are very active, even volatile. I'm getting some odd energy readings from them. There's no telling how the ship's systems might be affected."

"Can we compensate?"

"For the time being."

"That doesn't sound too bad considering how few choices we have," Janeway said. "Anything else?"

"The planet—it's a pre-warp civilization."

Janeway and Tuvok exchanged guarded looks of dismay.

Harry Kim watched them, his discomfort obvious. "I know that Starfleet prohibits contact between pre- and post-warp technological societies."

"Except in an emergency," Janeway said. "And this surely qualifies." She saw Tuvok frown but decided to ignore it. The ship *had* to get repaired.

"Folog's Moon?" Neelix mused. "No, they don't

have any atmosphere anymore. Sar Este Fourteen? It's the right size, but there should be warning orbitals and a gas giant. . . ."

Janeway waved him away. "Never mind, Mr. Neelix."

"Captain," Ensign Kim said. "The planet—the people below. They're hailing the ship, or trying."

"It appears that the first-contact decision has been taken out of our hands," said Tuvok.

Janeway nodded. "Open a hailing channel, Ensign."

"They're coming in on some strange frequency," Kim said. "It'll take me a moment to—there, got 'em. Audio only." His eyes met Janeway's. "You're on, Captain."

She stepped forward, took a deep breath, and said, "This is Kathryn Janeway, captain of the Federation *Starship Voyager.* I send greetings and request your aid. Our ship is in urgent need of repairs. We request your permission to send down a party for supplies."

In response the universal translator spat and whistled, producing birdlike twitterings almost beyond the range of Terran audibility.

But they did not, apparently, outstrip ultrasensitive Vulcan hearing. Tuvok flinched as a particularly high squeal climbed several octaves in as many seconds. "Mr. Kim, I request that you lower the volume."

"Yes, sir." For the first time Harry Kim reflected that possessing enhanced physiological abilities was perhaps not always a blessing.

The translator fought with itself, yielding gibberish and static from which only one or two words— "deputized" and "planet"—could be understood.

"Can you make anything of that?" Janeway asked, glancing at Tuvok.

He shook his head.

"Please repeat your message," Janeway said. "We regret that we are having difficulty receiving it."

Again the translator warbled. Then the gibberish resolved into comprehensible words and a smooth male voice could be heard to say, *"Voyager.* Greetings from the planet of Sardalia. You and your crew are welcome, most welcome. Come ahead. We will have people deputized to meet you. Please hurry, we await you most eagerly."

"Friendly, isn't he?" Janeway said sotto voce.

Tuvok stood and approached Janeway. "Captain, I suggest caution."

"Of course, Mr. Tuvok. That's why I'm going to send you and Commander Chakotay down to the surface. I can't think of two more cautious individuals, can you?"

CHAPTER
2

THE PLAZA WAS A GRACEFUL SPACE FILLED WITH THE
rustle of orange leaves on the wind and the splash of
water against stone, a quiet refuge in a bustling city.

Near the fountain at the center of the plaza stood
three tall, thin beings dressed alike in long silver
tunics and leggings that ended in tapered boots. The
two males wore their fine feathery purple hair in
elaborate bead-flecked braids. The female's hair fell
unconstrained around her oval face. All three had
large slanted golden eyes encircled by elaborate silver
tattoos.

By Terran standards, their arms and legs had an
elongated look, as if each limb, each digit, had an
extra joint somewhere. Their arms were clasped on
their chests in an oddly birdlike manner, and when
they walked their legs had a reversed bend that drew
their feet up flush against their knees. Nevertheless
their unusual proportions gave them a peculiar grace,
and their faces were remarkably humanoid, save for
the color and size of their eyes and the two delicate

vertical slits in the middle of the face where a nose would be.

Peculiar humming set the stones underfoot to vibrating as blue-white light filled the plaza. When the light had faded, two strangers, one garbed in black and gold, the other in black and red, stood suddenly on the mottled pavement before the fountain.

Their golden eyes widened with surprise, but otherwise the Sardalians maintained their composure and almost—but not quite—managed to convey the impression that they were fully accustomed to the daily materialization of unknown space travelers from thin air.

"Welcome," said the smallest, thinnest dignitary in an incongruous basso voice.

The Starfleet officers smiled. At least, Chakotay did. Beside him, Tuvok nodded gravely.

Chakotay thought that the tall, elegant natives of this planet in their glittering clothing resembled ancient Terran illustrations of children's tales, marvelous and fanciful. Repressing a smile at the thought, he sniffed the breeze appreciatively. There was a spicy tang to it that he liked very much, and a hint of salt and moisture that he associated with memories of a visit to a water planet.

The tallest Sardalian, evidently a female, held her many-jointed hands out toward them. Her voice when she spoke was rich and fluting. "You are from the spaceship, the *Voyager*? Welcome, yes, come and be welcome. Our city is called Vandorra. We often receive visitors here from above."

"Indeed," said the third official. He wore what appeared to be a silver badge of authority on his left shoulder. "We're a regular refueling stop for the G'mein and the Rika freighters." He paused, obviously expecting recognition at the mention of the names. When none was forthcoming he continued gamely. "And whom do you represent?"

"The United Federation of Planets," said Chakotay with a wry smile. What he said was true, but the words still felt funny coming out of his mouth. He had been a sworn enemy of this very federation only a short time before. "We're an alliance of approximately one hundred and fifty planetary governments and colonies."

"The Federation?" Golden eyes blinked languidly. "We've never heard of it."

"It's quite a distance from here."

"Ah, well, then that accounts for it. You are welcome. And which of you is the captain?"

Chakotay took another step forward. "I'm Commander Chakotay, first officer of the *Starship Voyager.* This is Lieutenant Tuvok."

A look of what might have been confusion clouded the Sardalian leader's face. Chakotay wondered if the Vulcan's severe appearance had alarmed him. Obviously, something was wrong.

"Am I to understand," said the Sardalian, "that neither of you is the captain?"

"That is correct," Tuvok said.

The confusion hardened into outrage. "Well, this is terrible. Against all of our protocols. It simply won't do, won't do at all. We must have your captain. What am I to tell the Lord Councillor? Oh, no, no, no. I simply cannot present a lesser officer. It's impossible."

Before either Starfleet officer could say a word the Sardalians folded their arms across their chests, turned as one, and retreated, muttering among themselves, leaving Tuvok and Chakotay alone in the plaza.

"So much for our welcoming committee," said Chakotay.

"How illogical of them to demand the presence of Captain Janeway." Tuvok sounded both puzzled and intrigued. He would, of course, never show annoyance. "Nevertheless, alien protocols must be observed. The captain must be told."

The first officer tapped his commbadge. "Away team to *Voyager*. Come in, *Voyager*."

"Go ahead." Janeway's voice was as clear as if she were standing in the plaza with them.

"Captain, we seem to have inadvertently offended our hosts. They demand that you beam down immediately. From what we've gathered, their customs forbid them from presenting junior officers to their lord Councillor."

"Chakotay, is it really that important?" The impatience in Janeway's voice was palpable.

"I'm afraid so."

Janeway's exasperated sigh could be heard on the far side of the plaza. "I'll be right down."

Lights flickered and dipped in the cavernous reception hall. The arched walls were embellished by richly embroidered tapestries and lustrous mosaics whose sinuous patterns and strange anthropomorphic shapes seemed to writhe against the dark stone.

The towering Sardalians, both men and women, were arrayed in great gauzy confections bedecked in gem-encrusted embroideries, their fine purple hair piled high and braided, trailing wisps of lights and shimmering silver plumes. The air was filled with their perfume as they stalked gracefully through the hall.

Janeway had insisted that Chakotay and Tuvok accompany her, and she was glad of their company now in this looming group. The scale of the room, of the very table and seats—more like padded perches—was oversize by Terran standards. Janeway couldn't help feeling a bit dwarfed.

"We bid welcome to our honored guests," said Lord Councillor Kolias, holding aloft a crystal goblet whose facets cast coruscating reflections against the walls and ceiling. "We Sardalians pride ourselves on hospitality and we can assure you, Captain Janeway, that you will have the full benefit of it."

Murmurs of agreement and the tinkling of glasses filled the room.

"More snuff, Captain?"

Kolias was the assiduous host, perched beside Janeway, serving and fussing until she longed to frogmarch him to a safe distance of at least two body lengths. He seemed to have no recognition of the concept of personal space.

However, diplomatic etiquette must be observed. Janeway held up her lacy sculpted goblet and smiled graciously as Kolias filled it with sparkling silver dust. She pretended to sniff it—and palmed a bit of the stuff for later analysis.

In a tall, reedy lot Kolias was easily the tallest and thinnest of all present: a walking skeleton towering over his comrades. His mane of braided purple hair was surmounted by an oddly peaked embroidered cap and his golden eyes were rimmed by elaborate silver tattoos that resembled fleurs-de-lis. How such a thin, enervated-seeming man had the energy to be so

loquacious was beyond Janeway's understanding—
and nearly beyond her tolerance.

Throughout the elaborate proceedings Janeway had
kept her expression pleasant despite her mounting
irritation. Maintaining the best of military poise, she
had let herself be presented to this councillor and
that, had met what seemed like the entire population
of the city, had responded to toast after toast. But she
had yet to discuss her specific concerns with the Lord
Councillor.

"Excuse me." A Sardalian male with blunt features
and an officious expression blocked Janeway's path.
His clothing was quite subdued compared with that
worn by the others in attendance: a tunic, robe, and
leggings in varying shades of blue and purple. The
silver marks around his eyes were thin, unembellished
lines. "You are the space captain?" His tone was
urgent.

"That's right," Janeway replied. What a refreshingly direct question, she thought.

"You must talk with me. There is great need—"

"Borizus," said a fluting female voice. "Just what
do you think you're doing?"

The girl stood half a head taller than Janeway. Her
amethyst hair hung to her waist in long polished
waves. Her skin was smooth and lustrous, her golden
eyes slightly tilted, and her silvery robes were en-
crusted with gems. But her tone was icy and her
manner toward her countryman was that of cold
anger mixed with undisguised contempt.

"How dare you intrude upon our guest's enjoyment
without being introduced?" she said. "Did you have
my father's permission to address these visitors? Did
you?"

Borizus bristled. "I don't require Kolias's leave to speak."

So this was Kolias's daughter, Janeway thought. *And spoiled rotten by the looks of her.*

"You're only second minister," the girl said. "That doesn't entitle you to take such liberties." She put her hand upon Janeway's arm as if to lead her away from something ugly.

But Janeway was not so easily deflected. "Excuse me." She pulled her arm free and turned to confront the man. "Sir, is something wrong?"

Borizus opened his mouth to speak. His entire manner cried out that yes, yes, there was something extremely wrong. But before he could communicate his problem, Lord Kolias himself was looming over the group, asking, "Just what is happening here?"

"Lord Kolias." Borizus's tone was ingratiating. His face changed in an instant to a smooth closed mask. "I merely wanted to invite our guests to tour the city's power facilities."

"You forget yourself, Borizus. They must first tour the Central Palace. But your enthusiasm is commendable." Kolias smiled tightly at Janeway. "Please forgive this transgression."

Janeway knew better than to become involved in local politics. She nodded with chilly courtesy and said to Borizus, "I hope there'll be time to see the power plant later."

He bowed and backed away.

Kolias proffered his multijointed arm. Janeway took it, allowing herself to be ushered toward the center of the room.

"It is a lovely evening, yes?" Kolias said.

Janeway felt a sudden urge to grab one of the lofty councillor's elbows and yank him down to her own eye level. *Enough small talk.* Instead, she smiled her brightest smile and said loudly in the voice she reserved for dealing with especially recalcitrant admirals, "Lord Kolias, on behalf of my officers and crew, I thank you for this splendid welcome. Your hospitality is both capacious and memorable."

There was the light tinkling of delicate notes upon the air. The assembled courtiers and guests were tapping their snuff glasses to indicate their approval.

"However," Janeway said. "We've already stayed too long and our ship urgently requires our attention. Therefore, we would like to meet with your top engineers as soon as possible."

Her words were met with a look of pained disbelief from the Lord Councillor and a mutter of disapproval from the crowd. Janeway didn't care. She had wasted enough time.

"But this is quite irregular, Captain," said Kolias.

"In that case, we bid you good night. We will discuss arrangements for later meetings from our ship." Giving her senior officers a nod to follow her, Janeway strode toward the huge, looming doorway.

"Captain!" It was Kolias, hurrying after her in his strange storklike way. "Please, wait. We're not accustomed to such abrupt departures."

Janeway's smile as she gazed upward would have melted the heart of an icebound moon. "Lord Councillor, perhaps I should apologize for our bluntness. It's part of our culture. However, the hour is late and we have much to do."

"But have you sampled our golange dust? The mosquibas powders?" Kolias sounded as though he were on the verge of tears.

"Wonderful, simply wonderful." Janeway kept the sharpness out of her voice. Would this Sardalian diplomat never get beyond trivialities? "Councillor, I'm sure you can appreciate my position. My ship is in dire need of repairs, and . . ."

"You must be exhausted. Let us not speak of such tiring matters now. Good night." Kolias folded his arms across his chest and turned away.

Janeway knew that she had been dismissed. She didn't like it. For a moment her gaze locked with Tuvok's, and she saw what she might have taken for sympathy if the eyes into which she stared hadn't belonged to a Vulcan. It galvanized her into action. Kolias may have dismissed her, but she had not dismissed *him*.

Pitching her voice at a near-shout so that it would carry, she said, "Lord Councillor, I'm afraid that I simply *must* beg your indulgence."

Kolias was already halfway across the wide ballroom, covering astonishing distances with his long spidery legs. At the sound of Janeway's voice he turned, but before she could say more he faltered, clutching his head and gasping for breath. Janeway watched in horror as Kolias stumbled and collapsed, nearly striking his head on the banquet table.

Yet his plight seemed to go unnoticed. No one in the crowd reacted except a lovely young girl with streaming lavender hair, who went quickly to his side. It was the same girl who moments before had so contemptuously dismissed the upstart Borizus: Kolias's daughter.

"Father," she cried. "Quickly. Inhale this." She held a faceted bowl filled with a pink powdery substance below his nose slit and tenderly propped up his head on her arm.

The stricken man sniffed, then inhaled more deeply. The contents of the bowl disappeared.

In a short time the Lord Councillor seemed to rally. His breathing came more easily, his eyes brightened, and he sat up. Joint by joint he racheted himself to his feet.

Janeway turned to Tuvok and Chakotay, and said quietly, "What do you think that was all about?"

"Some kind of a seizure, perhaps?" said the Vulcan. "I am no doctor, nor a judge of these people, but that man looked severely ill."

Chakotay shook his head as if to clear it. "These Sardalians seem obsessed by formality and the rules of their etiquette," he said. "But not one of them except the girl made a move when Kolias fainted just now. They didn't even look surprised. It was as if they expected it."

"Strange. And I haven't been able to get even one of them to introduce me to an engineer," Janeway said. "Nor to discuss our repair needs, the manufacturing of parts, anything." She eyed her officers. "So what have we learned about this place this evening?"

"The people seem peaceful and prosperous," Tuvok said. "It appears to be a pleasant place. But one wonders how they ever accomplish anything besides ritual socializing." He raised an eyebrow, an obvious sign of his desire to be finished with receptions and back at his post aboard *Voyager*.

"Captain." Lord Kolias approached, his odd jolting gait slowed to a hobble. He leaned heavily on his daughter's arm. "Forgive me. Marima here tells me that I have been remiss and must listen more closely to what you have been saying. A true host never ignores his guests' needs. Please tell me whatever it is that you may require and we will do our best to assist you."

Janeway's smile was swift and sincere. "Thank you,

Lord Kolias. We're desperately in need of replacement parts for damaged equipment. It would be most efficient if we could put an engineer in communication with our chief of engineering."

"It shall be done. I shall dispatch our best engineer to you tomorrow, Captain." He turned to leave, but a nudge from his daughter brought him back to the group. "Ah, yes, perhaps I should mention that we're interested in trade and in the exchange of knowledge, of ideas. Perhaps we could arrange for one of your crew members to stay here and teach us?"

"I'm sorry," Janeway said. "We have barely enough crew to run our ship. I'm afraid I can't spare anyone. And it is against our cultural system to barter crew members for materials. Please forgive our primitive customs."

"Of course," Kolias said. "We fully understand. Captain, our own cultural practices put great emphasis on hospitality, as you have undoubtedly noticed. Forgive us. We will help you repair your ship without other conditions." He bowed.

Janeway swiftly thanked the lord councillor and, with Tuvok and Chakotay, took her leave of the gathering. As she ordered *Voyager* to beam them up she felt odd misgivings nagging at her. She didn't trust the Sardalians. They were nice. Much too nice.

CHAPTER
3

RESTING HER HEAD AGAINST THE HIGH GRAY BACK OF HER ready-room chair, Janeway mused upon her strange odyssey. So many worlds, so many questions.

By dint of determination—and a bit of desperation—she had forged a crew out of the renegade Maquis and the survivors of *Voyager's* nightmarish trip from the Alpha Quadrant to the Delta.

Janeway had always had itchy feet—had longed for the adventure and exoticism of strange new places.

And here she was, seventy thousand light-years from home with a mongrel crew and patched-together ship. She wondered if some malicious god somewhere was laughing and asking if she was having fun yet.

Her eyes came to rest upon the holopicture of her lover Mark Mason and her beloved dog Molly Malone. She felt the same familiar longing, the same gut-wrenching tug every time she looked at them.

I will get back. I'll get home. I swear it. Please be there.

She forced her eyes up and away from the photo.

The visual scan of the planet Sardalia played across her viewscreen, and she fixed on it gratefully. Tuvok was right: It seemed like a very pleasant place. Three major landmasses were linked by colossal bridges that looked like golden spun silk. One continuous ruddy ocean surrounded the land. Delicate boats scooted along the sea-lanes under orange skies.

"Computer, magnify." She tucked a loose strand of reddish hair back in place, feeling more like herself.

The spires of Vandorra, surmounted by gold and silver caps, glittered in the sunlight. Graceful arched dwellings radiated outward from central hubs that might have been meeting halls. The immaculate streets of Sardalia's biggest city were thronged with people moving in a slow and orderly fashion. Vandorra was obviously prosperous, her people diligent and well rewarded.

Plant growth was abundant and well tended: There were parks everywhere, most buildings displayed at least one flower box, and most had cascading roof gardens.

But despite the beauty of the land and their own exotic grace the Sardalians on the streets appeared gaunt, even listless. Why was that? What was wrong here? Janeway remembered Kolias's sudden collapse. Her sense of uneasiness increased.

"Viewscreen off," she ordered brusquely.

The image died. Janeway tapped her communicator. "Engineering."

B'Elanna Torres's voice filled the room. "Captain?"

"B'Elanna, what's the status of our repairs?"

"I think we'll be able to work with the Sardalian materials Kolias provided, Captain. They're crude but usable. I'm analyzing the first samples now."

"Keep me posted. Janeway out."

The captain stood and stretched. She was fidgety. A walk through the ship might calm her.

The mutter and chirp of relays, call and respond of systems checks, and low murmur of officers running through their daily routines had always been a tonic for Janeway, and she availed herself of it now.

Striding along the corridors, Janeway also took comfort from *Voyager*'s sturdy bulk, her steel gray curves. A fine ship, with a fine young crew welded together by their common dilemma, determined to get home. Nothing would deter them from that goal, nothing. Janeway would see to it.

And yet everywhere she looked she saw crew members staring wistfully at their own viewscreens, some with open longing, others with tight, haunted expressions. Sad faces and sighs. Tear-filled eyes. No doubt about it, the planet Sardalia had exerted a powerful spell on *Voyager*'s crew.

Janeway preferred action to speculation—especially when the well-being of her crew was involved—and now she didn't hesitate.

"Janeway to Chakotay."

"Captain?"

"Meet me in my ready room in two minutes."

Chakotay was waiting for her, his brush-cut head bent over a viewscreen. At times he displayed an almost Vulcan composure, stoic and ironclad. His impassivity bespoke deep thought and deeply held beliefs whose most obvious stigmata were the sweeping feathers tattooed across a quarter of his brow: a tribute to his tribe, bestowed by his father.

"Am I disturbing you?" Janeway asked.

Her first officer got to his feet in a hurry, for once

23

looking a bit embarrassed, as though he had been caught doing something forbidden. "Captain. I was just looking at the planet."

"You too?" Janeway shook her head in mock despair. "Chakotay, I've been strolling the ship and everybody seems fascinated by Sardalia. A bit too fascinated, if you know what I mean."

A half-smile lit his face for a moment. "You have to admit that it's an appealing place."

"Yes, for a pre-warp society. But do I detect a melancholy note in your voice?"

Chakotay shrugged. But Janeway refused to let it go. She leaned closer to him, staring into his eyes.

"You're more attuned to the crew than I am," she said. "They're less guarded around you. So tell me, why this fascination? Why *this* particular place?"

"It's the first planet we've seen in a while that looks, well, homelike. The Sardalians aren't as alien-seeming as some races we've encountered. And Vandorra is a lovely city filled with gracious, welcoming people. Small wonder that the crew's drawn to it. It looks like a nice spot to live. Or visit."

"You're suggesting shore leave?"

"Why not?" His eyes twinkled.

Janeway refused to be charmed. "I can think of a dozen reasons, Chakotay, beginning with the gap—no, make it the chasm—between their primitive technology and ours."

The first officer nodded slowly. "But our personnel have been trained to be careful in these situations. And I don't have to tell you the kind of pressure they've been under. They'd probably benefit from feeling the ground beneath their feet, smelling fresh air, maybe even walking along a beach."

Chakotay was right, Janeway thought. What harm

would there be in a walk along a beach if it made her crew's eyes shine again? "All right. Schedule leaves, to commence immediately."

Her first officer's grin banished any lingering misgivings she might have had.

The announcement of shore leave was greeted with general delight—and a few cheers—by the crew. The Talaxian Neelix and his Ocampa companion Kes were among the first to sign up for a trip to the surface.

Delicate and elfin, Kes was a tiny blonde whose exotic beauty and sweet nature drew most of *Voyager*'s crew members to her, especially the males, much to Neelix's jealous displeasure. He had rescued her—with Janeway's help—from a brutal group of Kazon-Ogla and now was extremely protective of her. Kes returned—and reciprocated—his affection.

Just now Neelix was anxious to beam down and begin sampling the planet's food selection. He took his duties as *Voyager*'s chef very seriously, priding himself on the belief that his time spent as a scavenger and scout in the Delta Quadrant could be put to no better use than in the service of the ship. But as he strode eagerly toward the transporter room, Kes lagged behind.

"Is something troubling you, my sweet?"

Demurely she raised her eyes from the floor and gave him a searching look. "I hope the Doctor forgives me," she said. "He really wanted me to stay here and continue learning procedures. He's come to rely on me, Neelix. I hate to disappoint him. And besides, he never gets to go anywhere."

Neelix snorted. "He's just a program, Kes. He doesn't need a shore leave. And if he ever wants a vacation he can always go down to the holodeck and indulge himself."

Kes looked pained. "Neelix, please don't speak about him that way. It's true that the doctor is a hologram, but I've come to regard him as a real person. Just because he's not made of flesh and blood doesn't mean that you can dismiss him so lightly."

The Talaxian rolled his eyes. A hug from Kes melted him in a moment. "Sorry, dear. Although you will admit that he's easy to dismiss. After all, that's the nature of holograms. One command and they vanish, *poof.*"

Tom Paris approached. Neelix flashed him a sour look that said Paris was interrupting a private conversation.

"Neelix." Paris gave him a perfunctory nod and turned toward Kes. "You're looking lovely today."

Kes dimpled. "Hello, Tom," she said. "How's the arm?"

"Completely healed, thanks to the doc. And you."

"Are you going on shore leave alone?"

"No. I'm waiting for Harry Kim to meet me here. Maybe we'll bump into you on the surface."

"That would be nice."

Before Kes could say more the transporter sang its song, a halo of light enfolded them, and they were gone.

As B'Elanna Torres watched other crew members make plans for shore leave she felt a deep stabbing envy that surprised her. Harry Kim had invited her to accompany him ashore and, with barely contained disappointment, she had turned him down.

It wasn't fair, she thought. The planet below was a

treasure-house waiting for the right scientists: She and Harry could have had a marvelous time prowling around. The other members of the crew were competent but just not quick enough to see the possibilities in things. Harry, at least, showed a creative flair when it came to engineering.

Why should I stay here to oversee all of the nitpicky details and paperwork? she thought. *Any one of my subordinates could do that.*

The half-Klingon had never felt at home anywhere, except perhaps aboard a spaceship. Her brilliant and restless nature, coupled with her natural tendency toward rebellion, had resulted in her decision to leave Starfleet Academy during her second year. Joining the Maquis rebels had seemed like a natural next step.

Most of her Maquis friends and comrades were with her now, aboard *Voyager,* first among them being Chakotay. And she was even grudgingly coming to appreciate the company of many of the Starfleet officers she had encountered.

Never in her wildest dreams had B'Elanna Torres imagined that she would run the engine room of a magnificent ship like *Voyager.* It occurred to her that she might be one of the most contented members of the crew. She had her friends with her and enough engineering challenges to occupy even her agile mind. Her warring selves had achieved if not a lasting peace, then at least a workable truce. Although she was loath to admit it, this strange lost mission might have been the best thing that ever happened to her.

Impulsively, she tapped her commbadge. "Engineering to the bridge."

"Yes, B'Elanna?" It was Chakotay.

"Chakotay, I've been thinking. What if I went

ashore to supervise the collection of equipment and raw materials? I could expedite our collection process and perhaps discover other sources for our repairs. You know that nobody can prospect for components the way I can."

She waited eagerly for his reply.

"Negative, B'Elanna. We're down to skeleton crew as it is. I think you'd better concentrate on repairing the helm control. That's our highest priority."

"You don't have to tell me how good you are, B'Elanna. I'm the first to acknowledge it. And that's why we need you here. Chakotay out."

Torres directed an evil thought at her former Maquis commander. Hesitating only a moment, she buzzed the ready room. "Captain?"

"Yes, B'Elanna, what is it?"

"Captain, request permission to go ashore to supervise collection of materials."

Janeway's voice turned flinty. "B'Elanna, I think you're more valuable to us here, working on repairs. Besides, Kolias has promised us his best engineer to assist with repairs. He's due at eleven-hundred hours."

"But, Captain—"

"I'm sorry. It's out of the question. You can't be spared right now." The comm channel cut off.

Torres knew better than to argue with that tone. One of the things she had learned to respect most about Janeway was her tough, decisive nature. The captain wasn't a bad engineer, either, she'd give her that. Knew her way around a warp core, did Kathryn Janeway.

She turned, nearly bumping into a tall, thin alien with purple hair, so skeletal he looked as if she could snap him in two. For a moment she was tempted.

"Who are you?" she demanded ferociously.

His mouth worked silently for several seconds before he managed to stammer out his name.

"J–J–Jovic."

"And what are you doing here?"

"I was sent for."

Torres took in his flimsy purple garments, ratty hair braid, smudged silver eye makeup. She said dubiously, "You? You're the fine Sardalian engineer we were promised?"

He nodded a few too many times. "Yes. I'm a level-one fabricator. Lord Kolias sent me." He passed his awestruck gaze over the enormous arena that was Torres's special preserve. "May I ask, please, what is this place?"

"Our engine room."

Jovic's eyes went wide. His nose slits vibrated. "Truly? Where are the engines?"

"Here and there." Torres sighed. "I don't suppose you know anything about microrelays?"

"Micro-what?"

"Never mind. Let me sketch out for you what we need, and perhaps you can tell me if you think these parts can be made. Come over here and look at the computer."

"Computer?"

"This screen. Here." Torres fought back an impulse to yank the towering Sardalian down to her level. He might break.

Jovic sidled around the console and peered timidly at the computer screen.

"Now pay attention," Torres said. "I need the best durasteel you're capable of producing."

"Excuse me," Jovic said. "What is durasteel?"

* * *

Tom Paris walked down the corridor toward Harry Kim's quarters, grumbling to himself.

Where the hell is he? Doesn't that greenhorn know yet that if you don't get at the front of the transporter list, by the time you beam down it's practically time to beam back up? What are they teaching these kids at the Academy these days?

He was tempted to beam down alone: that would teach Harry something, all right. But friendship was still too precious a commodity to the newly rehabilitated Tom Paris to treat it lightly. A while ago he had still been under lock and key in New Zealand, a convicted traitor to the Federation.

Paris savored his commission, his rehabilitation, and his slowly healing sense of self-worth. Kathryn Janeway trusted him enough to give him back his Starfleet standing and make him her helmsman. He would never let her down. Never.

He rapped sharply at the door to Harry's quarters. "Hey, Kim! You in there?"

The door flew open.

"I've been waiting for you for half an hour." Paris leaned against the door frame and peered inside. Everywhere he looked he saw a jumble of equipment strewn from Kim's bunk across the gray carpet to the storage cubicle. "What is all this junk? C'mon, Harry, get a move on or all the best girls will be taken by the time we get there."

"I'll be ready in a few minutes," Kim said, waving vaguely at his bulging duffel. "I've still got to get these scanners packed, somehow."

Paris picked up one of Kim's tricorders, fiddled with it for a moment, and put it down with a look of disgust. "Why are you bringing all of this stuff?"

"I'll want to do tests on the water and soil." Kim's smile was beatific. "Just think, Tom. An entire new planet. There's so much to learn. That's what I joined Starfleet for."

Paris gave him a mordant nod. "A new planet. Precisely. Which is why I won't allow you to waste your time on soil samples when you could be riding shotgun with me, sampling the finest in Sardalian entertainment."

"Tom, don't you think—"

Paris yanked the tricorder out of Kim's hand and tossed it onto the bed. "I won't take no for an answer. Consider it a rite of passage. You'll love it. Now c'mon, or we'll miss our spot on the transporter schedule."

"If you insist." Harry Kim sighed, gathered up his bag, and followed his friend out of the room, pausing to stare longingly at the abandoned tricorder before Paris's hand on his shoulder yanked him out of his reverie and down the corridor. "I'm coming. I'm coming."

The central Vandorran marketplace was a festive array of purple, red, and orange-striped pavilions rising in scalloped semicircles atop tapered pilings. Although there were ladders set at the entrance to each stall, the distance between rungs made climbing hard work for diminutive folk like Neelix and Kes.

Nevertheless they scaled the heights, Neelix cheering them onward. "Just a little more, darling. It'll be worth it, you'll see. Hang on to my jacket. That's it. Up, up, up!"

With Kes clinging to his back, Neelix hauled himself up the last ten feet. He landed, barely winded, in front of a brilliant display that might have been purple sea urchins—or particularly dangerous handballs.

Neelix rubbed his palms together in anticipation and made a beeline for the front bins with Kes right behind him.

"Just look at these fruits," the Talaxian warbled, lofting a startling pink sphere bristling with orange spikes. "Those sublime clashing colors. Fabulous." He felt nearly as cheerful as on the day when he had taken that first wonderful bubble bath aboard *Voyager*. "I'll buy three dozen."

"Neelix," Kes said. "Hadn't you better go slowly?"

"This planet is a wonderland, a veritable cornucopia. We can load the ship's larder for months! I must sample the potted meats over there. And this fish! Look, look, have you ever seen a two-headed fish with black teeth before?"

"Never." Her expression indicated that she might not have cared to see it in the first place. "Neelix, do you intend to spend our entire shore leave in this marketplace?"

He turned, surprised. "Why, no, dearest. As I understand it, there are several marketplaces in Vandorra. I have a map here and we should be able to see them all in the time allotted."

"Neelix!"

"What is it, my flower? You look unhappy. Is something wrong? Have I done something wrong?"

Kes drew him aside. "I thought this was going to be a quiet time for us, on a beautiful planet."

"Of course." Neelix gazed about, mystified. "Us, and a few unusual vegetables."

"Vegetables!" The petite Ocampa seemed ready to stamp her foot in frustration.

"Kes, you know I have a huge responsibility to Captain Janeway and the crew of *Voyager*. The greater the variety of food I can offer, the more I can distract them from their sad plight." Neelix drew himself up proudly. "It's the least I can do for such a brave company. And we owe them our happiness. Remember that."

Sighing, Kes threw her arms around him and drew him into an embrace.

When they came up for air, Neelix's expression had turned sheepish and the tips of his ears were bright blue. "Oh. A quiet time. For us. Yes." And meekly he followed her as she led him toward the ladders.

CHAPTER
4

FOR A YOUNG ENSIGN ON HIS FIRST MISSION—EVEN AS
tangled a mission as *Voyager*'s had proven to be—
each shore leave provided an intoxicating chance to
learn more about strange and remarkable places.
Harry Kim gazed happily about the Vandorran street
market and drew in a lungful of fresh air, savoring the
marvelous alien tang of it.

*I'm a long way from Starfleet Academy, that's for
sure.*

He gazed in wonder at the oversize birdlike folk
crowding the narrow streets around him. They were
making mysterious gestures, speaking so quickly—
hurling nuggets of sound back and forth—that he
could scarcely understand what they were saying. It
seemed almost like a form of singing, communicating
by a series of high-pitched calls and responses.

The musician in Kim longed to record the sounds
and attempt to reproduce them later on synthesizer.
But he had left his tricorder aboard ship, along with
all the other tools he had intended to bring.

He shot a sidelong glance at Tom Paris, walking cockily along a few paces in front of him.

This is all old hat for him. Just another strange port on another strange world.

Harry Kim wondered if he would ever be as cool as Tom. He suspected that he wasn't built along those lines. But he could always hope.

A high booth selling bronzy gems drew his attention. Their facets alternated matte and reflective surfaces, and they were surprisingly warm to the touch. Kim bought a peculiar five-sided pendant for his mother and one for Libby, his girlfriend in San Francisco. Hefting the jewels in their small silken pouches, he thought:

I will see you again, my dearest ones. And what tales I'll have to share! You won't believe it when I tell you that I've been dead and revived, or captured by aliens and rescued. I've even fallen through a rift in time and space. . . .

Kim's thoughts were interrupted by the scent of something spicy and sweet on the air. He hadn't realized until that moment just how hungry he was. His nose led him to a tapered stall whose tall proprietor barely fit beneath the red-striped top of its tent.

Kim pointed at two smoked delicacies. They were, at first taste, spicy, then turned surprisingly sweet, melting away to nothing on the tongue. He bought and devoured two more.

At the corner a group of street players were frisking, tuning up—or was that actually their music? Kim attempted to follow the melodic line of it, but failed. Was it a two-octave interval? Harmonic fifths? Kim struggled to translate it into the musical concepts he understood.

He lost all interest in the musicians, however, when

a lovely woman whose long pale hair was nearly pink and whose gauzy tunic was dappled with ivory and mauve began singing a sudden plaintive chant, a cappella.

Her voice was both ethereal and sensual, by turns soaring to heights no Terran soprano could hope to match, then swooping earthward in a rich vibrato that went deeper than the deepest basso's volcanic rumblings. At first she sang as if in ecstasy. But her voice soon darkened.

Kim listened transfixed as she intoned:

"Bright were the years, the buildings, the halls,
    Light were the steps of the dance,
    Savory the meat and the drink,
    Good and rich was the life,
    But earthgrip, seagrip holds all fast.
    Lost are the dear ones
    Lost at last.
    Friend-loss, death-rapt
    Generations gone to dust,
    Forced underground
    From a curse
    Too foul to fight.
    Fifty mothers and fathers and sons
    Have passed, fallen to gravesgrasp.
    A well-wrought wall brought down by scourge.
    Oh, days of pestilence!
    On all sides we fell, and fell,
    And are falling, still."

She repeated the last two lines and a dozen people in the crowd joined in. When they had finished, tears welled in the singer's eyes and not a few cheeks were wet among the onlookers.

The singer turned away to gain composure as credits quickly filled her split-lipped bowl. Kim scrounged up a credit and tossed it in, hoping for a smile from the pretty singer. When she didn't look up he turned, disappointed, and allowed himself to be borne away by the tide of the crowd.

The song haunted him. How had that phrase gone?

> *On all sides we fell, and fell,*
> *And are falling, still.*

Kim hummed the melancholy refrain over until he felt that he had memorized the tune. Once back on the ship, perhaps he could reproduce its plaintive charm on his clarinet. He would have to transpose intervals, of course, but in its own compelling way the clarinet might render this particular song most effectively. Perhaps, beginning with this piece, he would make a collection of music from other worlds.

Yes, a collection of unknown music from the Delta Quadrant! Kim's heart beat faster at the thought. What a stir that would cause back on Earth. Humming louder, he scanned the crowd, anxious to share his new ambition with Tom Paris.

Kim found him nearby, with several sharp-eyed Sardalian gentlemen whose clothing had seen better days. They were clustered around a vertical gaming board.

"I should have figured I'd find you here," Kim said, shaking his head.

Paris gave him a mock frown. "Hey, I know that my mother is nowhere within seventy-thousand light-years, but that doesn't mean you have to fill in for her."

Harry had to admit that Paris looked curiously at

home as a gambler. *Talk about water finding its own level.*

He watched as luck went in Paris's direction and, grinning, the *Voyager*'s helmsman pocketed more than he had spent. But as any gambler knows, luck has a peculiar way of shifting.

"That's two red *cranachs* and a green one," said the game keeper. "You lose."

With a sour expression, Paris tossed a few credits into the pot. "Again," he said. "Double."

"Tom," Kim said. "Don't you think it's time to quit?"

"Hey, ease up, will ya?" There was a distinct edge to Paris's voice.

"Three greens and a yellow. You lose again, stranger."

Grim now, Paris threw his credits down.

Before he could make another bid Kim stuffed the credits back into his pocket, grabbed his arm, and pulled him away. "Let's go before you have to start borrowing from me."

Wearing the ghost of a smile, Paris allowed himself to be led down the street.

"Best *shiklak* pies in the district!" cried a vendor, standing before an orange and purple booth.

Kim steered both of them toward the colorful stand. "My treat," he said.

"I'm not hungry."

"Don't sulk, Tom." He reached up to the counter, bought two plump, steaming knobby pies, and handed one to Paris. "Here, before it gets cold."

Paris was about as enthusiastic as if Kim had placed a dead mouse in his hand. "You first."

Kim bit into the pastry and discovered that it was filled with a pink creamy paste that managed to be both smoky and tangy and reminded him of cinnamon barbecue sauce. "Hmmm. Not bad." It was certainly no worse than any of the food that Neelix had served up on the ship.

"Here, have mine."

If Kim hadn't grabbed for the pie Paris would have dropped it into the gutter. He took a deep breath. "Tom," he said. "If you don't lighten up I'm going to go back to *Voyager* and get my tricorders."

Paris grinned sheepishly. "Sorry. I hate losing. You'd think I'd be used to it by now, wouldn't you?" He shook his head. Kim could almost see the black clouds dispersing. "Here, give me that pie back."

"Tell your future, gentlemen?" cried a reedy voice. "You are far-travelers, yes? And farther to go. Shall I read what you'll find on your long road?"

The speaker was a long-limbed, gimlet-eyed woman, her thin face lined by years, her sparse hair half-covered by a threadbare purple kerchief.

Just another fakir, Kim thought. And yet there was something about her that piqued his interest. His mother had always believed in fortune-tellers, ever since one had told her that she would have a son. He nudged Paris with his arm.

"How about it, Tom?"

"Yeah, sure." Paris shrugged. "Why not?"

The fortune-teller's stand was adorned by frayed draperies that sported faded scenes of feudal glory. The interior was dim, lit only by a single lamp, and smelled of aged perfumes and musky incense. Kim felt his curiosity diminish considerably as he passed over the threshold.

He had been warned in Starfleet Academy against entering unknown unsecured rooms alone or with only one other companion. Strangers were easy marks for seemingly friendly locals. Many a space traveller had been jumped, robbed, even killed, on shore leave. The lucky ones woke up in jail.

Kim hung back at the entrance. "I don't know, Tom. Maybe this isn't such a good idea."

"C'mon, don't wimp out on me, Harry. You don't have any dark secrets you're afraid of, do you?"

"No. Don't you?"

"Hell, all of my dark secrets were revealed long ago."

"What if it's a setup?"

"I'll protect you. Get in there."

Propelled by a shove, Kim found himself standing before two long, worn bars topped by cushions. A raised platform held a high pile of dusty cushions, a bowl half-filled with incense, and a string of well-handled beads.

The crone stalked in, settled herself in the cushions, and gestured for the two men to sit down in front of her. They perched themselves on the cushioned bar, legs dangling.

"How much?" Paris said.

"A credit each."

He smiled and put two credits on the platform.

"What would you know?" the old woman asked.

"When will I meet my own true love?" Paris said, grinning broadly.

The woman held a chunk of incense to the candle flame. It flared briefly and crimson smoke rose to fill the tent. The mildly bitter fragrance of the smoke seemed to put the fortune-teller into a trance.

Just as Kim was beginning to grow restless she opened her eyes, peered closely at Paris while fingering the worn string of beads, and nodded. "Are you finished with the blond-haired woman yet?"

Paris's smile shrank. "A blonde? Which one?"

"A petite young one with pointed ears."

Paris's own ears were turning bright scarlet. He seemed speechless.

Kim decided not to comment.

The fortune-teller gave a witchy leer and turned to him. "And you?"

Might as well ask the big question. Kim took a deep breath. "Will we ever get home?"

Frowning, the fortune-teller stared deeply into his eyes, stroked her beads again, shrugged, and said, "Some of you. But not all."

Before Kim could stop to ponder what that meant, the fortune-teller had leaned closer. "But this I tell you now, for free. There will be trouble, and you must be on guard. Beware the water. 'Ware!" She pointed to the booth's entrance. Kim didn't need to be told twice.

"Let's go, Paris."

The two men jumped down and hurried out into the waning sunlight.

"Weird, huh?" Kim's eyes sought Paris's. He didn't want to show the older man that the crone had frightened him. "Maybe it's time to get a drink?" That, Kim thought, was probably the sophisticated thing to do.

Paris gave him a mirthless grin. "Yeah. Absolutely. And maybe two."

CHAPTER

5

THE BAR WAS DARK AND SMOKY, LIT BY A FAINT ROSY light. There were no booths, merely cushioned perches. A musician sat in a corner, playing strange, plangent chords on a stringed metallic box. Otherwise, the place was empty.

Tom Paris looked around and found his environment to be acceptable.

He approached the bar. It was neck-high and he felt oddly childlike before it. "What's on tap?" he asked.

The bartender stared down at him, brushed purple hair out of his eyes, and said, "Pardon?"

"Your beer? Brew?"

"Don't you want snuff?"

Paris nearly made a face, then remembered that diplomacy was important, especially in a strange bar. "Maybe later. We'd really like something to drink."

"Well, I could see if we've got any *demara*. We usually keep some around for the children." The bartender paused as if he couldn't believe that any self-respecting adult would want such stuff. "If we have it, how many do you want?"

"Two."

"Two *demara*. Right." The Sardalian's nose slits vibrated a moment. He turned away and began rummaging under the bar, out of sight.

Paris's spirits lifted. Then he glanced toward Kim and his sense of well-being immediately soured. Harry was fiddling with some paper, attempting to make musical notations. *Always working, that kid.*

"Two *demara*." The bartender handed Paris two slender glasses filled with purple liquid in which flecks of gold glistened.

Paris took a tentative sip. It was oddly sweet, with an almost bitter, pungent aftertaste. *Like Denebian brandy. Maybe.*

"Harry," he called. "Put that away and try some of this."

Kim looked up, eyed the potion, and said, "Uh, no thanks."

It was time to take a firmer approach. Paris leaned decisively across the table. "Harry, that fortune-teller shook me up as much as she did you. But you'll put that behind you and enjoy yourself now if I have to rope you, tie you, and pour this into your stubborn mouth." He set the glass down, not gently, in front of his friend. "Now drink this. Or else."

Kim shot him an irritated look. "Thanks." But he brought the flute to his lips and took a tiny sip. A slow smile spread over his face. "Hey. Not bad. Sort of like sweet sake. Sort of." He finished the remainder in two gulps. "Good. I'll have another."

The towering purple-haired bartender grinned.

Paris nodded proudly. "That's my boy. Better make that two more, barkeep."

"Just a moment," said a lilting voice. "I'd like that put on *my* bill, please."

The bartender's amber eyes widened. "Yes, ma'am!"

The owner of the voice was an ethereal beauty with large amber eyes and long violet hair that fell in gentle waves around her rounded face. Delicate silver tattoos curled sinuously at the corners of her eyes. She wore a shimmering tunic and white leggings that ended in soft boots. "My name is Marima," she said. "May I join you?"

Paris nearly fell in his haste to get down from his perch. "Please. Take my seat."

Kim was right beside him. "No, mine."

"Why don't I take my own?" she said. Pulling a high perch over, she folded her joints prettily upon it, tucking her arms across her chest. "What are you drinking?"

"Demara."

Her nose slits vibrated for a moment. "I see. Well, you *are* strangers here, after all. And what are your names?"

"I'm Tom Paris and this is Harry Kim."

She nodded her welcome. "I'm delighted to see you enjoying our hospitality. How do you find our city? Does it mystify you? Delight you with its exoticism and strangeness?"

"We haven't seen much besides the inside of this bar," said Kim.

Marima's eyes narrowed. "Well, then tell me about your travels," she said. "You must have seen many wondrous things. Have you gone a long way? How fast does your ship fly?"

Just another rich, spoiled thrill seeker looking for a

contact high. But she is beautiful. "Oh, let's not talk about all that technical stuff," Paris said quickly.

"Of course, I'm really most anxious to hear your impressions of Vandorra. We must be unlike anything you've ever encountered." She held her head up, preening.

"Well," Paris drawled. "This seems like a very nice place. And not nearly as strange as some that we've seen."

Her eyes narrowed again as she said, "Well then, our fine arts and cuisine?"

"We haven't had much chance to sample them yet," Kim replied. "But we've enjoyed what we've had. Reminded us of home."

"Home?" Her smile faded. "You mean to tell me that you don't find Sardalia unimaginably strange and unique?"

Paris tried to steer the conversation back into safer waters. "I'd rather discuss more stimulating matters. Why don't you tell us all about you?"

Now she smiled again, but the effect was polite. Cold. "I don't have time now. In fact, I'm running late. If you'll excuse me." She stood up.

"Wait," Kim said. "We've barely had a chance to talk."

"I'm sorry."

Paris watched her walk away. *Guess we didn't make the grade.* The thought nettled him and he got to his feet, calling after her. "Marima, wait. We were just getting friendly. Where are you going?"

She sighed and turned. "If you must know, I'm going harvesting with some friends, on a dare."

"Harvesting? What's that?"

"Why, *harvesting.* You don't know? Well-traveled strangers?"

"Of course we don't. Can't you explain?"

"Well, I don't have time, I'm already late." Her eyes flashed back and forth as if she were debating something. Then, decision made, she shrugged. "Do you want to come?"

"Sure." Paris lit up at the thought of a harvest trip: ripe fruit, cozy hayrides, cuddling in dark corners.

"It's risky."

"We're accustomed to that," Paris said. "I'd love to come."

"I don't know, Tom," said Kim. "Better check with *Voyager,* first."

Paris frowned. "Am I or am I not on shore leave?"

"I see your point. Okay. Let's go."

"Harry, three's a crowd. Besides, aren't you forgetting your prior engagement?"

Kim's face was guileless. "What prior engagement?"

"Soil testing. Scanner reading. Musical notation. That sort of stuff."

"Weren't *you* the guy who forced me to leave my tricorders onboard *Voyager?* Wasn't it you who told me that in order to fully appreciate a new planet I had to do more than just make silly scientific tests?"

Paris gave up. "Never mind." Turning to Marima, he said, "We'd be delighted to join you." His voice took on a mordant cast. "Both of us."

The cab that took them to Vandorra's waterfront was cozy enough, with a plush golden interior and Marima tucked snugly between the two Starfleet officers. But as they got out—and Marima paid the tab—Tom Paris stared in surprise and dismay at their surroundings.

Rickety docks and pilings swayed to the hypnotic

rhythm of the planet's oceanic tides. A few ramshackle buildings lined the waterfront. Most of them looked condemned, or about to be. A pervasive odor of old fish, sour mud, and rotting wood filled the air. Paris took in a lungful of it and frowned.

"Is this the right place?" he said.

Marima's laughter was a cascade of silvery notes. "Of course. Why would I bring you to a wrong place?" Gracefully she leaned over the side of the wooden walkway, grasped two handrails, and in one silken movement pushed off, executed a liquid somersault, and swung out of sight beneath the pier.

Paris rushed forward, certain that he would see Marima lying broken on the rocks below or floundering helplessly in the red foaming surf.

Instead he saw her laughing face as she scrambled blithely down a curving slender ladder that wound beneath the pier.

"Are you coming?" she called. "Or are you spacers afraid of a little adventure?"

Paris gave a quick disgusted sigh and began descending, stretching to reach the rungs calibrated to the Sardalians' elongated frames. Kim, coming after with even shorter legs, was forced to jump from rung to rung. Paris prayed that his friend didn't miss and land on his head, plunging them both into the heaving waters below. Where did this damned curving ladder lead?

With some relief Paris reached the last rung and saw that there was something more than water below: a dark bronze ship bobbed at anchor, hidden beneath the pier. He swung himself onto the deck. A moment later Kim stood beside him.

The vessel's name was *Fair Wind,* inscribed in silvery letters on its prow. Spidery struts supported a segmented hull. Paris thought that the ship would resemble a flea scuttling along the surface of the water.

Five or six Sardalians were already aboard. Marima greeted them eagerly. Her friends were a rakish bunch, the women sporting elaborate silvery tattoos, their purple hair hung with glittering orbs and perfumed gemstones. The men wore similar tattoos but favored braids worn over one side of the head. Everyone wore the same sort of purple-gray wet suit and boots.

"Here. Put these on." Marima handed Paris and Kim a pair of the clammy flexible garments.

The wet suits hung in their hands like limp, empty bodies.

"Yuck," Kim said.

Paris nodded grimly. "I second the emotion. What do we need these for?"

"They'll keep you warm and dry."

"I'm already dry," he said, grinning. "And I intend to stay warm."

Marima smiled. "That may not be as easy as you think. The changing rooms are over there." She indicated two small enclosures.

Sighing in defeat, Paris lugged the sour-smelling suit into the tent and began to wiggle into it. From the sounds emerging next door, it appeared that Harry Kim was doing the same. He emerged half a second ahead of Kim. Paris noted with wry amusement that he had had to roll the sleeves and legs back almost as much as Harry had in order to wear the elongated suits at all.

Beneath his feet the deck planks began to vibrate noisily as the engines started up. Slowly and a bit awkwardly, the *Fair Wind* lurched away from its moorings. At slow speeds the ship obviously didn't maneuver well.

Once clear of the pier, the ship's struts extended until they held the passenger compartment high above the water.

"Appears to be a primitive hydrofoil," Kim muttered, safely out of Marima's earshot. "I wonder what her top speed is."

"I think *I* could outrun her," Paris said.

"When was the last time that you walked—or ran—on water?"

Paris's only reply was a smirk.

Marima approached with several lumpy confections in her hands. "Eat these before they melt," she said. "You may find them mildly intoxicating."

The glutinous candies were cool and spicy. Paris felt a sudden warm flush come over him, and the lemony sky spun above his head. By the time he had regained his equilibrium, Vandorra's spires were mere spiky ghosts on the red horizon. In a moment they slipped out of sight behind the planet's curve.

The *Fair Wind*'s struts shifted, drawing the ship's body down for better maneuverability. She moved quickly into deep water and the wind picked up. Soon the boat was rocking side to side on heavy seas.

A chiming metallic purple and green ball the size of a shuttlecraft floated past, and then another. Gusts of wind sent the ship veering sharply toward a third buoy. The pilot compensated, steering around it.

"What are those?" Kim said. "Buoys?"

Marima's nose slits vibrated briefly. Her smile, when it came, looked a bit strained. "A marker for territorial boundaries."

Kim would have liked to ask more. But he was swept suddenly by a powerful wave of nausea. He clutched his middle with one hand and clapped the other one over his mouth.

Tom Paris grabbed him. "Come on. Over here." He dragged Kim to the side of the vessel, just in time.

An hour passed, an agonizing eternity for Harry Kim. The throes of seasickness were a new and unwelcome sensation. The only thing he was grateful for was that B'Elanna Torres wasn't there to see his humiliation. He could just imagine her look of disgust as she said, "Come on, Starfleet! Get over it." But how he longed to be back on *Voyager*'s bridge.

A hoarse cry caught his attention.

"Darra! Darra off to port!"

Kim stared through widened eyes at a sea filled with buoys blinking yellow and red, yellow and red. At first he took the thrashing objects beyond them for more buoys that had been destabilized by the *Fair Wind*'s wake. Then he looked more closely and saw that they weren't buoys, not at all.

Tom Paris swore softly. "What the hell are those things?"

Marima's golden eyes were bright with excitement. "They're what we came for. The *darra.*"

"Them?" Paris said. "They're the harvest?"

A strange skin-prickling vibration filled the air.

Off the bow were huge seagoing animals, ovoid in shape, their scaly skins a bronzy ocher dotted with bright iridescent spots. A ring of what might have been eyes—orange and baleful—surrounded a transparent membrane through which pale apricot-colored brains could be seen, pulsating slowly. The *darra* seemed to be great clumsy creatures floundering in the ship's wake. But not helpless.

Their fins—at either end—were serrated like

blades and their gaping mouths revealed parallel rows, top and bottom, of double-tipped triangular teeth.

The ship closed with them.

Trumpeting angrily, the *darra* slashed and bit at their attackers, using their well-developed rear fins to balance nearly upright. They were formidable opponents, but they were no match for the Sardalians' guns and grapples. The water was soon stained deep orange with the animals' blood.

Paris and Kim hung back, horrified by the carnage.

"This is a slaughter, not a harvest," Kim said.

"You insisted on coming," Paris said. He winced as a Sardalian stun gun sent another *darra* tumbling into the collection nets that fed the ship's distensible lower hull.

Kim turned on Marima. There was no trace of hesitation—or infatuation—in his voice now. "What is this?" he said. "Why are you slaughtering those animals?"

Intent on the harvest, Marima gave him a distracted look. "I'll explain everything to you later."

"Marima—"

She turned her back on him, obviously fascinated by the spectacle of a thrashing, bellowing *darra* being hooked and hauled into the ship's lower hold.

An unusually short Sardalian, his braid half-undone, gave a sharp cry of alarm. "Micaszians! They're attacking. Micaszian ships. Take cover!"

Several swift sleek boats could be seen to starboard, moving to encircle the hydrofoil. Without warning they loosed a volley of shots.

"Harry, watch out!" Paris yanked Kim down beside him as a shot went over their heads.

"Projectiles," Kim said. His tone was half-astonished, half-exalted. "They're firing primitive projectiles! Can you believe it? I wonder if they're using gunpowder, even."

"We'll ask them later, okay?"

Their companions produced their own weapons and began to return fire.

"Guns on a pleasure boat?" Paris said. "Looks like they expected to be attacked."

"Tom, if you were a poacher, wouldn't you travel well armed?"

A staccato burst of projectile fire drowned out Paris's reply.

Instead of retreat, the *darra* remained on the scene. They thrashed in the foaming water, vibrating wildly between the antagonists and creating enough turbulence to sink two of the warning buoys nearby. Somehow they were unaffected by the gunfire overhead.

The *Fair Wind*'s engines roared. The ship was swinging about in a desperate attempt to outrun her pursuers. Paris couldn't see any way out of the ambush. They looked good and trapped, surrounded by superior firepower and more maneuverable craft.

"I think we should surrender," Kim said.

"If we get the chance."

Boom!

A shot landed just short of the bow, sending up a huge splash that drenched all onboard and nearly swamped the ship. Kim and Paris clung to a webwork of fine mesh. Their shipmates were grabbing for handholds, coughing and gasping.

The intensity of the shelling increased. The air was peppered with explosive projectiles as the shelling increased. One of the hydrofoil's support struts took a direct hit and collapsed in a cloud of winking embers. The craft began to lean at an alarming angle.

"I don't think they're interested in our surrender," Paris said grimly. "Harry, can you swim?"

"It's a fine time to ask." Kim gave him a wide-eyed panicky look.

The shots were hitting all around the ship, rendering the *Fair Wind*'s guns inoperative.

Now a fresh barrage of shots hit the hydrofoil, destroying the ship's main struts and steering mechanism. The body of the ship tore free from its remaining supports, plummeted down toward the water, and hit the surface hard.

Two well-placed shots punctured the hull with explosive force.

With a rending shriek the *Fair Wind* broke apart. The *darra* leapt away through the red water as the ship's passengers, crew, and remaining cargo spilled into the churning, treacherous sea.

CHAPTER
6

"DON'T TOUCH THAT!"

B'Elanna Torres lunged in front of the storklike Sardalian engineer Jovic as he reached toward the control panel for the inertial damping field generators. One wrong move and the entire crew could be crushed against the bulkheads during the ship's next acceleration. It was the third disaster Torres had averted since Jovic entered engineering.

She glowered at him.

"Jovic, I've asked you several times not to touch anything. But if you continue to ignore my requests I'll be forced to ask you to leave."

"I'm sorry, B'Elanna Torres." Retreating from the heat of ire, Jovic bumped up against a wall console with such force that he set off two alarms.

Torres had had enough. She cut off the klaxons and tapped her communicator. "Security to engineering."

In a moment two husky officers were standing at the door, phasers drawn.

Torres smiled. "Please escort Mr. Jovic here to the transporter room. Make certain that he beams back down immediately. And don't let him touch *anything.*"

"But, but—!" The sputtering Sardalian was led from the room, right past Chakotay.

"Hold it," said the first officer.

The security men and their charge came to a full stop in front of him.

"This man is our guest," Chakotay said. "Where are you taking him?"

"The transporter. Lieutenant Torres's orders."

"We'll see about that." Chakotay strode into engineering. "B'Elanna, what the hell is going on here?"

Torres didn't bother to mince words with him. "That Sardalian is an idiot. I would've been better off instructing a Neanderthal. I simply can't work with him. He doesn't understand anything. He's so astonished by the ship that he can't even focus his attention on me."

"Do you blame him?" Chakotay said. "This is all new and fascinating."

"That's very nice for him. But I'm attempting to conduct major repairs on a crucial operational part of the ship, not run a nursery school for pre-warp engineers. And I'm seriously afraid that Jovic is going to do some real damage the next time I turn my back."

"Are you saying that he can't do the work?"

Torres saw her opening and lunged for it. "Yes, Commander. That's exactly what I'm saying."

"All right. We'll return Mr. Jovic to Vandorra and have a chat with Kolias about asking the engineering guild to provide a better replacement."

* * *

Elsewhere on the ship, Captain Janeway was exercising her own brand of self-control.

"Fascinating, simply fascinating." Kolias said. He stalked alongside her in his disconcerting birdlike way, his golden eyes aglow. "Your ship is an absolute marvel, Captain. And I do appreciate your hospitality. Very kind. I wouldn't have missed this for anything."

Janeway hoped that her smile looked convincing. She had reluctantly agreed to Kolias's visit, because reciprocal hospitality was of such high importance to the Sardalians. Her refusal to host the lord councillor of Vandorra aboard *Voyager* might have damaged her chances of obtaining the materials that they so badly needed for repairs. Even more reluctantly she had agreed to be Kolias's personal tour guide. Obviously a lower-ranked officer simply wouldn't do.

Janeway had been careful to restrict much of their tour to the crew's quarters and mess hall, the areas least likely to arouse technological curiosity. Nevertheless, the long-legged Sardalian had exclaimed in wonder over every element of the ship that she had shown him.

Next stop on the list was sickbay, a site that Janeway would have gladly skipped had Lord Kolias not begged and pleaded to see it. With misgivings she had finally acquiesced.

"Right this way," she said, leading him into the turbolift. "Sickbay." The lift doors closed and the cab sped between decks.

"Voice-activated elevators," Kolias said, glancing around. "Marvelous." He tucked his arms in front of him.

Not for the first time Janeway wished that she had found some way to keep Kolias off the ship. The lift doors flew open and she gestured. "Down this hall."

Sickbay was immaculate and silent. Janeway glanced into the doctor's cubicle, but of course it was empty. The emergency medical holographic program hadn't been activated yet. Thanking her good luck, she issued a silent prayer that she could keep the opinionated hologram out of sight.

"And this?" Kolias said.

"As you requested, here is our sickbay."

"Your medical facilities? But where is the staff? The laboratory? All I see are tables and these machines on the walls. How do you care for your sick and injured?" There was a strange urgency in the Sardalian's query.

"Most of our equipment is stored until needed," Janeway said. "Because we're shorthanded we often pull staff from other departments in the ship."

"They are doctors in addition to their other tasks?"

"Well, not exactly."

"What do you do in the case of medical emergencies?"

There was a shimmer in the air.

Damn. As the doctor materialized, Janeway tried—and failed—to decide whether his frown appeared before or after the rest of him.

"Please state the nature of the medical emergency," the doctor said.

Janeway sighed. "There is no medical emergency, Doctor."

"Then why did you call me, Captain?"

"I didn't."

Kolias stared in amazement. "Where did he come from?"

"Somewhere else, of course," said Janeway, avoiding the Sardalian's gaze.

Frowning until his forehead was almost as wrinkled as B'Elanna Torres's, the doctor said, "It's really not like you to play games with me, Captain. If there's no need for my presence I'll just turn myself off."

"Please," Kolias said. "Don't go." His nose slits quivered alarmingly. All trace of his diplomatic calm had evaporated. The Lord Councillor looked and sounded as though he were close to hysteria.

Janeway stared at him in surprise. "I beg your pardon?"

The doctor, too, seemed nonplussed. "Is there a medical problem I can help you with? Are you ill?"

Kolias's golden eyes were bright with an odd, fervid emotion. Was it fever? Desperation? Janeway couldn't imagine what was bothering the man. But her speculations were cut short by the chirp of her commbadge.

"Captain?" The voice was inflectionless and yet managed to convey great urgency.

"Go ahead, Tuvok."

"Captain, all of the crew on shore leave have made the required check-in except for Lieutenant Paris and Ensign Kim. They do not respond to our hail and are considerably overdue."

"Have you attempted to scan for them?"

"Affirmative. Even our long-range sensors can find no sign of their comm badges."

"I see. I'll be right there." Janeway paused, considering protocol. But with two crewmen suddenly missing she had little patience for the arcane rituals of diplomacy. "Lord Kolias, I'm afraid that I'll have to cut short our tour. I'll take you to our transporter room on my way to the bridge."

The shore was rocky and deserted, rimmed by crumbling green cliffs whose sheer walls fell to the beach without obvious footholds or paths.

Land. Dry land. Hallelujah.

Tom Paris wiped the seawater from his eyes. He took a quick look around and felt his spirits plummet.

Water, water, everywhere, dammit.

He sat down hard upon pebbly orange sand. Barely fifty yards away, rusty waves pounded the crescent shore. Paris stared at them with grudging respect: He had struggled through them up the rocky, sliding bank that passed for the beach until he had pulled himself safely out of their grasp.

He twisted to look behind him.

The cliffs rose up like sentinels. The only way out appeared to be by sea.

As if to discourage even that faint hope a particularly large wave dashed itself to foam upon the shore. Paris muttered an imprecation.

Harry Kim sank down beside him and began to knock seawater out of his ears. "Well, here we are," he said.

"Yes. Here we are. Terrific little shore leave," said Paris. "Just wonderful. We get invited along as guests at a slaughter. Our host's ship is set upon by pirates, and disintegrates, dumping us into the drink, and we wash up on an unknown beach miles from nowhere on this strange planet."

"Well," Kim said. "At least we didn't drown."

Paris gave him a disgusted look. "Harry, if you insist on being such an optimist, I won't bring you along the next time I get shipwrecked. Not even if you ask nicely."

"Look, it could be worse," Kim said. "We're alive. And we still have our communicators."

"Okay, I'll admit that this beats drowning at sea. But just barely."

Kim tapped the commbadge that he had attached to the front of his wet suit. "Ensign Kim to *Voyager.*"

There was no response.

He tapped it again, harder. *"Voyager,* come in."

The only sound was that of waves slapping against the rocky shore.

Kim's confidence began to erode visibly. "Something's wrong. Paris, try yours."

"Paris to *Voyager.*"

The silence stretched out over seconds to a minute, then to two.

"Voyager?" he said. "Is anybody receiving this?"

A far-off sea creature issued a trilling series of high mocking cries.

"Neither of these communicators is working," Kim said. "I thought they were nearly indestructible."

"Maybe there's an especially corrosive element in the seawater," Paris suggested. "Hey, look there!" He pointed. A familiar figure was struggling up out of the surf not far away. "Marima!"

Paris reached her first. She was shaking hard, obviously exhausted by her ordeal in the cold water. Gone was her flamboyant glamour; the water had seen to that. Marima resembled nothing so much as an oversize hatchling, drenched and miserable. Her hair was a purple mass plastered against her skull and her eyes were nearly swollen shut. Gasping for air, she groped forward, her nose slits quivering.

"Marima, can you hear me?"

Her only response was a tiny whimper. She took a few more tottering steps.

As her legs gave way, Paris dived to catch her. He barely made it, breaking her fall just before her head hit the ground. She was as light as a small child in his arms.

"Just rest now," he said. "It's okay, take it easy. We've got you."

She coughed hard, turning her face away from him.

"Easy now. You're safe." He lowered her gently to the sand. The girl's teeth chattered and her body shook visibly. "Gods, you're freezing."

"No," she said, her voice faint and thready. "It's not the water. It's the fever. The disease."

"Disease?" Paris stared at her in confusion.

Kim peered over Paris' shoulder. "What disease? What's she talking about?"

Slowly, as though each word were an enormous effort, Marima said, "We call it the gray plague. A hereditary illness. It's crippling. Incurable."

"That's what's causing the shakes?"

She nodded. "The gray plague attacks in sudden waves. Seizures. I haven't had one for a long time."

Kim knelt down beside her. "Don't you have any treatment for it?"

Her eyes darkened as though a shadow had passed through them. "There's an enzyme in the blood of the *darra* that can force the disease into remission. But we don't know how to synthesize it—so we need the blood."

"That's why you were harvesting the creatures?"

"Yes. But we were careless. We wounded too many. Such a shameful waste."

"How often are the harvesters attacked?" Paris said. "And who are the Micaszians?"

Marima started to answer, but before she could speak a spasm caught her and ripped the breath from her lungs. Slowly she fell back against Paris's arm, unconscious.

Paris exchanged a dismayed look with Harry Kim.

He set Marima down carefully, and without a word stood and began to strip off his wet suit. That accomplished, he covered the Sardalian woman with it. "Yours, too, Harry."

"Huh? What do you mean? Why?"

"Harry," he said, disgustedly. "This is no time for stupid modesty."

Blushing, Kim quickly contributed his wet suit to Marima's insulation. Then he glanced at Paris. He pointed to his friend's ribcage. "What's that mark you have there?"

"This scar?" He patted the livid line bisecting half of his chest and grinned a small but affectionate grin. "Nothing. I got it in the prison revolt on Mala Figura II."

"Get serious."

"Okay. I single-handedly fought off a pack of Mugato."

"Tom—."

"I survived, all right? Drop it."

The chill wind raised gooseflesh on their naked bodies and grains of sand bit into their skin.

"Hell of a way to spend a shore leave," Paris muttered. He tried to keep his tone jocular, to prop up Kim's spirits, and perhaps even his own. But he knew that their situation was no joke. They were stranded in a strange place without functional communicators or warm clothing.

His stomach rumbled. Paris added food to the list of survival concerns. Squinting out to sea he saw dark clouds rolling toward them. Night was coming. How long could he and Kim—and Marima—hold out?

CHAPTER
7

DESPITE JANEWAY'S PLEAS OF URGENT BUSINESS IT HAD taken her a maddening amount of time to return Kolias to his planetside offices. He had flapped around with so many questions: When could he return and speak to that charming doctor? Would the doctor perhaps attend a small reception in his honor? Would Janeway and the doctor be available to attend a celebration the following day?

The Lord Councillor had gone, finally, trailing questions and invitations. If he had lingered one moment longer, Janeway might have been tempted to shove him into the transporter herself.

Now free of annoying diplomatic concerns, she confronted her two senior officers in her ready room, and she didn't waste a syllable. "Cancel all leaves immediately. Assemble a search party and begin a sweep for Paris and Kim."

Chakotay and Tuvok nodded, both carefully avoiding her angry glare.

"Yes, Captain," said the first officer.

"I want Paris and Kim found quickly. Give it your full attention, Mr. Tuvok."

"Right away, Captain," the Vulcan said. "I will assemble a security team immediately."

Janeway tapped her viewscreen impatiently. Those crew members were her responsibility and she wouldn't sleep well until they were safely back aboard *Voyager*. "Another thing. That second councillor at that reception—what was his name? Borizus. He seemed to want to tell me something, perhaps to warn me. I'd certainly like to find out what that was all about. And he seemed refreshingly free of the Sardalian love of ceremony. Chakotay, find this Borizus and invite him up here for a chat. Don't take no for an answer."

"Yes, Captain."

"And give me hourly reports on the search. No, make that half-hourly. Get on it, gentlemen. Dismissed." Janeway bit the final word into small jagged pieces.

Neelix and Kes had spent a long romantic dinner in a beautiful restaurant suspended like a spun-glass orb between two graceful curving towers. Below them the lights of Vandorra winked like giant diamonds strewn in careful rows.

"Fabulous," Neelix said. "Absolutely wonderful." He sat on a mountain of cushions that ever so barely enabled him to reach the table, and mopped a smidgen of dessert from his lips with a voluminous lavender napkin. "Despite their primitive technology these people manage some very sophisticated culinary effects. I can't remember having a meal like this since we joined the *Voyager* crew."

"I've enjoyed all of your cooking," Kes said loyally. She was balanced on a similar tower of pillows.

Neelix reached across the table, stretching to squeeze her hand. "My flower."

A tall, taciturn waiter brought the bill. As Neelix paid it he said, "I'd like to speak to the chef."

The waiter's nose slits quivered. "Is there a problem?"

"No. I'd just like to ask him about that last delightful bit we had."

"The *gaba* surprise?"

"Yes."

His nose slits were positively vibrating. "I'm sorry, he never shares his recipes."

"I can manage the recipe," Neelix snapped. "In fact, I can improve it. It's the meat source I'd like to know about."

"I'm sorry, he *never* shares his resources, either."

Neelix held up a white and pink bill—his last bit of Sardalian currency. He waved it from side to side. "Do you understand the concept of a gratuity in this culture?"

The waiter palmed the bill and said quietly, "Try the market near the three towers."

Winking, Neelix said, "Thank you. Come, Kes."

They took the big, slow, manually operated elevator to the ground and walked out the huge arched doorway into the cool night air.

The fine meal, the refreshing breeze, and Kes at his side put Neelix in a nostalgic mood. "Did I ever tell you about the time I followed a group of Kazon-Ogla pirates back to their squalid nest and . . ."

Kes gasped and staggered back against her lover's chest.

"Darling," Neelix cried. "What is it? What's wrong?"

"I don't know." She stared into the darkened plaza but appeared to see nothing. Sweat glittered on her smooth pale brow, drenching her golden bangs. Breathing hard she said, "Neelix, I just feel this terrible flash of fear and anger."

The Talaxian gathered her into his arms. "A panic attack? Kes, dearest, you're safe with me."

"It's not *my* fear," Kes said. She fought free of his embrace. "It's like a huge storm sweeping down over me. Oh, it's awful, the killers, make them stop it, they'll kill the children. . . ." She sank to her knees on the cold stone pavement, crying out in a long, wordless, terrified protest.

"Kes, I'm going to get help."

She shook her head furiously. "No." Her breathing slowed and her eyes cleared. "No. I'm all right. It's going." She stood up. "It's passed." She took a deep breath. "Whew."

"Are you certain?"

"Yes, quite certain."

Neelix's eyes glinted with concern. "What was that?" he said. "Could you tell?"

Wordlessly she stared at her lover and shook her head.

"A warm drink is what you need." He led her to a tea stall and ordered a steaming cup.

Kes drained it in two gulps and held it out for a refill. Only after she had finished a second—and then a third—did the color return to her face.

"Oh, much better." Her smile had regained some of its former radiance. Wearily she rested her head against his shoulder. "I'm sorry to spoil the evening, Neelix."

He kissed her lightly on the forehead. "Don't be ridiculous. No evening I spend with you can ever be spoiled. Now, shall we return to the ship?"

"Oh, no, it's such a lovely night." She patted his cheek. "You know what I'd really like to do?"

"Name it!"

"Go for a walk in one of the marketplaces."

He gave her a melting look of adoration. "My sweetheart."

"Chirp!"

The commbadges on their chests signaled in unison and a familiar voice said, "Tuvok to all personnel. Shore leave is canceled. Repeat, shore leave is canceled. Report back to the ship immediately."

Kes's blue eyes widened in alarm. "Something terrible must have happened. Neelix, we've got to go back right now."

But Neelix was not to be put off the trail so easily, now that his interest had been rekindled. "We will, sweetie, we will, just as soon as I find the source of those delicacies. Ah, look there. A tower, and another. And there's a third beside it." He hurried between the lofty buildings and found a small marketplace brightly lit.

A pigtailed merchant wearing a purple apron held up a small piece of meat and said, "Try our sauteed *gaba* sir? One bite and you'll be hooked."

Before Kes could protest further, Neelix accepted the morsel and popped it into his mouth. He chewed slowly, savoring the unusual taste.

"Mmm, yes," he said. "Rather reminiscent of Brill cheese toast."

Kes crossed her arms in front of her. "Neelix, I hope you remember all the trouble that your Brill cheese caused with the ship's neural gel packs!"

"Shhh, beloved. You're distracting me. Let a master do his work." He turned to the merchant and helped himself to another taste. "Hmmm. Definitely a hint of minty aftertaste, with a distinct metallic finish. Very nice. I'll take a kilo." He pulled out a credit slip and stared at it uncertainly. "Sir, I don't suppose you accept Talaxian money?"

The pig-tailed merchant stared at him blankly. "What's this, a joke?"

"Hardly. It's a Talaxian credit slip. Money from my homeworld. I'm afraid that I've run out of your currency."

"Sorry," said the Sardalian. "I can't accept this."

Thinking quickly, Neelix said, "What about trade?"

"What have you got to offer?"

The Talaxian grinned broadly and cast a thankful glance up toward the heavens. "What haven't I got?"

Janeway regarded the Sardalian standing before her with satisfaction. Borizus, head of Vandorra's engineering guild, was no more charming than he had been the last time they had met. But he had responded to her summons with alacrity. Now perhaps they would get somewhere.

"I think you'll forgive me if I dispense with small talk," Janeway said. "I wanted to give you an opportunity to meet with me privately. You seemed quite anxious to do that the other evening, at the reception."

She waited.

The Sardalian shifted his weight from one series of knees to another, and scowled. "Did I? I'm afraid I can't remember."

"Are you sure?" Janeway probed him with her gaze. "You were interrupted by Kolias's daughter."

"Perhaps I had too much snuff. I don't remember that evening very clearly."

She kept a level stare fixed on him.

"Did Kolias tell you not to talk to me?" she asked.

Borizus bristled at the question. But then he made a gesture much like a shrug and said, "Kolias doesn't rule me. In fact, we don't often meet. What skills he has lie in the administrative—and political—sphere, while mine are more practical."

"I don't understand. I thought he was your superior."

"He is that, yes."

"And therefore you must do as he says, is that it?"

"Kolias outranks me," Borizus said sharply. "But he doesn't think for me. He couldn't think his way out of a crisis if his life depended upon it." The Sardalian's nose slits quivered. "Some say that he's the perfect choice for lord councillor. He loves the receptions, the parties, the protocol. Everything that doesn't really matter."

"And you don't?"

"I'm an engineer by trade. I'm concerned with practical matters. When I see a problem I want to fix it."

"Even if the problem is a lack of effective governing?"

Borizus's eyes narrowed until they were nearly closed. "I'm loyal to Kolias."

Janeway saw that she would get nowhere with him. She changed her approach. "As a professional problem solver and head of the guild, do you see any problems that you wish to discuss with me?"

He shook his head. "No. Nothing."

I'll bet. "You certainly seemed concerned about something the other evening." *But somebody has gotten to you and either intimidated you or bought your silence. Damn.*

"Why did you send for me?" Borizus asked.

Janeway decided to dangle some bait he might bite at. "We're in need of a liaison between your people and our engineering department. The last man sent proved less than competent."

Borizus seemed surprised right out of his glower. "An engineer—a subordinate member of *my* guild— was sent to this ship without my knowledge?"

"Kolias arranged it."

"I see." The scowl was back, deeper than before. "Perhaps he meant to tell me but was distracted by personal concerns."

"Such as?"

"His daughter is missing.

Taken aback, Janeway stared at the Sardalian. "She is? That lovely girl? For how long?"

"Two days."

The same length of time that Paris and Kim had been gone. Was it merely a coincidence? Janeway thought of the young woman who had come so quickly to her father's aid, and then thought of Tom Paris's predilection for attractive females. Was there a connection? Janeway would have bet a year's replicator rations on it. "Perhaps, then, Kolias *was* distracted."

Borizus ducked his head down between his shoulders in a sour gesture. "Or perhaps he sent one of his pets here, hoping to outmaneuver me. Obviously it didn't work."

"No." Janeway paused, wondering briefly about the power struggle that she had blundered into. But that was nothing she needed to be concerned with. It was none of her business, after all. She said, "Well, now that you're here, would you care to consult with our chief engineer? We have urgent need of your finest metal alloys."

The Sardalian nodded. Janeway tapped her commbadge. "Janeway to engineering. B'Elanna, I believe that I've found a replacement for Jovic."

"I hope he's not as clumsy."

"I'll overlook that, Lieutenant. I'll send him down with security. And—B'Elanna—he's the head of Vandorra's engineering guild." Janeway cut the channel.

Almost immediately her commbadge beeped again. "Neelix to Captain Janeway."

"Go ahead."

"I've lost my belt pouch. I believe I left it at the restaurant in Vandorra. Or it could have been in the marketplace, I suppose."

"And I take it that you want to go back to the planet and look for it?"

"Yes, Captain."

"Are you aware that I've canceled all shore leave?"

"Yes, Captain."

"Is it really that important? Can't you replace this belt pouch, or replicate it?"

"Captain, I wouldn't ask this, but it contains the only holocard of my late parents, my lucky *korin,* and two of my favorite recipes. Irreplaceable is really too light a word to use here."

Janeway sighed. "Very well, Mr. Neelix. I can spare

you for half an hour. But please be extremely cautious. We've already misplaced two crew members somewhere on that planet."

The Talaxian sounded positively cheerful. "Oh, not to worry, Captain. Caution is my middle name."

Why, Janeway wondered, did she doubt that last statement very much?

"Make it fast, Neelix. Janeway out."

The night had been cold and bitter. Harry Kim had spent most of it pacing along the rocky shoreline, alternating watch with Tom Paris while Marima slept fitfully beneath her coverlet of wet suits, mumbling and occasionally crying out. She was quiet now.

Kim scanned the brightening horizon once again. This was a stupid place to die, he thought. His eyelids began to close and his mind to fog into sleep. His head fell forward, and the movement awakened him. Groaning, he forced his eyes open.

Strange birds had appeared overhead, coasting effortlessly in lazy circles. They reminded Kim of the hunting hawks and other birds of prey of Earth.

But these were large, too large to really be birds. And that central tube that lay across the spine of the wings like some insect's elongated thorax, what was that?

Giant insects? On Sardalia?

Even that thought couldn't keep him completely awake. Again Kim felt himself slipping away toward unconsciousness. At the last moment he jerked himself awake.

Above him the skies were empty, gradually lightening as dawn approached.

Start walking, he thought. *Got to keep moving, keep the blood flowing to my legs.* Yawning, he got up and peered toward the horizon. His yawn died aborning.

There, on the water. What was that? A smudge, where no smudge had been before.

A small, traitorous voice in Kim's brain told him that it was merely the shadow of a cloud or perhaps a hallucination. *It's nothing. Go back to sleep.*

He rubbed his eyes. The speck was still there.

"Paris," he called softly. "I think I see something."

His crewmate was up and beside him in an instant.

"Where?" Paris squinted into the growing light and took a step closer to the shoreline. "Hey, that looks like a ship!"

So, Kim thought. It wasn't a delusion. Or if it was, at least it was a shared one. "We've got to get their attention."

"Grab a wet suit and start flailing."

Kim swung the rubbery garment through the air until he thought his arms would come off.

"It's working," he cried. "They're coming closer."

Paris turned toward Marima. "I'll get her up and move her toward the ship.

Kim nodded, busily pulling on his wet suit.

The ship was close to shore now. It was a sturdy-looking vessel, Kim saw. A smaller craft put out from it and soon it was near enough for him to make out the faces of those piloting her. They wore the usual purple topknots and their eyes were encircled by silver lines.

As soon as they were in range he shouted: "We were shipwrecked. We have someone in urgent need of medical attention!"

The grim faces of their rescuers' faces seemed oddly familiar.

"Save your breath," Paris said. "These are the same people who destroyed *Fair Wind* and stranded us here."

CHAPTER
8

B'ELANNA TORRES LOOKED INTO THE GLOWERING FACE OF
the new engineer, Borizus, and felt her Klingon half
raise its hackles in instinctive dislike.

Down, girl.

Aloud she said, "You're Borizus? Well, I hope
you're more careful than the last engineer they sent
me."

The Sardalian glared at her. He was an imperious
male, obviously accustomed to giving orders, not
taking them. "Are you certain that you're in charge
here?" he said, sniffing loudly. "I've never met a
female chief engineer, much less an alien one."

Yeah? I'll bet I could run rings around you. "What
you have or haven't experienced is of no concern to
me," Torres snapped. "What matters is that you
provide us with the materials necessary for us to effect
repairs. That's the only reason you're here to begin
with."

He gestured at the control console. "First explain
how this works."

Torres mastered the urge to kick him out of engineering and halfway back to the transporter room. "I don't think you understand," she said tightly. "I give the orders around here, not you."

As if he had not heard her the Sardalian reached out and placed his hand against a diagnostic sensor control. Immediately the board lit up like an old-style fireworks display.

Borizus jumped, obviously shaken. But that was small compensation. Angrily, Torres cut off the sensors and with the other hand tapped her communicator.

"Torres to Chakotay."

"Go ahead, B'Elanna."

"Look, this Borizus is no improvement. He won't listen to anything I say, he doesn't seem to give a damn about cooperating with us, and he doesn't really believe that I'm an engineer. He just wants to set off alarms and demands that I show him how things work."

Chakotay's response was sharp. "Of course the man's curious. He's an engineer. It stands to reason that he'd wonder how a starship works."

"I don't trust him."

"Well, try to get over it, B'Elanna. He's the best they've got. We can't keep rejecting their engineers and expect them to provide us with the raw materials we need. Chakotay out."

Torres turned to the Sardalian, took a deep breath, and said, "All–l–l right. Let's get down to business."

Borizus grunted his assent.

Smiling tightly, Torres held up a warning hand. "I'd just like to make it clear that if you touch anything,

anything at all, without first asking my permission, I'll stun you into unconsciousness. Understood?"

Harry Kim struggled with wave after wave of seasickness as the deck heaved and surged beneath his feet, and his stomach heaved right along with it. He almost wished that he were back on the beach, shipwrecked. This was misery, pure and undiluted. The only thing that remotely helped his stomach's equilibrium was a determined concentration on amassing information. Desperately he focused his attention on Assurna, the Micaszian ship's captain.

"Why did you attack us?" he said. "And then why did you track us and save us?"

"We didn't want to kill you," Assurna replied. She was a wiry woman with deep purple hair and amber eyes. "We wanted to get you away from the *darra*. That was our primary concern." She stared past Kim at the semicomatose Marima. Her nose slits quivered. "As strangers you couldn't possibly be expected to know of our laws. But the daughter of Lord Councillor Kolias knew quite well that she was trespassing in our waters."

"So why not return her to her father and lodge an official protest?" Kim asked.

"This has happened before." Her tone was one of patient condescension. "Don't you think we've already tried official protests? They don't work. The raids on the *darra* continue. So we'll use the girl to drive a bargain with the Sardalians for more reasonable culling of the *darra* and better-enforced boundaries for the spawning grounds."

"What about the others who were aboard the *Fair Wind?*" Kim asked.

The Micaszian gave a gesture much like a shrug. "Lost."

"Drowned?"

"Or eaten," said Assurna "The *darra* aren't fussy. They've got hearty appetites. In times of hardship they'll even happily eat each other."

A chill raced down Kim's back as he absorbed that particular bit of information. He and Paris had been in that water, too.

Tom Paris pushed his way into the discussion, saying, "You've got to get Marima some medical attention. She's terribly ill and she's not getting better."

Assurna's hard expression didn't change. "We already know that. And of course she's not improving. That's the nature of the illness."

"Look," Paris said. "If you want a hostage use me, not some unconscious, half-dead girl. Call my ship, talk to my captain. I'm sure we can work something out."

"It's Kolias we want to reach, not your captain. And for that purpose his daughter and none other will do."

"But Marima may not last very long as a hostage. Don't you understand? She may be dying."

"We'll take that risk."

"I don't get it," Kim said. For a blessed moment the nausea receded. "Why are you so protective of the *darra?* You're practically willing to commit murder to save what seem to be big omnivorous fish."

The Micaszian ducked her head between her shoulders, scowling. "You off-worlders don't understand *anything.* We in Micasz venerate peace and hate bloodshed of any form. It's the Vandorrans who are the aggressors. We're sailors and sea farmers who prefer to keep to ourselves. I assure you that the last thing we intend is to harm—much less murder—anyone."

"Then why are you doing this?" said Paris.

"When the gray plague—the hereditary illness from which Marima suffers—was first diagnosed, and the enzyme in the *darra* blood was found to control the disease, the *darra* were hunted nearly to extinction. It was decided generations ago that the *darra* must be protected for the good of all Sardalians. We in Micasz had a tradition of sea farming and so, logically, we took over the maintenance of the creatures."

"Maintenance?" Paris raised a skeptical eyebrow. "You make them sound like machines."

"We raise them in protected enclaves, care for them, and cull only as many of them as are absolutely necessary to supply the special enzyme that all Sardalians need. But now a faction has emerged in Vandorra, our rival city, that disputes our methods." Again she gazed at Marima with cold disdain before turning her back.

The sick girl stirred, protesting weakly. "You protect the *darra* while dribbling out the enzyme, keeping us all miserable, always sick, half-dead. Look at me!" Her eyes were fever-bright as she attempted to rise, joints crackling. As she fell back she cried, "Such noble peaceful people, the Micaszians. You care more about those fish than about us!"

Assurna spun to face her. "In your greed and fear you'd kill them all, and us with them," she snapped. "Stupid girl, you strike at our sea farms—you saw those buoys, you knew you were entering our domain—and slaughter indiscriminately. You Vandorrans would carelessly destroy the precious little supply we have. What will you do when the *darra* are all gone? You're the criminals here, you and your father, the mighty Lord Councillor, who condones and encourages your behavior."

"We're all dying by inches," Marima cried.

A sudden upward surge in his digestive tract convinced Harry Kim that he was, too.

"Oh, you're still alive," said Assurna. "And, for the moment, the *darra* as well. Don't forget that they too have rights." The Micaszian leader turned to the Starfleet officers. Her voice held a note of entreaty— and warning. "You may come to have increased respect for them once you've learned more about them. And I'll make sure that you have considerable opportunity to do just that. You'll begin by feeding them." Her expression was unreadable but her boot-heels rang against the deck as she strode away.

Paris leaned close to Kim. "Looks like we've stumbled onto a private fight," he whispered.

"No maybe about it," Kim replied between clenched teeth. A big wave rocked the boat and his stomach took a sickening plunge. But he managed to choke out: "And what's more, I've got a nasty feeling that we're on the wrong side."

B'Elanna Torres swore pungently in Klingon and slammed down her microwelder with such ferocity that Chakotay, checking on her progress, was certain she had broken it.

"Hey!" he said. "Take it easy. Those don't grow in hydroponics, you know."

She gave him a snarl that might have been a smile. "Sorry. This is just so damned frustrating. These Sardalian alloys are so crude it takes three times as

81

long to work with them as our regular materials. That's the third time that a linkage I've been soldering has corroded beyond recovery."

The first officer folded his arms across his chest and assumed an expression of mock severity. "I can't believe that I'm hearing the brilliant B'Elanna Torres, she who can fix anything, being brought low by a tiny consideration like crude metals."

"Stuff it, Commander."

He smiled tightly. "Insubordination, B'Elanna?"

"That used to be the order of the day in the Maquis."

"I'll overlook it—this time. Besides, I don't know why you're complaining. I remember you working with not much more than a spanner and a prayer during our Maquis operations. And you managed. By comparison you've got an embarrassment of riches here."

"I suppose." Her tone was grudging. "Don't goad me, Chakotay. It's been a bad day."

"Tell me about it. And where's your friend?"

"Borizus? He's on dinner break. I sent him with Lieutenant Carey to sample Neelix's latest creation."

Chakotay shuddered in exaggerated sympathy. "Poor man. You really don't like him." He was rewarded with a ferocious grin before Torres bent back to her task.

But he was oddly reluctant to leave engineering. Perhaps it was a touch of nostalgia for their Maquis days. "Can you use another set of hands until Carey returns?" he said.

"Can I? Grab this scanner and hold it steady as I weld. If the indicator moves past yellow, yell."

Chakotay cupped the scanner in his palm and watched Torres's nimble fingers work the sooty metal, microwelding it into shapes, coaxing it, bullying it. Sour cloying smoke and ash floated up, coating them both. The first officer held off coughing—but just barely—until Torres had shut down the welder.

"Let it cool," Torres said. "If the welds hold we're in business." She set down the welder and wiped her hands, sharing a corner of the rag with Chakotay. "And how goes the search for Kim and Paris?"

"I wish I had some good news to tell you," Chakotay said, frowning. "There's just no trace of them."

"Nobody saw them? They didn't buy anything? Eat anything? Go anywhere?" Torres's tone was frankly contemptuous. "Come on, Chakotay. I can't believe that in twelve hours Tom Paris didn't manage to get into at least one fight in a bar."

"I know."

Chakotay's commbadge beeped. "Tuvok to First Officer."

"Here."

"We have got a lead on Paris and Kim."

The first officer exchanged a quick hopeful glance with Torres. "Go ahead."

"It seems that a bartender on Vandorra's water-front recalls serving both men."

Torres chuckled mordantly.

"And?" Chakotay prompted.

"He remembers that a young lady joined them. They left the bar together."

"That's a good trailhead. Anything else?"

"Yes, Commander. The young woman was Kolias's daughter."

CHAPTER
9

DARRA SURROUNDED THE MICASZIAN VESSEL, ADULTS and their young, scores of glistening ocher animals whose silver spots winked in the sunlight.

"Come, my beauties," Paris said in a comic basso profundo. "Dinnertime." He tossed a bucketful of squirming multilegged worms into the water and watched the sea beasts gather, churning the water with their tails as they dined. "You are some ugly bastards, aren't you?"

"They only surround the boat at mealtime," Kim said. "And as soon as they're finished eating they vanish."

"Reminds me of mealtime at home," Paris said. "When I was a kid."

"And I was just about to suggest that this behavior demonstrates a form of rudimentary intelligence."

Paris grinned mirthlessly. "Hey, you must be feeling better if you're insulting me."

"I was, until I looked into the feed bucket. Can't say that their chow looks very appetizing."

The hold of the ship was crammed full of the wriggling spiderworms and it was the feeders' duty to collect the food before tossing it overboard. Both Paris's and Kim's buckets were close to overflowing with the noisome bugs.

Paris had gallantly offered to work Marima's shift as well as his own. Now he was beginning to regret his chivalry.

Marima came on deck moving slowly, knees occasionally buckling in several places. She clung to the deck railing with both hands as she forced her way toward the Starfleet officers.

Paris watched her progress with a mixture of admiration and pity. "Hey, what do you think you're doing?" he called.

"You're very kind, Tom, but I can't let you take on all of this for me."

"Go lie down, will you?"

"No. I'm feeling better." She shuddered, attempted to fight it, and failed. "Really."

"Sure."

"Let her help if she wants to," Kim said.

Paris sighed, wondering if it was crueler to chase her away or to allow her to participate. *What the hell.* "All right, Marima, I'll let you hold the bucket for me, how's that?"

She nodded, looked down at the worms and made a face. "Ugh. Disgusting."

"Be glad you don't have to eat them."

She nodded again, but the nod became uncontrollable as the shaking overwhelmed her. "I'm sorry. I can't—" Her eyes rolled back in her head as she collapsed. Harry Kim broke her fall, sitting on the deck with Marima's head in his lap.

Paris called to the guards. "Hey, there's a sick woman here. Can't you do something for her?"

The Micaszians didn't seem to hear him.

"I don't think they care," Kim said.

"We'll see about that. Hold on to her, Harry." Paris set down his bucket and walked boldly up to one of their captors, a reed-thin male with an elaborate purple topknot wrapped in a flamboyant purple kerchief.

"Excuse me."

The Micaszian glowered down at him but gave no other response.

"Y'know," Paris said. "It's really poor policy to allow one of your hostages to die. Especially when she's the daughter of the lord councillor of Vandorra."

The guard grunted and turned away.

"Hello? Am I getting through?" Paris tapped him roughly on the hip.

The Micaszian exploded in a fury of motion, arms slashing out at Paris with killing speed.

With instincts honed by years spent in waterfront bars, Paris ducked, found an opening, and struck back hard.

The Micaszian staggered.

Paris hit him again, hammering the alien's face and neck.

The guard reeled under the blows but caught his balance against the deck railing. Braced, he launched himself at *Voyager*'s helmsman, slamming Paris across the face and upper body.

Paris lost his footing and toppled backward. His head struck something hard, and after that he found it difficult to concentrate. He was dimly aware of someone calling his name and of blows landing on him but they were very far away as the world around him darkened and was still.

B'Elanna Torres lowered the replacement relay housing into its conduit cradle. Ten hours of hot, sweaty effort had refined the crude Sardalian alloys into something she could work with. Now, just a few more welds and she would be ready to test her results.

"Say a prayer, Borizus."

Snorting with contempt, the Sardalian said, "Pray? To whom, for what?"

"That this works," she said, and thought: *So I can get you out of my hair.*

The casing connectors clicked into place and she sealed them with a quick thrust of the welder. Just one more piece and she would—

Wham!

A heavy weight—Borizus—slammed into her.

"What the hell?"

Torres lost her grip on the welder. As she watched in horror it went wide off its target and melted the carefully reconfigured metal into a shapeless, glowing puddle. Crying a savage oath, Torres disconnected the tool's power source.

Livid, she whirled, ready for battle.

Borizus was sprawled motionless on the floor. His florid complexion had gone ashen gray.

"Borizus," Torres said. "Can you hear me? Borizus?" She knelt to check the Sardalian's vital signs, then realized that she had no idea what they were.

The fallen man groaned faintly.

She tapped her commbadge. "Engineering to sickbay. Emergency. Intership beaming on my command." She leaned over and grabbed Borizus's shoulders. "Now."

The air around her hummed, engineering faded out, and the neutral walls of sickbay materialized. A moment later, the transporter effect released her.

The holographic doctor stood frowning down on her and her unwieldy burden. "What seems to be the problem, Lieutenant?"

"He collapsed. On me." She half-dropped, half-shoved Borizus into the doctor's arms.

"Hmmm." The doctor lowered the Sardalian onto a diagnostic bed and peered at him, eyebrows arched in surprise. "And what, exactly, *is* he?"

"Sardalian. A native of the planet below. More than that I can't tell you. Just get him back on his feet, will you?"

"Cure an unknown species just like that? Certainly, Lieutenant. Are there any other miracles that you'd like me to work while I'm at it?"

Torres's gaze might have melted latinum.

She reached for her commbadge to order herself beamed back to engineering, then thought better of it. If she walked back she would save the ship's energy stores. One thing her service in engineering had made her painfully aware of was *Voyager's* precious limited resources.

"Doctor, if you want me I'll be in engineering," said Torres. "Attempting to recast the replacement part that melted when this gentleman fell on top of me. He's just cost me days of work. Take care of him, Doctor, before I kill him." She strode out the door, hearing its gentle whoosh and wishing just once for the hearty satisfaction of being able to slam it behind her.

* * *

The patient was a humanoid unfamiliar to the doctor. Nevertheless his program could compensate for this problem by matching tissue types, providing equivalences, and cross-referencing. Quickly the doctor selected a temporary life-form identification subroutine and inserted the label "Sardalian, male" onto a file.

The patient groaned and opened his eyes.

Supplementary socialization programming suggested that some verbal contact with the patient was in order.

"What is your name?" the doctor asked.

"Borizus."

The doctor's program added the patient's name to the temporary file label.

"What is this place?" said the Sardalian. He appeared to be rather primitive in his apprehension and awareness, and the doctor altered his nomenclature/language referents appropriately.

"I'm a doctor. You're sick and I'm tending to you." Scanning the patient with a tricorder, the doctor began an analysis of readings.

The patient made a sound that correlated most closely with human/Terran expressions of impatience. "Don't waste your time. No doctor can help me."

"No?" replied the hologram. "Perhaps no doctor of your own species. But my medical resources and data base are immense and far-ranging, I assure you."

The patient stared at him with obvious interest. "You say you have great medical knowledge?"

"I believe that is what I just said, yes."

The patient Borizus began to sit up, waving his arms. "Doctor, I think—"

All diagnostic indicators lit up.

The doctor decided that the patient was becoming

too agitated and selected a sedative, injecting it with practiced skill and speed.

The Sardalian fell back, inert.

And so to work, the doctor thought.

A seemingly chronic inflammatory and debilitating condition of unknown origin was the cause of the patient's distress. It required additional study.

But Lieutenant Torres had told him to get the temporary patient "back on his feet." That seemed to indicate dealing only with the immediate presenting symptoms. Therefore, the doctor eradicated the weakness and pain of the patient and awakened him. Three hours had passed.

"Sickbay to engineering."

"Torres here. Go ahead."

"My patient is ready to be returned to you."

"Thank you, Doctor. I'll notify the transporter room. Torres out."

Moments later a humming sound filled the room and light danced in blue particles around the Sardalian, reducing him to molecules and removing him in the wink of a tricorder.

The doctor thought that the entire process seemed like an unnecessarily elaborate—not to mention messy—way to travel. Then, his services no longer necessary, he turned himself off.

Kathryn Janeway resisted the urge to pace her cabin, telling herself that she was supposed to be resting. But how could she rest when two key members of her crew were missing?

"Janeway to bridge."

The first officer's voice responded immediately. "Chakotay here."

"Why are repairs moving so slowly?"

"B'Elanna just called me. There's been an accident in engineering. Borizus collapsed, knocking the microwelder out of B'Elanna's hands at a critical moment."

"How bad?"

"She lost two days' worth of work."

Janeway closed her eyes in dismay. "Can we assign other personnel to assist her?"

"I don't think it will help."

"Two days' work gone . . . I can hardly believe it. Perhaps bringing the Sardalians aboard was a bad idea. But B'Elanna hasn't exactly been cooperative. And she really doesn't seem to be working at the top of her form."

Chakotay's voice was gentle when he replied. "I think B'Elanna is distracted. She may be upset over Harry Kim's disappearance."

"Oh." Janeway paused to absorb that. The feelings of her crew were important—to a point. "Well, we're all very concerned about Harry. Tell B'Elanna that we'll find him and that we're doing everything we possibly can. And to get moving on those repairs."

"You know that she doesn't like—or trust—the Sardalian engineers."

"She doesn't have to. I'll certainly admit that their methods are primitive. But the basic materials they provide are useful, Commander."

"Well, after her experience with Jovic and Borizus, she's convinced that the Sardalians are out to get her."

"Sheer paranoia." *I ought to have a talk with her.*

"Maybe. And you know how excited B'Elanna can get. She just told me that she'd rather work without any help from the Sardalians. She'd even like to start from scratch, go down to the planet and collect the material she needs by herself."

"What?" The starch was back in Janeway's voice in an instant. "Out of the question. All that would accomplish would be to slow down repairs even more."

A priority signal overrode all other communications. "Sickbay to Captain Janeway."

"Go ahead, Doctor."

"Captain, a most curious thing has happened."

Janeway gritted her teeth. "Enlighten me. Quickly."

"A tricorder is missing. The computer inventory doesn't tally with the actual count."

"How long has it been missing?"

"Unknown. But I suspect that it was taken recently, between the time that I was last activated and now. There are signs that somebody has been rifling through sickbay equipment."

"Have you queried Mr. Neelix?" Janeway said.

"Neelix? To be honest, it hadn't occurred to me to do so. Is there any reason why I should?"

"It might be a good idea. In the past, some of the most surprising objects have had a peculiar habit of gravitating to the galley. And, Doctor, are you certain that your inventory figures are accurate?"

"Of course." The emergency medical holographic program sounded astonished that she would even ask such an insulting question.

"Forgive me, Doctor—"

"Do you think that I can't keep track of my own equipment?" the hologram continued. His voice began to rise. "That I'm not aware of objects that are missing? I run a tight sickbay, Captain. I may not be kept up to date on events in other areas of the ship but I assure you—"

"Doctor, will you excuse me? I have another priority message coming in." Janeway cut off the commbadge and reopened a channel to Chakotay. "I'm sorry, Commander. There was a slight tempest in sickbay. The doctor can't find one of his tricorders."

"Sounds serious," the first officer said lightly. "Shall I inform Tuvok?"

"Let's wait." Janeway permitted herself a weary smile. "I know that we decided to encourage that hologram to develop more of a personality, but I'm not sure that the result has been an unqualified success."

Chakotay chuckled. "I'd say it's a little too late to do anything about the doctor now. He'd be insulted if you tried to reprogram him."

"Well, as captain I'll reserve that option, just in case he gets too annoying."

Harry Kim peered off the bow of the Micaszian ship.

The water was smooth, glassy, and empty.

He whistled a declining scale in C and waited. A sudden boiling of the sea announced the arrival of hungry *darra*. Soon the water around the boat was filled with thrashing bronze-hued sea animals impatient for their meal. The air shook and crackled with their expectant vibrations.

Kim swung the feed bucket high in the air to make certain he had the *darra* creatures' full attention. Every reddish eye was riveted on him.

Marima stood poised, hands clutching the guardrail.

"Now watch this," Kim said. He cantilevered a

portion of the squirming spiderworms out over the water.

The *darra* scooped them almost daintily off the bracket that Kim extended, and into their mouths.

"Party tricks," Marima said. She leaned against a pile of discarded buckets and watched him, obviously unimpressed. "So they've learned to gather when food is dispensed. That doesn't take much intelligence."

Kim frowned. "What about this?" He whistled twice, the signal for no more food.

The *darra* began dispersing immediately.

Kim turned triumphantly to Marima, only to be met with a dismissive shrug.

"And now they're finished feeding and are leaving," Marima said. "No great mystery there."

"They recognized my whistle," Kim said. "And they understood when I signaled that feeding was over."

"Perhaps you've trained them the way that a pet can be trained. That still doesn't prove much. I have a pet—a purple *mogwik*—that likes to play hide-and-seek in the Great Hall. But I don't mistake its playfulness for advanced intellect."

Kim sighed. "You're a tough audience."

"I have to be," she said. "I'm Lord Kolias's daughter." She smiled gently and patted Kim on the shoulder. "Don't be too disappointed."

"I'm not." *But I won't stop trying to convince you that the* darra *are intelligent, either.*

"So, Borizus, up and around?" B'Elanna Torres attempted to sound welcoming as the Sardalian glowered his way back into engineering. "I managed to prepare the piece that you melted for remodeling—it only took me two hours to get the matrix set. You're just in time to watch me recast it."

Borizus grunted in what could have been either pleasure or disgust.

"Look, it's really fitting together quite well." Torres set the piece into place, set the timer, and stepped back.

The numbers counted down to zero and the entire casing was bathed in a nucleonic bath that caused the melted pieces quickly to re-form.

The Sardalian engineer watched openmouthed, obviously astonished.

Torres restrained a self-congratulatory smile. "I thought that might get your attention," she said.

"This is a ship of miracles," replied the Sardalian fervently. "Everywhere you turn there are amazing things."

"If only that were true. Now listen, Borizus. So far I've been able to work fairly well with that metal alloy. I'll need an additional five shipments of it as soon as possible."

He nodded. "I should have that for you in a few days. I've instructed the factory to put aside all other work. However, it might be best if I were there to oversee the work. Those metalsmiths get lazy when they're not prodded regularly."

"By all means." Torres was delighted at the prospect of not having his gloomy presence looming over her shoulder. "I'll call security for an escort for you. . . ."

"I believe that I can find my own way to your transporter room."

Torres gave him an incredulous look. "You'd get lost in a minute."

"To the contrary, I know that in engineering we are

on Deck Eleven, that the bridge is on Deck One, and that the transporter is on Deck Four."

"Well," Torres said, impressed. "You've certainly learned your way around the ship, haven't you? But I don't think the captain would care for my allowing a guest to go unescorted."

Was that a flicker of anger in his eyes? Some powerful emotion passed swiftly over the Sardalian's face and was gone. Torres decided she had had enough of the prickly engineer and his black moods. She tapped her communicator.

"Torres to Tuvok. Mr. Borizus would like to return to Vandorra. He'll need an escort to the transporter room."

"Acknowledged," the Vulcan replied. "I will dispatch a security detail immediately. Tuvok out."

CHAPTER

10

TOM PARIS AWOKE, STRETCHED, AND REACHED FOR HIS Starfleet uniform.

He opened his eyes and his vision exploded into a thousand jagged shards. Quickly, Paris shut them again.

Rubbing his aching head he wondered, *What the hell did I do last night?*

Then he felt the unfamiliar aches in his limbs, the crusty layer of dried seawater on his limbs, and remembered. He also remembered something about a very large Micaszian with whom he had had an even bigger misunderstanding.

He probed the lump on the back of his head. It was tender, but he didn't think he had a concussion. His hard head had saved him from real damage more than once.

Paris glanced over at the next bunk where Harry Kim lay in peaceful slumber. Good old Harry, he thought. Finally sleeping. No need to wake him yet.

So, just another morning as a hostage on a hostile

ship on a strange planet. What was his next move? Get up and feed the *darra*. Right.

Voyager's helmsman got carefully to his feet, picked up the feed bucket, and made for the door. Spiderworms, here I come, he thought.

But as he walked out the door of the bunk room, a Micaszian with two fat purple sidelocks hanging over the right side of his otherwise clean-shaven skull shoved him back roughly.

"Time to feed the animals," Paris said. He swung the bucket by its handle and fought down the urge to swing it right into the guard's jaw. "Can't have our fishies getting hungry, can we? Want me to save you a helping?"

The guard held up a warning hand. "Stay here."

"What about the *darra?* Who'll feed them?"

"We'll take care of them." The Sardalian's tone said that it was no longer Paris's business.

"I'm not sure that I understand."

"You don't have to."

Paris didn't like the sound of that. He briefly considered butting the man with his head—after all, it was the hardest part of his anatomy—but then he remembered the lump on the back of it. He thought, too, of Harry Kim, still asleep. It was one thing to bring down trouble upon himself, quite another to involve the blameless Harry in it. Sighing in disgust, Paris retreated to his bunk.

Kim sat up, blinking. "Did I miss feeding?"

"Relax," Paris said. "We're off duty."

"We are?" Kim frowned and slid out of his blanket. "But the *darra* will go hungry. I don't understand."

"Neither do I."

The ensign peered out through the grimy porthole. "Just look at them out there."

Paris stared over his shoulder. *Darra* filled the waters around the ship. The adults were frolicking with their young, tossing them high into the air from tail to flippered tail.

"They're playing," Kim said. "Look at them, Tom. I can't believe that's not intelligent behavior."

"Yeah, but maybe that's all just a nurturing instinct. Be careful, Harry, okay? Don't make these weird fish into more than they are."

"So you don't think they're intelligent?"

"To be honest, all they look like to me are big seagoing eating machines." Paris sank down on his bunk, put his suddenly aching head down with great care, and closed his eyes. "Wake me when it's feeding time for humans."

Paris was soon snoring gently. Harry Kim stared at his friend, wondering how he could sleep at a time like this.

Kim couldn't help but worry about the *darra.*

They'll begin to starve. And then they'll kill and eat one another. But nobody seems to care.

He remembered that when he was a child his mother had told him that Mr. Nobody never accomplished anything. But he was somebody, and that was what mattered.

I'll feed you, guys. Hang on. Kim got up, crept out of the prisoners' bunk, and eluding the notice of the guards, made his way belowdecks.

The holding pen was brimming with its noisome cargo. Kim filled his bucket.

Nearly on tiptoe, he walked slowly up the deck toward the deserted bow.

Off to starboard he could see the *darra* frisking in

the red waters. Was it his imagination, or did they notice him and move closer in anticipation?

He swung the bucket up and tilted it to pour its squirming contents into the sea.

An arm got in the way of his swing, an oddly jointed, extremely elongated arm. It belonged to Assurna. Scowling, she pulled the bucket out of his hand and slammed it onto the deck.

"What are you doing?" she demanded. Her nose slits shivered. "Do you want to kill them all?"

Kim stared at her in angry confusion. "I'm feeding them. They'll starve otherwise, or eat one another. You told me that yourself. Or don't you care?"

"Fool. It's the end of the feeding season, the beginning of breeding. They'll die if they eat now."

Pointing at the assembled *darra,* Kim demanded, "Then why are they gathering?"

"They're animals. They like the taste of the food."

The science officer in him cut in. "You said that it's the beginning of breeding. Are you imposing artificial schedules on them?"

Assurna nodded sharply. "It's more efficient this way. When the food's cut off they begin to breed."

"Why don't you let the *darra* decide when to breed?" Kim demanded. "Or better yet, let them forage for themselves instead of making them dependent on you. What did they originally eat?"

"Each other. Us. Anything."

"Oh." He stared out at the hungry *darra* and felt helpless. Their many eyes seemed fixed intently upon him.

I'm sorry. I tried.

"How did you get down into the hold without the guards seeing you?" Assurna said.

"It wasn't difficult."

"I'll fix that."

Kim felt like telling her to guard the hold all she liked. *I can guarantee you none of us will be sneaking down there now that the* darra *won't be feeding.*

He said nothing of what he was feeling. He merely glared at the Micaszian and excused himself.

Borizus made good on his word and returned to *Voyager* with several kilos of matte purple-black alloy bars.

B'Elanna Torres ran a tricorder over the shipment, checked the readings, and nodded her approval. "Crude stuff, but we can work with it. Let's get it into the metal shop and I'll start recasting right away."

"Recast?" Borizus said, frowning.

"Got to filter out the impurities." She expected him to rear back in anger, but all the Sardalian did was nod.

"Filtering," he said quietly. "I see."

Well, Torres thought, perhaps he wasn't so impossible after all.

She marched into the fabrication works, trailing Borizus behind her. "It should only take a few moments to set up the recasting specifications."

The crucibles gaped, awaiting fresh metal. The mere sight of them raised Torres's spirits even higher. It was so good to be *doing* instead of theorizing.

The raw metal sank into the deep maw of the mixers and out of sight, to be superheated and whirled until all impurities fell away and were discarded. At this point, hardeners and matrix-enhancing strengtheners could be added.

After the newly mixed metal had been supercooled and re-formed, the resulting alloy would be ready to work with.

Torres switched on the mixers.

Humming, the crucibles vibrated into silvery blurs.

Minutes stretched as the crucibles heated, whirled, and re-formed the metal.

Torres waited impatiently, tapping her foot, until the metal had cooled and then once again been warmed to room temperature. The indicator light flicked from red to blue, which meant that the metal was safe to touch. The mixer lids clicked open and Torres reached in eagerly to scoop up the dull gray alloy.

Hefting it, she pronounced judgment. "Looks good."

Next it went into the hardener to be annealed, and from there to the fabricator to be shaped to specific templates.

When the metal was again safe to touch, Torres pulled it from the shaper and with Borizus's help piled the newly fabricated parts neatly upon a null-g cart.

Anticipation made her blood pound. At a near-run she hurried back to the main engineering bay.

The metal casings fit perfectly. As Torres prepared to snap the last connectors into place and weld them, she felt a slight thaw on her feelings toward the Sardalian. After all, he couldn't help being ill, could he?

Over her shoulder she said, "Borizus, this may have worked out better than I thought. The last-minute repairs gave me a chance to cull some of the original casting impurities out of the matrix. You may have inadvertently done us all a favor."

The Sardalian said nothing.

Torres didn't care. She was intent upon making the final painstaking seals. "There." She snapped off the welder. "I think that does it. We just have to test it. Borizus, this is the moment of truth."

There was no answer, not even a sour grunt from the tall Sardalian engineer. Torres began to wonder if she had really hurt his feelings.

"Now don't sulk, Borizus. I know I was a bit rough with you before, but you understand why, don't you? And now that you've brought me this metal supply I've been able to finish recasting the trigger connectors. I'll be able to move on to the thruster controls."

More silence.

He's really pushing it, Torres thought, and glanced up from her console. "Look, Borizus—"

He was gone. She was alone in engineering.

Torres recalled an earlier conversation with Borizus, and her comment, *Well, you've certainly learned your way around the ship, haven't you?*

Cursing, she reached for her communicator. "Engineering to Captain Janeway."

"Bridge here."

"Captain, Borizus has left engineering without notifying me. He's loose somewhere on the ship."

"What? Who's with him?"

"He's alone."

A moment later Kathryn Janeway's voice echoed through the corridors and companionways of the starship. "This is the captain. This is a stage-one alert. A Sardalian named Borizus is wandering the ship without clearance. He is not armed or considered dangerous at this time. But use caution. If you see him detain him and notify security immediately. Janeway out."

Torres nodded with grim satisfaction—she hadn't trusted Borizus from the start—and got back to work.

* * *

Kathryn Janeway exchanged a wordless glance with her security chief. Tuvok's face was placid as usual, but his eyes looked, well, troubled.

"Do you think he's an agent for Kolias?" she said. "Sent here to spy on us and that's why he sneaked away from B'Elanna?"

Tuvok nodded gravely. "Perhaps. His behavior is certainly suspicious. We must not rule out any possibilities."

Janeway leaned toward the Vulcan. "I can't help believing that Kolias is behind this. Borizus is his subordinate, isn't he? Possibly the Lord Councillor knows more—much more—about the disappearance of our crew members than he's willing to let on."

"Your suspicions may be warranted."

Janeway gave him a relieved look. "Get another security team on the search for Borizus. And keep scanning Kolias's communications."

"Aye, Captain."

Sickbay was a cool, quiet refuge of orderly calm and Kes was grateful for it. Here she could work freely without the distraction of the many minds and personalities that comprised *Voyager's* crew plucking at the edges of her empathic awareness. In sickbay she was at liberty to absorb as much information as the emergency medical holographic program—or the doctor, as she preferred to think of him—could throw in her direction. At the moment he was tossing tidbits about his most recent patient, Borizus.

"Interesting case," said the doctor. "An unusual body type. His weakness was apparently due to a chronic problem. I would have enjoyed studying the condition more thoroughly."

Kes marveled at the hologram's scientific curiosity. "Did you get any tissue samples?"

"Yes, although I haven't yet had time to analyze them. There's simply too much to do here."

"As usual." Kes was so accustomed to his complaints that half of the time she scarcely heard them. "Doctor, why don't we just scan the planet's surface for Kim and Paris?"

He weighed her query thoughtfully. He always did, never dismissing her questions, no matter how elementary. It was one of the things Kes liked best about the doctor.

"I believe that it would take a very long time to make such a detailed scan," he said. "If Kim and Paris are traveling—or being moved—that would further complicate matters."

"But don't they have anything distinctive about them? Moles or extra ribs or rudimentary tails? Something—anything—that would stand out in a crowd of Sardalians?"

"Well, let's investigate, shall we?" The doctor brought Ensign Kim's file up on the wallscreen. "As you can see, Mr. Kim is an unspectacular specimen: average blood pressure, blood gases, skeletal configuration. Nothing distinctive at all, aside from that epicanthic fold. And even that does us no good, since some Sardalians appear to have a similar eyelid structure."

"And Paris?" Kes said. "What about him? If we can find one of them we can probably locate the other."

Nodding, the doctor said, "Computer, show the file on Lieutenant Thomas Paris."

A schematic, overlaid by a grid of words, appeared on-screen. The doctor peered at it and frowned. "No, that's only my recent notes on Lieutenant Paris's burns. I want the main file on Tom Paris."

The flat female voice of *Voyager*'s computer replied immediately. "No further information is available on Thomas Paris."

The doctor frowned. "Have you searched the entire ship's memory?"

"Affirmative. Nothing more is on file."

"But that's impossible. Every single member of this crew has a comprehensive medical file." He paused, thinking. "Computer, show medical log extract seven-point-nine-eight-two-point-five."

A file flashed onto the desk screen. It was the same schematic that had appeared moments ago.

"Hmmm. So all I have is a partial treatment record on Mr. Paris. But I do see a brief notation to look for his main file. I must have noticed that it was missing."

"Why would Tom's records be missing? Do you suspect that someone removed them on purpose?" Distractedly Kes tucked a strand of blond hair behind the pointed tip of her right ear. "Why would anybody do that?"

"I don't know what to think. First a tricorder goes missing, and now this." The doctor shook his head. "Well, no matter. When you're finished cataloging those specimens I gave you, you can go, Kes."

"Same time tomorrow?" she said eagerly. There was so much to learn, so much to do.

The doctor favored her with a frosty smile. "Yes," he said. "Of course."

CHAPTER
11

"GET UP," THE GUARD SAID. "WE'VE GOT A NEW WORK detail for you."

Harry Kim blinked dazedly at the sudden disruption of his dreams. Beside him in the next bunk, Tom Paris was already sitting up. "What's going on here?"

"You'll find out. Get moving."

Kim and Paris found Marima already up and waiting outside the cabin. She flashed them both a nervous look, but otherwise remained composed, as they were led into the deeper recesses of the hold. The air was rank with the smell of old fish.

"Here." The guard handed them three bloody aprons. "Better get some gloves from that bin over there."

"I don't think I like this." Kim said.

Paris nodded. "I *know* I don't."

"Stop whispering," said the guard.

Both Kim and Paris had difficulty fitting the thin, elongated gloves meant for Sardalians over their own hands. Finally, they gave up.

"What is this place?" Marima demanded. Her tone had a ghost of the haughty daughter-of-the-Lord-Councillor in it.

Not now, not here, Kim thought.

Marima glared at the guard. "Where have you brought us, and why?"

His smile was ugly. "It's simple. You want more *darra?* Fine. Start by butchering the ones that were killed in your raid. Perhaps this will satisfy your need for *darra* blood."

Several wicked-looking knives were laid out upon a stained, makeshift cutting surface next to a series of manacles.

Paris pointed at the chains. "Why do we need these things?"

"We can't allow you to wander the ship with these knives, can we?"

The guard shackled each one of the hostages to the table. Only then did he allow them access to the knives.

A large vat sat in the corner. Jutting from it was at least half of a small, dead *darra.* The bronzed skin had gone flat brown and the iridescent spots had vanished.

The guard grabbed it and swung it up onto the table, where it landed with a moist, sickening *thunk.* "Now pay attention. This is how we do it. Slice between the flukes and the dorsal fin, like so. Make it a good, deep cut, and the flesh will practically divide in your hands. Try to avoid the pelvic fin—it's razor sharp."

Blood flowed over the knives and the cutter's hands, a thin orange flood spilling into shallow collecting basins whose narrow grooves sent it flowing down long flexible tubing toward refrigerated storage tanks.

It was a quick business to collect and store the blood. Only the meat was left.

"You'll want the smaller knives for the meat," the guard said. "Try the half-cleaver."

"This is disgusting," Marima said. "Evil."

"No," said the guard. "It's practical. And you're a fine one to be calling *us* evil." He pointed delicately with the tip of his curved knife. "Mind, also, the stomach, the eye spots, and the bell. Sometimes there are hidden stingers in there. And in the mouth, the cutting teeth and crushing teeth can do real damage if you grab them the wrong way."

"I thought you revered these fish," Kim said. He was beginning to feel queasy again.

"We do," the guard replied. "But we're practical people. A dead *darra* is no good to anyone if it's allowed to rot."

"And then what will you do with it?"

"Eat it. They're very tasty, you know. We process the blood and then the meat is used by the crew—or if there's enough, we freeze it for later."

The day stretched into twilight and then night before they were finished. Harry Kim's hair was stiff with blood and other bodily juices of the *darra* when the guard released him and his companions from their shackles.

Although Kim scrubbed mightily with the seawater and scraping tool that Assurna had provided, he felt only slightly less sticky as he crawled disgustedly into his bunk.

He fell asleep easily and quickly, but his dreams were haunted. He was swimming in a pure, clear water. But strange clouds began billowing, turning the water from a faint blue to an opaque orange. He was treading, gasping for air in great floods of orange *darra* blood as the undertow threatened to grab hold of him and sweep him away.

"Sickbay to Captain Janeway."

With misgivings, Janeway said, "Go ahead, Doctor."

Instantly the doctor appeared on-screen. "Captain, some sort of madman just tried to take me prisoner."

"What?"

"Yes, he tried to force me to accompany him down to the planet's surface. I tried to explain to him that I was a hologram, but the fool just wouldn't listen."

"Doctor, can you describe him?"

"He was the Sardalian that I treated in here several days ago."

"Borizus?"

"Yes."

"Is he still in sickbay?" Janeway's glance darted to Tuvok in hopeful anticipation.

"Negative. When I returned he had gone. The gratitude of some patients!"

"Doctor, that man is on the loose onboard *Voyager* without authorization. We're trying to catch him."

The aggrieved tone slipped back into the doctor's voice at near-warp speed. "Well. Why didn't you tell me that in the first place? I could have knocked him out with a mild sedative. Why, I ask you, am I never informed of the important developments on this ship?"

"You must have been turned off when I made the announcement."

"Perhaps. Well, Captain, if you can imagine, he came in groaning as though in terrible pain. I asked him what the problem was and he pointed to his head."

"Doctor," Janeway said crisply. "Could you speed it up? I'm extremely busy."

"When I came closer he pulled a scalpel out of its tray and tried to hold it against my neck. Preposterous." He paused. "Captain, you really should make a note to have all important announcements stored in my memory buffers."

"Fine. We'll discuss this later. Janeway out." Gripping the arms of her command chair, she turned to Tuvok. "You heard that, I assume? Borizus was seen in sickbay within the last fifteen minutes." She fought the urge to rest her head in her hands.

"I will advise my search team," said the Vulcan.

Janeway couldn't restrain a muffled curse. "Damn! We nearly had him."

Next to her, Chakotay nodded sympathetically. "We'll find him, Captain."

Frustration made Janeway restless. "Tuvok," she said. "Keep scanning the planet. I'll be in my ready room."

"Aye, Captain."

After Captain Janeway had left the bridge Tuvok again slowly scanned the center of Vandorra, searching for readings on Paris or Kim. As he expected, there was no sign of them.

The stoic Vulcan turned to the records of surface-to-ship communications and saw that the captain—and crew—had received a flood of invitations for social and cultural events.

Why, he wondered, were the Sardalians so eager for social interaction when their real interest seemed to be an exchange of technological information? Hadn't that fact been confirmed by the episode with Borizus? These people seemed almost as illogical as humans.

Back to the sensors and the comfort of their cool, indisputable schematics. Tuvok stared at them carefully. Those clusters of buildings along the shore seemed to be laboratories. In fact, there seemed to be an entire district completely devoted to scientific and medical investigation. Just what were the Sardalians researching so ardently?

The Vulcan security chief mistrusted the Sardalians. His captain would have called his reaction "instinctive," but Tuvok disdained such inconsistent unscientific impulses, although he admitted that they did exist in certain non-Vulcan species. He preferred to believe that his opinion was based, as always, upon irrefutable logic.

There was a strange edge to the Sardalians' friendliness, a tinge of desperation. That, coupled with the disappearance of *Voyager* crew members on shore leave, left Tuvok both curious and suspicious.

He tapped his commbadge. "Tuvok to Janeway."

"Go ahead."

"I recommend that security efforts be intensified even more, immediately. I would like to commence a steady twenty-four-hour scan of all surface communications."

"A hunch, Tuvok?"

He ignored the amusement in her voice. It was beneficial for the captain, he told himself, to relieve her stress through the human act of "teasing." "I have observed that the Sardalians have sent you no fewer than fifteen invitations to separate receptions. The number of invitations for the doctor are twice as numerous. In fact, he may be the most popular member of the crew as far as the Sardalians are concerned."

"He'll be surprised. And I'm surprised, considering that they have yet to meet him."

"Kolias met him, did he not?"

"What's your point, Tuvok?"

"Captain, I do not trust these people. Despite their pleasant facade I believe that they are withholding important information from us, information about themselves. And we do not know if Borizus is a free agent or acting under orders, possibly from Kolias, which seems likely."

"I concur. Very well, Tuvok. Add as many crew members to the security details as you deem necessary. And keep them looking for Borizus. I want him caught. You have the bridge."

"Then you are taking a rest?" He didn't bother to disguise the approval in his voice; the captain routinely overworked herself. If he had been accused of a personal concern for Kathryn Janeway, perhaps even a feeling of friendly regard, he would have refuted the charge, stating that his concern was merely for the well-being of the ship. If the captain didn't function well, *Voyager* wouldn't function well.

Janeway's tone was a sharp reprimand. He remembered yet again that she stubbornly detested his attempts to protect her schedule—and energy. "I'm taking a *short* break, Mr. Tuvok. A coffee break, more to the point, if there is anything remotely like that blessed substance still available on this ship. I'm heading down to the galley now."

"I believe you have a replicator in your quarters."

"It's not working."

"I will report that to maintenance. And—Captain?"

"Yes, Tuvok?"

"I remind you that you have a reception to attend within the hour in Vandorra."

Janeway sighed.

"Perhaps," the Vulcan ventured, "Commander Chakotay or I could attend in your place, with appropriate apologies."

The captain's hesitation alone indicated that she was tempted to accept the offer. Tuvok waited, anticipating that Captain Janeway would see the inescapable logic of his suggestion.

"It *is* tempting," she said. "But, no, I'd better not. Remember how offended the Sardalians were when I sent you down before? Besides, I'd rather have you onboard, scanning for Paris and Kim. At least somebody will be getting some work done."

"Then, Captain, refuse to attend as a way of indicating your displeasure over this incident with Borizus."

"Tuvok, so long as we require their cooperation I don't dare offend them. No, I'll go to their damned reception. But first I'll have my coffee." The comm channel cut off.

As Tuvok glanced down at the sensor display again he resolved to intercept any other invitations that might arrive for the captain—and lose them.

Harry Kim had just performed Mozart's Clarinet Concerto in A before a packed house at San Francisco's old Davies Symphony Hall. He had played well and the crowd was applauding wildly.

"Thank you," he said, keeping his tone humble. "And now I'd like to play something for you that I first heard on a planet called Sardalia in the faraway Delta Quadrant."

The audience was rapt as he made his way through the sinuous melody.

> . . . *"We fell, and fell,*
> *And are falling, still."*

At the end of the tune the crowd went crazy, cheering, whistling, roaring its approval. A beautiful young girl with cascading dark hair stood up on her seat, blew him a kiss, and began to pelt him with roses.

Soon Kim was covered with the silky ruby-colored blossoms. Their rich perfume made him dizzy and giddy, and he laughed happily until a thorn caught him in the neck.

"Ow!" Kim came awake with a jolt. It was dark in the cabin, the middle of the night, and Tom Paris was beside him, poking him and whispering, "Wake up!"

"I am up." Kim glared at him. "What do you want?"

Paris clapped a hand over his mouth. "Shh! Listen."

Someone nearby was speaking loudly. "What do you mean you can't help us?" It was the voice of Assurna, the Micaszian ship's captain, cutting through the silence of the night. "Don't be ridiculous. We've told you our terms."

Paris cast a warning glance at Kim. "This doesn't sound good. She's raising her voice."

"What do you think is going on?" Kim said.

"She's trying to negotiate something, that's for sure." Paris crept closer to the main cabin, ducking down to avoid the gaze of the guard.

Assurna continued her protest. "But I tell you she's

his daughter! What do you mean that you require proof? What sort of proof, an ear? An eye? Despite what you may think, we're not barbarians." Her voice grew shrill. "I demand that you put me through to Lord Kolias's office at once. He'll believe me."

A long pause punctuated by small sounds from Assurna indicated that she was listening intently.

When next she spoke there was a note of weary hopelessness in her voice. "Very well, if you say that he isn't there then I'll make another attempt to reach him later."

Kim stared at Paris. "I'll bet she's trying to work out our release—but it sounds like somebody isn't cooperating on the other end. That's crazy."

"Strange land, strange people," Paris said. "I'd say our chances of survival aren't improving."

Kim gave his crewmate a grim look. "I wish I could find something positive to say, but for once I'm afraid I have to agree with you, Tom."

Kathryn Janeway had her jaw set and a dangerous intensity to her gaze as she strode along the corridor of Deck Five. The captain of *Voyager* was determined to find some drinkable coffee or else bloody well know why not. She had searched both the officer's and general mess, but answers—and coffee—had proved maddeningly elusive. Not one replicator seemed to be functioning.

"Janeway to bridge. Tuvok, how's the search for Paris and Kim going?"

"Inconclusive, Captain. Our ground teams have found nothing. We are continuing to scan."

"Call me as soon as you know anything."

"Of course, Captain."

The implacable patience in his voice irritated her. "What about that Sardalian engineer?"

"He is also proving . . . elusive."

Was that an actual note of frustration? Janeway couldn't resist goading her security chief. "How can one Sardalian elude the entire ship's internal sensor system?"

"Unknown, Captain."

"Well, I like a mystery even less well than you do, Tuvok. Find him."

Rummaging through the galley in the officer's mess, Janeway was unable to locate the bottle of her favorite vanilla extract, perfect for topping off coffee. In fact, she couldn't find the emergency coffeemaker either.

She searched the mess storage once again, suspicion growing. It was gone, really gone. First her crew, then the tricorder, and now her favorite vanilla extract. That was a few too many things missing to suit the captain of *Voyager*. But she had a sneaking suspicion where she might find some of them.

Janeway tapped her commbadge. "Janeway to Neelix."

"Yes, Captain?" The Talaxian sounded faint, far away, and distracted.

"I want to see you."

"Er, you do? I'm a bit busy right now, Captain. Why don't I call you back in a little while?"

To Janeway's astonishment, the Talaxian cut the communication from his end.

"Computer," she said. "Locate Mr. Neelix for me."

"Mr. Neelix is in his quarters," the flat contralto voice replied.

"Mr. Neelix," said Janeway, her tone deadly calm.

"Uh—yes, Captain?"

"The mountain is coming and Mohammed had better damned well prepare himself."

"Mo—who, Captain?"

"Janeway out."

She strode purposefully out the door, intending to explain Starfleet protocol—and obedience—until the Talaxian's ears were blistered.

At the entrance to the turbolift Janeway nearly collided with B'Elanna Torres as she emerged from the lift.

"Captain! I was on my way to see you."

"What is it, B'Elanna?"

"I still think I could speed up our repair process if I were allowed to go down there and supervise the metals collection myself. There are so many impurities in the alloys they supply. I'm sure I could make better selections. And now, with Borizus's latest behavior, I don't trust any of those Sardalians any more."

Janeway folded her arms across her chest and stared at her chief engineer wearily, both impressed and appalled by her tenacity. *You never give up, do you?* Aloud, she said, "B'Elanna, I just can't spare you. You've instructed your engineering staff on what to look for below. I should think that would be sufficient."

"I think you just don't trust me to deal with the Sardalians. Captain, don't you think I'm competent?"

"Of course I do, B'Elanna. That's beside the point."

"I know you had your doubts . . ."

"Those were settled long ago. Do you think I would have made you chief of engineering if I didn't trust you? But you're absolutely crucial to the repair of the helm control. I don't see how you can be spared right now."

Torres dug in, hands across her chest. "You know I see possibilities in things that few others do."

Janeway had to give her credit. The woman *was* one of the most gifted engineers she had ever encountered. Her concern was commendable, but right now she just wasn't using her head. "That's exactly why I need you here," she said. "B'Elanna, don't you think that I would send you down to the surface in a minute if I thought it would help?"

"But—"

Tuvok's voice cut in. "Yellow alert. An intruder is in transporter room one. Security detail to transporter room one on the double."

"On my way," Janeway said. She stepped into the turbolift with Torres right beside her. "Deck Four."

Moments later she and Torres were racing down the corridor toward the transporter room.

Tuvok was waiting for them.

"Have you frozen the controls?" Janeway asked.

"Yes. But he has managed to jam the door lock."

"I'll fix that," said Torres. "Is he armed?"

"Unknown. Nothing we would recognize as a weapon is registering on my tricorder scan."

Three security guards pelted around the curve of the corridor and skidded to a halt, coming smartly to attention as they saw Tuvok and Janeway.

"Sir. Captain."

"When Lieutenant Torres opens the doors, you are to enter and secure the chamber," Tuvok told them.

"Aye, sir."

Torres had the panel off the door controls and was busily rerouting the main circuit. "Almost there," she said.

"On my signal," said the Vulcan.

Torres nodded. "Okay."

"Now," Tuvok said.

Torres keyed the lock mechanism and the doors flew open. Weapons drawn, the security guards raced inside with Janeway and Tuvok on their heels.

Borizus was crouched, frozen, upon the transporter grid, his eyes wide with surprise.

In his hand was the purloined tricorder.

Tuvok walked toward him and silently extended his palm.

The Sardalian engineer surrendered the tricorder, not meeting the Vulcan's implacable gaze.

The captain tapped her commbadge. "Janeway to the bridge."

"Chakotay here."

Her voice was crisp and curt. "Please call Kolias and tell him that I'll be unavoidably delayed."

CHAPTER

12

"I'LL ASK AGAIN," JANEWAY SAID. "WHY DID YOU STEAL the medical tricorder?"

Borizus sat in the brig, remote and taciturn, his long arms folded upon his chest. His expression was stony, a set, defiant mask. Only his nose slits quivered occasionally.

Tuvok sat at the small table near the door, flanked by security men. His face did not betray weariness, but his gaze was slightly distracted. The Vulcan had relentlessly grilled the Sardalian using every tactic he knew, with no useful results.

Janeway had tried her hand next, but made no better progress. She gazed thoughtfully at the Sardalian and longed, for the third time in several hours, for direct access to a Starfleet's Judge Advocate general. How gladly she would have consigned Borizus to their tender mercies: penal colonies, diplomatic protest, trade restrictions. For half a cup of Columbian coffee, Janeway would happily have tossed Borizus out the nearest airlock.

But Starfleet and its legal options were thousands of light years away. Here in the Delta Quadrant Janeway had exactly two alternatives: to keep Borizus locked up aboard *Voyager* for the duration of their journey back home—however long that might be—or to return him to Sardalia and the chastisements of his own authorities.

Neither choice would provide her with the information she needed. The time had come for a bluff.

"You realize that we have recourse to severe penalties for theft." She leaned closer, her voice pitched at an intimate level. "We can send you to one of our penal colonies to do hard time. You would never see Sardalia again."

Tuvok turned, his attention sharply focused on his commanding officer. Janeway ignored the question in his eyes. "Do you hear me, Borizus? Do you really want to spend the rest of your life on this ship, in this room? It will happen."

Was that a crack in the Sardalian's mask? Janeway bore down hard. "I promise you, Borizus. We'll keep you locked up until your teeth fall out."

The Sardalian was growing distinctly pale. His nasal slits vibrated as his respiration—and distress—increased.

Janeway nodded in mock sympathy. "Yes, it's a shame that you'll never be able to see your home or loved ones again. If you have any children, I'm sorry for them. They'll never see their father again." She paused, shook her head sadly, and drifted away from him to stand at the viewscreen, hands laced together behind her. "It's such a cold, dark universe out there. And to spend your existence among hostile strangers, far from home . . ." She left the sentence unfinished.

Borizus grunted. It was the first sound he had made in two hours.

"Of course," Janeway said. "I might be inclined toward leniency if you showed any signs of cooperating with us." She let the suggestion hang upon the air.

Borizus unfolded his arms and rested his hands on his knees. Looking down, he muttered in sepulchral tones, "This is all that fool Kolias's fault."

Janeway felt her pulse quickening. "How so?"

The Sardalian kept his gaze averted. "I told him that we should negotiate directly with you. But that's never been his style. He's a poor leader, an imbecile."

"He seems to be ill."

A shrug. "Who isn't ill on Sardalia?"

Janeway pushed a little harder. "Why don't you tell me about it? Is that why you wanted the tricorder?"

Borizus glared at her. "Let Kolias tell you," he said bitterly. "He's Lord Councillor, isn't he? I'm merely a subordinate. Therefore, I follow orders. I can do nothing without his leave."

"So you admit that you were operating under his orders?"

Again Borizus shrugged. "I don't want to go to your prison. We Sardalians require special treatment in old age. I don't want to suffer and die here, among strangers."

"I don't blame you." Now she radiated exaggerated sympathy and understanding: Borizus was just a flunky, intimidated into silence by his superiors. "And of course we're certain that *you* didn't initiate the plan to steal our equipment."

Slightly, ever so slightly, Borizus's expression eased. He craned his head up above his shoulders. His nasal slits barely moved.

Janeway laid it on even thicker. "Why, after all, should you take the blame for Kolias's schemes?"

"Why indeed?" Borizus warmed to the argument. "He's a successful politician. He allows others to take responsibility for his designs. It's ever so with politicians, leaving the real people, the real workers to take the blame."

Janeway moved in for the kill. "And what design did he have on us?"

Borizus gave her a quick, dark look. "To learn that, you must ask him."

"But I'm asking you."

The Sardalian shrugged nervously, refolded his arms across his chest, and lowered his head.

Damn. Janeway flashed Tuvok a look of pure frustration. "Lock him up again," she said. "I'm going to have a little chat with Lord Kolias."

The golden city of Vandorra twinkled in the dying sunlight, its spires glittering with reflected light. Intent upon her target—Kolias—Janeway scarcely noticed the city's beauty.

She did, however, observe a group of people clinging together silently in the shadows of the Great Hall.

There were about eighteen or twenty of them, their faces painted ashen white and their lavender hair covered by pale hoods. Their clothing, too, was white, giving them a sepulchral appearance that was heightened by the looming shadows of dusk.

They stared at Janeway without a quiver of animation or acknowledgment of her presence. It was as if they were looking right through her. Janeway wasn't accustomed to being ignored. Then she corrected herself. *They're not ignoring me. Their attention is merely . . . elsewhere. What a strange, spooky bunch.*

She half-expected them to float away silently, dissipating on the cool evening breeze.

She risked a greeting. "Hello."

Golden eyes stared at her and through her.

"Excuse me?" Janeway asked. "Is there some problem? Something wrong?"

Not a flicker passed among them.

Suddenly chilled to her marrow, Janeway turned and hurried past them into the warmth of the Great Hall. The towering guards, resplendent in their purple robes, nodded at her as she went past them.

"Captain Janeway?" A slender woman whose pink hair was plaited with crystalline lights stood at the foot of a massive flight of stairs. "Lord Kolias requested that I convey you to the reception. But isn't the doctor with you?"

Janeway stared at her in some perplexity. "Was he expected?"

"The invitation was for both of you."

"Well, he couldn't make it."

The woman's nose slits quivered gently. "This way."

Janeway followed her guide into the banquet hall. The reception appeared to be in full swing. Bell-like tones cascaded through the air and the scent of rich spices filled the room with sweet pungency.

She scanned the crowd until she found Lord Kolias settled on a high-backed perch upholstered in rich ruby cloth. Briskly she moved toward him.

Kolias rose as she approached. "Ah, Captain," he said. "At last. You *have* kept us waiting. And where is the doctor?"

Again, the emphasis on the doctor, Janeway thought. What was going on here? "He couldn't join us."

The Lord Councillor stared at her. "But I've invited his local colleagues. To honor him." Kolias indicated several well-turned-out Sardalians in the crowd. "They'll be so disappointed. Are you certain you can't persuade him to change his mind?"

"Absolutely. It's out of the question."

Kolias's nasal slits began to vibrate.

"Lord Kolias," Janeway said. "We *must* talk."

"Oh, we will, Captain. We will." He settled himself back on his perch and gestured to a page carrying a bowl of snuff.

"I mean *now.*" Janeway took a step toward him, coming between Kolias and the snuff. "There are certain issues that absolutely must be settled."

Was that a flare of irritation she saw in the Lord Councillor's eyes?

"This is not the time . . ."

"It's never the time, is it?" She gazed at him coldly. "I'm afraid, Lord Councillor, that I have to be blunt with you. If we don't discuss my concerns in private I'll lay them all out for you—and the assembled guests—here and now." She paused, letting that sink in. "The reason I was late was because of the criminal actions of one of your own people."

Kolias grew pale. "A Sardalian offended you? Tell me his name and I'll personally see to his punishment."

"His name is Borizus."

Lord Kolias stared at her as if unable to believe what he had just heard. "The second councillor? God's eyes! And what has he done to displease you?"

"He's stolen equipment—or attempted to steal it—from my ship."

"This is a very grave charge, Captain."

"I know, sir. I wouldn't make it if I hadn't caught

him in the very act." She stared at the Lord Councillor, thinking, *your move, Kolias.*

Kolias rose, towering above his fellows. "We must discuss these matters in private." He nodded, gesturing for Janeway to accompany him. Two assistants cleared a path for them through the crowd.

They moved quickly away from the banquet hall and down a high arched corridor. A small hallway led into a plush, well-appointed room. Kolias settled onto the lavender cushions of a capacious seat with an air of relief and ownership. These were his personal apartments, Janeway supposed.

"Where is Borizus now?" asked the Lord Councillor.

Janeway said, "I have the man in custody onboard my ship. Frankly, I'd be grateful if you took him off my hands."

"Of course. But what did he steal?"

"A tricorder." She paused as what might have been a look of incomprehension flitted across the Sardalian's face. "A diagnostic tool from our medical clinic."

"I see." Kolias didn't seem very surprised.

"Also, Lord Councillor," she said. "Are you aware that two of my crew members are missing?"

Kolias's gaze froze. His nasal slits moved slowly in and out. "I had heard something of this when I visited your ship. A shame about your crew."

"We haven't been able to find them. And we've been doing a lot of looking."

"I'm aggrieved to hear it."

"We'd certainly appreciate any help you might be able to give us. I understand that your own daughter is missing as well."

The Lord Councillor's pain surfaced quickly in his eyes. "Yes. I haven't heard from her in days."

"Then we have a problem in common," Janeway said. "Let's work together and help one another."

"Of course," said Kolias listlessly.

Janeway leaned toward him. "I've got two men lost on this planet. I need to know whether they're in any danger."

Kolias managed to look both thoughtful and wounded at the same time. "Captain, we are an innately peaceful people. I hope—and assume—your crew members are well. Perhaps, if you're concerned, you could have your doctor come down to analyze any potential risks to your people."

"Kolias, you seem extremely interested in my ship's doctor—"

"Pardon, lord." A junior councillor bustled into the room. "Forgive this intrusion, but I must speak with you. A matter of the highest urgency." His body language implied the need for privacy.

Kolias turned to Janeway and said, "Will you excuse us, Captain?"

"Of course," she said reluctantly. "I'll just go stretch my legs."

She sauntered back toward the reception hall.

In the center of the room two elongated dancers were making spidery movements within a tent of pink and gold transparent silk. They were accompanied by several musicians who pressed elaborate bronzed tubes to their nose slits and coaxed forth strange bleats and whispers.

Janeway watched, pondering the incongruity here. The Sardalians obviously loved beauty and luxury. They ate well, pampered themselves, cared deeply about their arts. Why, then, did they all look so weak and unhealthy? The Lord Councillor's complexion had appeared gray beneath a light coating of rouge, and his subordinates were similarly pasty. The group of nobles gathered in the hall seemed gaunt and weak. Several were clinging to chair backs or each other in an effort to remain upright.

Maybe it's normal for Sardalians to look like they're always on the edge of collapse.

She knew that if she questioned him directly Kolias would prove elusive. "No, no," he would say. "We're all fine. Nothing is wrong. And what a shame about your crew."

What a shame about your crew.

Janeway started, stung yet again by the recurring thought: What if Kolias *were* responsible for the disappearance of Paris and Kim? Was he holding them as pawns in some sinister trading scheme that he had not yet made apparent?

Starfleet tacticians had long ago drilled into her the habit of investigating problems from as many angles as possible. This was one angle whose slant Janeway didn't like, not at all.

And why were they all so anxious to see the doctor? Something was extremely wrong here.

Turning her back on the glittering proceedings, she made her way out of the banquet hall and nearly tripped over a sleepy-eyed page curled into a nestlike arrangement of cushions.

"Where's the washroom?" Janeway growled.

He jumped to his feet, nasal slits flapping, and stared at her.

"The washroom?"

"Just down the hallway, then. Mind the stairs."

Janeway found the facilities. At a glance they seemed to be functional despite their elaborately gilded and painted surfaces. Once inside she bolted the door and opened a shielded channel directly to *Voyager*.

"Janeway here."

"Captain?" The first officer's voice was a steady reminder to her of all that she cared about.

"Chakotay, I want you to monitor the Lord Councillor's movements and communications."

"Every communication, Captain?"

"Everything. If he gets a complaint from the garbage collectors, I want to know about it. I don't trust him and I'm more convinced than ever that he had something to do with the disappearance of Paris and Kim. And pay special attention to any messages concerning medical matters."

"I'll get on it right away."

"Good. Janeway out."

On her way back to the banquet hall she heard rustling from behind a lush canopy. Was someone following her? Attempting to eavesdrop?

There was definite movement behind the banded drapery. She crept nearer. The fabric rustled again.

Janeway flung the curtain aside, expecting to see some red-faced subcouncillor brandishing a sword.

Instead, a purple-skinned quadruped came bounding out at her with a rocking-horse gait and nearly bowled her over.

It had two sets of bright orange eyes, a long, tapered snout, and no apparent ears whatsoever.

Instinctively Janeway held out her hand, palm open. "I won't hurt you, little one."

A shudder ran through the beast and it blinked its many eyes many times. Cautiously it approached, snout quivering, until it was almost within touching range.

Just a little closer. "C'mon," Janeway urged. "I really don't bite."

With a bound the creature landed at Janeway's feet and rubbed its head against her legs. Making an odd bubbling sound, it arched its back. Polished silver orbs had been braided into ridges of thick amethyst fur along its flanks and neck.

"You little sweetheart," Janeway said, patting the downy hide and savoring its silky feel. The orbs chimed faintly with each stroke. "You're somebody's favorite pet, aren't you?" For a moment Janeway was reminded of Molly Malone, her own sweet dog so far away, and the thought brought an expanding lump to her throat.

The creature jumped back playfully and sped away around a corner, out of sight.

At the same moment, a coltish young Sardalian child, all legs and arms and streaming lilac hair, clattered down the far end of the hallway, calling, "Dai! Dai, come here, you bad *mogwik.* Come back here!" Before Janeway could make a move, the child had bolted through a doorway and was gone.

But the pup had dashed in the other direction. Sighing, Janeway started after it. At least she could return somebody else's pet to its owner.

There. A flash of purple fur.

She darted around a column.

The *mogwik* stood in the hallway, watching her.

"Dai?" she said softly. "Come here, Dai."

The animal seemed delighted that she had joined the game. It took off at a dead run.

She chased it through several storage rooms, under an arched and fluted doorway, and down a long, winding stone gallery. Finally she cornered it against a broad tapestry.

"Dai, sit!"

The pup doubled back between her legs.

Janeway spun, but the *mogwik* had disappeared.

Perhaps in here, she thought, gazing into a massive, carpeted room. She stepped down two broad steps and entered the chamber.

It was empty. Neat rows of pictures were hanging on the gray stone walls.

"Dai?" She whistled as she would for her own dog. "Here, baby."

There was no answer but the sound of her own breathing. Janeway turned to go.

Wait. Those pictures.

They were primitive representations of people slaughtering what looked like fierce ovoid animals with many teeth. The animals appeared to hover in the air—or were they swimming? Janeway looked carefully. Yes, some sort of aquatic animal, fighting for its life as hunters attempted to butcher it. In other pictures the hunters could be seen devouring the meat. Was this the "innate peacefulness" of the Sardalians to which Kolias had referred?

Slowly Janeway toured the room. The works reminded her of both the cave paintings she had seen on Betair Seven and the art that was such a ritual part of the religion of the Nesclun Moon Pygmies.

She studied the works with particular attention. Although she was no student of galactic art history, these were obviously highly significant paintings.

Smaller rooms deepened from the main show hall and contained more refined artwork of later periods, primarily portraits of dignitaries and their families, or so they seemed to be.

A tiny alcove held one object: a viewscreen. Janeway studied it with some curiosity. It seemed rudimentary but was apparently functional. She waved her hand in front of it, but was disappointed when neither her body heat nor movement triggered the machine. Hesitantly she tapped the front of the screen as she had seen professors do with antique display units on Earth. Nothing happened.

She began to turn away, but her eye fell upon a silvery disk set into the side of the screen. Janeway pressed it and the screen sprang to life.

A blizzard of red and gray particles danced on the screen and solidified into a photo of the Great Hall. Martial music played as a stentorian voice intoned: "Our history is one of pageantry, bravery, great sea hunts, and battles with the *darra* for control of the water."

Proud music pumped away behind the sonorous voice as the lecture continued. "Over time we have learned to resolve our problems without violence, to farm the *darra,* to respect and not plunder the seas. To make the most of our precious resources."

Images chased one another across the screen: a parade of Sardalian progress. Big cities under construction, great ships setting sail, bridges being built.

"There seemed to be no limit to our achievements. Our cities blossomed. Trade prospered. We were even visited by travelers from the stars. And, in response, we began to develop our own plans for interplanetary travel."

Schematics for crude rockets appeared. Kolias was shown, briefly, welcoming a group of short, squat, hairless humanoids.

Visitors from another system? Janeway wondered.

"We have met every challenge, overcome every obstacle."

Abruptly, the images darkened and the music moved into a minor key.

"But now the greatest obstacle of all has appeared. The gray plague has struck, devastating families, reaching into every aspect of our lives. No more serious threat to our civilization exists today."

Scenes flashed across the screen of Sardalians lying weak and dazed in beds. Of great ships idled, and white-faced citizens holding vigils by the Great Hall.

"Some saw it as a curse; others, as retribution from the gods. Even now, many of us find it difficult to address.

"We don't know where it came from. Perhaps it has always been with us. But we will fight it and triumph as we have triumphed before. Each day Sardalian scientists make progress in their quest to find a cure. Please support their efforts. And take hope. We will find an answer."

The screen went dark.

Stunned, Janeway pondered what she had just heard. The gray plague? A threat to Sardalia's civilization? What did it mean?

Her speculations were interrupted by a sudden nudge from behind, just below her knees.

Her purple-furred friend was back.

Absently, she petted its quivering snout. *Answers.* There were certainly questions here that she wanted answered.

Janeway twined her fingers into the *mogwik's* fur. It pulled away in alarm but she held fast.

"Oh, no," she told it. "I'm not going to chase you anymore." She swept up the struggling animal and made her way back to the main hall.

Kolias stood near just inside the banquet hall's

grand entrance. His eyes widened as she approached. "Captain," he said. "Where in the world did you find that *mogwik?*"

"In your museum, Lord Councillor. And only after much work."

The lilac-haired child appeared from behind a fluted column. "Dai!" she cried. "You've found her."

Janeway deposited the *mogwik* into the girl's outstretched arms.

"Tulila, I thought you would take better care of Dai," Kolias said sternly.

"I will, lord. I promised Marima I'd look after her. I won't let her get away again." Clutching the animal to her chest, the child scurried off down the corridor.

"My daughter's pet," said Kolias.

"I see."

"Captain, we were begining to become concerned as to your whereabouts." Was that nervous suspicion she detected behind the Lord Councillor's solicitous mask of goodwill?

"I've had quite an interesting time in your museum," Janeway said. "And learned a great deal."

Kolias's nose slits began to flutter.

She thought briefly of the group of spectral Sardalians she had passed on her way to the reception. "Lord Kolias, when I arrived here I encountered a group of your citizens dressed in white. They were massed silently near the front of the Great Hall, staring. What were they doing?"

"That was an official protest," Kolias said. His nasal slits were a blur. "It'a an honored tradition in Vandorra, a means by which citizens may express their opinions."

"But what were they protesting?"

"Who knows?" The Lord Councillor sounded uncomfortable. "It could be any number of things. Someone is always dissatisfied."

Janeway sensed that he was hiding something. Her appetite for subterfuge, never expansive, had been nearly exhausted in the brief time she had been on Sardalia.

"Lord Kolias," she said. "I'd really like some answers. *Now.*"

"But, Captain, you speak so harshly." His nasal slits were positively vibrating. "Is something else wrong? Has someone else offended you?"

Janeway aimed right for the chink in his etiquette. "Yes, Lord Kolias. *You.* You have offended me."

"And how have I done this?"

"You've failed in your duty as a host."

Kolias's face reddened. "Have I?"

"Yes. You've refused to respond to my questions honestly."

"Captain, please. I thought I'd made my intentions clear in the matter of Borizus."

Janeway refused to be deflected. "And still you refuse to answer."

"I don't understand. Perhaps you're not feeling well? Is this sort of behavior typical of your people?" He looked genuinely perplexed, as though the only cause he could find for this grievous breach of etiquette was illness—possibly of a psychological variety.

Janeway bristled at the implication. "The only problem with health that I'm aware of seems to concern *your* people, Kolias. And the gray plague. Is that why you're so anxious to have *Voyager's* doctor visit you?"

The Lord Councillor's cheeks flushed deep vermilion. "You should not have mentioned that word in this company. We never discuss such things in a place like this." He pulled his head down between his shoulders. His expression had turned as hard and unyielding as a graven mask.

Hmmm. Time for Plan B. Janeway modulated her voice to its softest, most ingratiating tone. "Forgive me, Lord Kolias. I've offended you and I apologize most humbly. I am, after all, a stranger here."

"Whose ways are most blunt and unfamiliar!"

"Yes, yes, forgive me, please. Not for anything would I insult a fine gentleman like yourself and the people assembled here." She made certain that her nod encompassed the courtiers as well as Kolias. *It's just like my holonovel, where I play Lucie, the governess of Lord Burleigh's estate. Bowing. Scraping. Curtseying. All in a day's work, I suppose.* Janeway kept her expression pleasant and held out her hands, palms open, toward Kolias.

The Lord Councillor seemed mollified. His head emerged from between his shoulders and he nodded. "Well, let us put that behind us. Captain Janeway, I urge you to choose your words carefully in our company."

"Of course. And may I ask another question?"

"What is it?"

"Can you imagine why Borizus might have stolen our medical equipment?"

Kolias met her gaze firmly. "I have no idea, Captain. None whatsoever. Please return him to us so that we may deal with him appropriately."

"Of course." Plainly it was time to go. Janeway took the escape route that Kolias had helpfully suggested. "In truth," she said, "I'm feeling a bit fatigued, Lord Councillor. Perhaps I should return to my ship now. Please excuse me. Carry on with your splendid evening."

"Good evening, Captain."

She hurried out of the room. Once safely out of sight of the guests, Janeway tapped her commbadge.

"Voyager. One to beam up."

A shaft of humming light came and took her away.

CHAPTER
13

Marima made her way across the deck, hand over hand along the railing, and settled down carefully beside Tom Paris.

"Hey, stranger." He smiled and offered her a spoonful of the thin, pink, fishy gruel that was his midday rations. Paris suspected that it was made from *darra* parts, but he really didn't want to know.

She shook her head in refusal. "Just wanted to feel the sun." Leaning back, she closed her eyes and rested her head against the outer wall of the cabin. Her lavender hair looked stringy and unkempt.

Paris stared at the girl. Lines had been etched into her pale skin by her pain. Grimly he wondered how far the disease had progressed. He knew that each night she was wracked by convulsions. It was obvious that she was growing weaker, despite her assurances that each attack was not in itself life threatening. Paris didn't think that she looked strong enough to weather another big one. With relief he watched her slip into a light sleep.

He lifted his head to look for Harry Kim, although he already had a suspicion of where he would find him.

Sure enough, Kim was leaning against the deck railing, badgering the Micaszians with concerns about the *darra,* forcing them to lean down and talk to him, fraternizing with the enemy, including Assurna.

Kim seemed fascinated by the big sea creatures. He couldn't ask enough questions: Was there anything that the *darra* wouldn't eat? Did they sleep? How many young did they spawn? How long did it take to raise them? Did they stay together in pods? How long did the average *darra* live?

It was driving Paris mad. Harry Kim seemed like a data-hungry machine. "Harry," he called. "Give it a rest, will you?"

Either Kim chose to ignore him or he was too deep in discussion about *darra* breeding habits to hear him.

Paris was about to raise his voice even louder to make his point when he saw something that drove all thoughts of *darra* right out of his head.

A winged man, floating through the air above the ship. Long purple wings of incredible delicacy were strapped to his back. His legs seemed to be lashed into a sack of some sort.

I'm cracking up. Losing it. A flying man?

As he stared in fascination, Marima stirred beside him and opened her golden eyes. "Paris?" She looked up, following his gaze. "Oh."

"What's keeping him up?" Paris said.

"Air currents. He can hang from those wings for hours so long as the wind holds."

"He's tied into a harness?"

"Yes. The Micaszians like to use this to aid navigation. It's an old tradition with them."

"Then it's not recreational?"

"No. At least, I don't think so."

"That's dumb." He turned to shout in Kim's direction. "Hey, Harry, look up."

For a moment Kim glanced upward, but almost immediately turned his attention back to the guard. Paris doubted that the glider had even registered on him.

As Paris watched, the glider swooped down to circle over the ship, and he felt the hot needle of envy in his soul. Not that he wished to be hanging in midair between two wings, no, thank you. But it reminded him of *Voyager,* and how badly he wanted to be back on that ship's bridge, awaiting Kathryn Janeway's command.

The glider made one more lazy circle and landed neatly upon the foredeck.

Show's over. Stop mooning, Thomas. Paris stood up and sauntered over to bedevil Harry Kim a bit. "Hey, Harry. Planning a change of career?" he said. "Thinking of giving up the operations game and becoming a *darra* herder instead? Want to settle down here at sea?"

Kim frowned sharply. "Real funny, Tom. I just think this is a rare opportunity to learn about these unusual animals. Besides, it keeps me from paying attention to my stomach."

He turned back to the Micaszians and Paris heard him ask eagerly, "Have you tried to increase the number of offspring they have or increase their breeding cycles?"

"It's not possible," Assurna replied.

"How do they reproduce?"

"Parthenogenically, by budding. The lack of food seems to trigger the breeding hormone."

"So that's why you cut off the worms," Paris said. "How many offspring do they have?"

Assurna gave him a deeply suspicious look, as if she could countenance Harry Kim's questions but knew that Paris's were just idle chatter. "One per season," she said slowly. "And it's years until they're mature enough for our purposes."

"What about breeding them at regular intervals?"

"Too complicated a procedure, catching and releasing the *darra*. It risks too much injury to them. And us." Assurna nodded in dismissal and without another word stalked back toward the pilot's cabin.

"There's got to be a better way," Kim said stubbornly. "I know there is."

Paris shook his head in mock dismay. "That's just the scientist in you talking."

Kim shot him a sidelong glance that was probably meant to be a warning. "Don't you have any scientific curiosity about anything, Tom?"

He pretended to strike a thoughtful pose. "I don't know. I never thought about it. Wait—yeah, okay. I'll tell you what I'm curious about, Harry. I'm curious about how we're going to get back to *Voyager*. Does that count? And I'm beginning to think we should just get a big white flag and wave it. How about if you turn your scientific curiosity to that dilemma?"

"I already have." Kim sounded resigned. "I took a look at their radio equipment. It's just too crude—I couldn't jigger it to reach any of *Voyager*'s lowest comm wavelengths. They'd never hear us."

Paris frowned. He hadn't even considered the ship's rudimentary radio. He patted Kim on the shoulder. "Well, just keep thinking, Harry."

"Anything to avoid the heaves. Hey, where are you going?"

"I want to keep an eye on Marima." Paris gave him a sad half-smile and resumed his post beside the sleeping girl.

Janeway paced the length of her ready room as her thoughts swept over the uncooperative Kolias, her missing crew members, and the desperate need to finalize repairs to *Voyager* and resume their journey.

Her musings were interrupted by a general announcement. "Attention everyone. An important announcement."

It was Neelix, commandeering intership communications without regard for regulations or protocol.

As usual. Janeway reminded herself that Neelix *had* been tremendously helpful to the crew of *Voyager*, acting as guide, cook, and self-appointed morale officer. His enthusiasm was admirable. *If only he respected—or even remembered—Starfleet procedures.*

The Talaxian's voice bubbled over the ship comm. "Dinner will be served half an hour later tonight so that your chef may give the proper amount of time and effort required for a new delicacy. Oh, you're in for a treat if I do say so myself! I repeat, dinner will be delayed half an hour."

Neelix.

Janeway suddenly remembered her unsatisfactory exchange hours ago with the Talaxian, and further, some unfinished business regarding missing vanilla and coffee pots.

"Computer," she said. "Locate Mr. Neelix."

"Neelix is in his quarters."

Janeway tapped her commbadge again. "Chakotay, you have the bridge." Briskly she strode out of her ready room and into the turbolift.

"Deck Four."

The door to Neelix's quarters was locked tight. Janeway buzzed for admittance.

"Just a moment," said a muffled voice that sounded like Neelix and Kes both talking at once.

Sighing, Janeway tapped her communicator. "Captain Janeway to Neelix."

"Yes, Captain?"

"Open your door."

"Yes, ma'am!"

The door flew open to reveal bedlam.

There were small mauve animals resembling giant slugs with goatlike faces meandering all over the room, chewing on the rug, the light fixtures, and whatever else was left exposed. Neelix was trying frantically to herd them back into a penned enclosure in one corner of the room. The things left a red slimy trail as they moved, and were making faint mewing sounds. The odor they exuded was reminiscent of burning rubber.

"Mr. Neelix," Janeway said. "Would you mind telling me just what is going on here?"

The Talaxian beamed up at her. "Ah, Captain, such a pleasant surprise."

"Not for me. What is all this?"

"These," he said, gesturing proudly, "are *gaba.*"

Janeway disentangled herself from one of the snail-things as it began to chew on her boot. "You know that we have strict regulations against keeping pets on this ship."

"Of course I'm aware of restrictions." Neelix clutched his chest, deeply wounded. "These aren't pets, Captain. These are food. And just wait until you taste them lightly sauteed in phrinx lard with a touch of jelled garboonian rind."

"Live food?" Janeway's eyes widened.

"I know." Neelix held up an admonishing hand. "I know what you're thinking. I, too, initially considered purchasing the meat already dressed. But it just doesn't keep well, Captain, not at all. I finally decided that the only way to go was to beam up a small pod of the hatchlings and cull from them as necessary."

"Hatchlings?" The captain took a deep breath. "Neelix, this ship is neither a zoo nor a cattle farm. To begin with, we don't have the resources to feed these . . . things."

The Talaxian shrugged happily. "Oh, their needs are minor, I assure you. They'll eat practically anything." As he spoke, a gaba was demonstrating its omnivorousness by polishing off the remains of his bedspread.

A certain dangerously quiet note entered Janeway's voice. "I'm not negotiating here. This is simply unacceptable."

"Now, Captain, you really mustn't judge a dish until you've tasted it. Keep an open mind. You humans are *so* provincial when it comes to food."

She fixed a stare on him that had shriveled more than one Starfleet cadet. "It is the captain's prerogative to judge whenever and wherever she pleases as to the good of the ship. It is your job, as crew, to respond—and quickly, Mr. Neelix—to that judgment. Now I want these things out of here and off my ship before dinnertime. And I want my favorite vanilla flavoring returned—*and* the coffeemaker for the officer's mess."

"But—"

"And to facilitate this operation I'm assigning Mr. Tuvok to assist in the animals' return."

A look of dismay crossed the Talaxian's face. "Oh, not Mr. Vulcan . . ."

I'm sure he'll share that sentiment. "Neelix, I don't want to see or hear from you until this mess is cleaned up. Clear?" Janeway didn't wait for a response. The door closed smartly behind her, nearly cutting off the head of a *gaba* reaching hungrily for her trouser cuff.

In the corridor, safely unobserved, she shook her head, wondering whether to laugh or cry. The beep of her communicator was a welcome distraction.

"Captain?" The first officer's steady voice filled the corridor.

"What is it, Chakotay?"

"As you suspected, large portions of the Sardalian population appear to be chronically ill, many near death."

"Yes, they're suffering from the gray plague."

"From what?"

"Meet me in the ready room and I'll explain. And send Mr. Tuvok down to Neelix's quarters to assist with dispersal and decontamination."

"I'm not sure I understand."

"Once Tuvok gets there he'll know what I'm talking about. Janeway out."

When she got to her ready room, Chakotay was standing by the scan console, studying the screen intently.

Janeway was at his side in an instant. "You've found a trace of Paris and Kim?"

The first officer's tattooed brow was wrinkled in frustration. "For a moment I thought I had something. But it's gone."

"Can you recalibrate and trace?"

"There's nothing there to trace. It was like a phantom, a sudden blip."

Janeway made no attempt to disguise her disappointment. "I know they're alive somewhere down there. I can feel it."

Chakotay nodded. "And we'll find them. I feel that, too. But what was that disease you mentioned? Gray plague?"

"Yes. Very strange. While I was on Sardalia this last time I stumbled across what seemed to be a sort of museum. Paintings in a primitive style that showed the people hunting fierce aquatic animals. And a visual presentation about a threat to Sardalian life called the gray plague. It seems to be a disease of epidemic proportions."

"Is that what caused Kolias's collapse when we were at that first reception?"

"Yes, and it's behind the general debilitation of the other citizens, too. I'd bet on it."

Chakotay gave her a look of sudden sharp concern. "Do you think this is something that could be communicated to our crew? Could they catch it?"

"We'll have to consult with the doctor. Unfortunately, we know very little about it at present."

"This ties in with several protests I've observed in Vandorra, some rather violent, staged outside the Great Hall."

"Violent demonstrations? I want to see them," Janeway said. "Route those tapes to my private screen. Did you note any reaction from Kolias to these demonstrations?"

"None."

Janeway's commbadge chirped. "Torres to Captain Janeway." The chief engineer's voice sounded unusually agitated.

"Go ahead, B'Elanna."

"Captain, one of the main microrelay ligatures is gone, along with its isolinear chip panel."

"Missing? How long?"

"It's difficult to say. I hadn't checked this portion of the system in some time."

"Any speculation on who did it?"

"If Borizus had come anywhere near it I'd swear it was him," Torres said. "But I don't see when he had the opportunity. He's still in the brig, isn't he?"

Janeway turned to Chakotay. He nodded. "Kolias wants him back, of course," he said. "But I thought we ought to delay a bit."

"B'Elanna, can we replace the ligature?"

"I'll have to have a new one cast. But that takes time and requires more alloy, which only delays our other repairs."

"Better get started, then," said Janeway. "I'll have Tuvok send down a security team to stand by in engineering. And we'll start scanning the ship—and the planet's surface—for that missing part."

An oath from the usually self-contained Chakotay startled Janeway.

"What is it, Commander?"

"I just checked the transporter log. The record doesn't match the system's energy outlay."

"You think somebody made an unauthorized beam-down?"

Chakotay's dark eyes met hers. "Not only that. I think it happened while Borizus was still at large on the ship."

"Was he capable of operating the transporter controls?" Janeway asked.

"I don't know. B'Elanna told me that he'd learned his way around in a remarkably short amount of time."

"And he *is* an engineer. I can see that I'd better go talk to him again."

The first officer's face was grim. "If that ligature is in the hands of his engineering guild—with all of its chip panels intact—then we've got to retrieve it," Chakotay said. "This may be a pre-warp civilization, but that doesn't mean they couldn't dissect and analyze the panels."

"And," Janeway added, "if they can figure out any of the technology behind them it will have devastating effects on the development of Sardalian society." Her gaze was bleak. "You're right, Commander, we've got to locate and reclaim that ligature as soon as possible. And, unfortunately, I think I know just the woman for the job."

"B'Elanna?" Chakotay shook his head. "Are you sure?"

"I'm getting sure. Quickly."

Janeway's commbadge beeped and Tuvok's voice said, "Captain, I am receiving a direct transmission from the planet. It is unusually direct and potentially hostile."

"Put it on."

"Spaceship Voyager," said a sly tenor voice. "Listen carefully. We are prepared to offer you terms on the missing object that you seek."

CHAPTER
14

HARRY KIM ADJUSTED THE ILL-FITTING TUNIC HE HAD been given and pulled up his leggings yet again. He would never get accustomed to life on the water, he thought. Even the dry biscuits his captors had given him did little to calm his rebellious stomach.

Give me Voyager *in an ion storm, any day.*

Beside him, Paris was eating with what appeared to be real enjoyment. He paused, obviously feeling his companion's eyes on him and looked up, his lips quirking. "What's the matter, Buddy? No appetite?"

Kim threw him an exasperated look. "How can you enjoy this stuff?"

"Food is food, Harry m'boy. And it's positively ambrosia when compared with some of Neelix's more creative feasts."

Kim was forced to concede that point. Still, their situation, their location, and the rations seemed designed to kill all but the most stalwart appetite.

The Micaszian captain, Assurna, appeared on deck and walked toward them. As she drew closer it became obvious that she was highly agitated. Her nasal slits were vibrating wildly. "We've finally heard from Kolias's people. They won't bargain, not even for his daughter's life."

Kim and Paris exchanged uneasy looks.

"Where does that leave us?" Paris said.

Assurna's face smoothed into a stony mask and her head began to recede between her shoulders. "We can't bring you back with us, and we can't release you."

"But we're not even from this planet," Kim said. "You can't just kill us in cold blood."

The mask cracked a little bit. "Believe me," Assurna said. "If there were another way . . ."

"Did you tell them that you have two members of the crew of the starship?" Paris said.

"Yes."

He gave her an exasperated look. "And?"

"They said that was of no consequence."

"And what about the other members of the *Fair Wind*'s crew? Maybe they'd be more useful bargaining chips."

The Micaszian captain drew her head even further down between her shoulders. "You're the only survivors that we've been able to find."

Kim took a moment to digest that.

Paris, quicker, leapt back in. "But if you kill us—at least Marima—won't that be considered an act of war?"

"*You* crossed into our waters," Assurna spat. "You were the aggressors."

"When the dust clears it might be difficult to remember who started the fight," Kim interjected. "If anybody around here is still alive."

"The *darra* are precious. They're the key to the survival of our race."

"Give or take a few people killed in skirmishes over them?" Paris said. "Does that make sense?"

"We won't allow the *darra* to be hurt or culled before their time. Piracy is an act of war, too." Assurna turned to leave them, but paused for a moment as her head lifted slightly. Craning her neck so that she could look back at the hostages, she said simply, "I'm sorry."

Before either Starfleet officer could reply, she strode away out of earshot.

Janeway was on the bridge, facing down an unknown Sardalian voice. "Who is this?" she demanded.

The speaker on the comm link was smug and evasive. "We will speak only to your captain."

"You *are* speaking to her."

"How can we be certain of this?"

"Get to the point or I'll terminate this conversation. What do you claim to possess?"

"Your missing equipment."

Janeway gestured sharply to Tuvok, but the Vulcan was already scanning the signal, tracing it back to its point of origin. "What are your terms?" Janeway demanded.

"We require full access to your engineering and medical technology."

"How do we know that you really do hold any property of ours? All we have is your word to go on."

The voice gloated openly. "You have powerful observing devices. No doubt you can see us already."

And an image appeared on-screen. At first all that Janeway could make out were a few indistinct figures, shrouded in cloaks and veils, looming in the background of a small room.

Then the microrelay ligature, panels gleaming, came sharply and undeniably into focus.

"How did you get this?" Janeway demanded.

There was no answer.

Tuvok leaned close. "Captain—"

"Cut audio." Janeway waited a beat until a nod from Chakotay told her that her words would not be transmitted to the surface. "What is it, Tuvok?"

"We have traced the location of this transmission to the Great Hall. More pointedly, it appears to be originating from Kolias's offices."

Janeway stared at him. "So it's Kolias who's behind this!"

"It appears so."

"And that ties in with everything that Borizus told you," Chakotay said.

"He certainly alluded to the Lord Councillor's complicity in his attempt to steal our medical tricorder," said Tuvok. "And he has maintained the implication that Kolias has been masterminding all of his actions. Of course, it is a clever—and convenient—explanation."

"I think this is pretty damning," Chakotay said. "Can we confront Kolias now?"

Janeway shook her head. "First, let's see about that microrelay ligature. Tuvok, can we get a transporter lock on that part and beam it directly into engineering?"

"Not without transporting several Sardalians along with it," Tuvok said.

"Fine. We'll just transport them right back again."

The Vulcan peered at his console again and

frowned. "Captain, they are moving the ligature. I can no longer guarantee transporter lock."

"Damn. Audio on." Janeway confronted the comm link and her voice was icy. "I'll need additional time to confer with my senior officers regarding your terms."

"Are you not the captain?"

"We'll discuss your offer in one hour," Janeway snapped. *"Voyager* out."

She whirled to face Tuvok. "Have you gotten a lock on that part yet?"

"We have an approximate fix, but indications are that it is in transit, making attempts to achieve an accurate transporter lock extremely difficult."

"Damn." She tapped her communicator. "B'Elanna? Get up here right away. I want to see all of my senior officers in the ready room. On the double."

In under five minutes, *Voyager's* senior staff—those who were not missing on the planet's surface—had assembled. Janeway turned a grim face to her senior crew.

"As some of you already know, we have good reason to suspect that Lord Kolias has been lying to us, that he has been involved in the disappearance of our crew. And now we have cause to believe that he may have been behind the disappearance of our microrelay ligature as well."

Torres frowned. "That bastard. I thought from the start that he was way too nice."

The captain repressed a smile. Torres might be a bit outspoken, but at the moment her opinion came dangerously close to matching Janeway's own. "Comments?" she said.

"I've got to say that it all seems to fit together,"

Chakotay said. "I've been monitoring Kolias's communications, as you asked, and I've been getting more than a little suspicious. There's an awful lot of cloaked and scrambled messages coming and going, even for a top dignitary. The Lord Councillor of Vandorra definitely seems to be up to something."

"And I have a feeling that I know what it is," said Janeway. "It appears that there's a scourge loose upon this planet, something called the gray plague."

"A plague?" For a Vulcan, Tuvok sounded dismayed.

Janeway continued. "It's a congenital disease. Not, apparently, contagious. But they don't like to talk about it."

"It's no threat to us?" Torres asked.

"There doesn't seem to be any way that it can be."

"But you don't really know, do you?"

"No," Janeway said, her chagrin showing. "It's just a reasonable assumption, that's all." She never liked operating in the dark. "However, it's no secret that the Sardalians are extremely anxious to make use of our medical equipment."

"Although providing medical assistance is not, in itself, a violation of the Prime Directive," Tuvok said, "there is a strong possibility that such assistance would change the balance of power on the planet."

Janeway nodded. "I'll take that under advisement."

Torres looked troubled at that. "Forgive me for saying so, Captain, but it seems to me that only Starfleet could consider medical aid as interference."

"Lieutenant, that is treasonous talk," Tuvok warned.

She glared at him. "What are you going to do, lock me up in the brig with Borizus? If you do that, Tuvok, there'll be nobody left to supervise repairs."

"While you are a member of this crew you will abide by Starfleet regulations."

"You don't outrank me, Vulcan! And you don't tell me what to do."

"Stop it, both of you," Janeway said. "I want observation and informed comment, not bickering." She looked toward her security chief. "Tuvok, do you have anything to report?"

He leaned forward. "There *is* some sort of illegal poaching of sea creatures going on. By tapping their rather crude mass-communications system, both Chakotay and I have overheard Kolias threatening council members of a rival Sardalian municipality called Micasz. What is more, he—or someone in his office—seems to be in coded communications with what I take to be sea raiders. There are contesting factions in disagreement here, and the argument appears to be heating up. It is unclear which one Kolias represents."

"Sea raiders?" An image flashed into Janeway's mind of those primitive paintings: fierce aquatic creatures with double rows of deadly teeth. "Were you able to tell what they were after?"

"Unfortunately, this was not discussed. But I did learn that Kolias's daughter, Marima, is also missing."

"Yes," Janeway said quietly. "I know."

Torres slapped her palm against the table. "Well, that ties it, doesn't it? His daughter, Kim, and Paris, all missing. I think we need to have a talk with him. Up here, where ritual etiquette won't get in the way."

"Are you suggesting that we abduct him? Commit an outright act of war?" Chakotay said.

Janeway held up her hands. "We have no intention

of committing a hostile, much less illegal, act. But that doesn't mean that B'Elanna's entirely wrong."

"Captain?" Tuvok stared at her as though she had just sprouted a second head.

"We'll invite Kolias up here for a reception—"

"Not another bloody reception!" Torres said. "Captain, do we really have time?"

Janeway overrode the interruption. "—And fail to transport his courtier because of a transporter malfunction, for which we will be extremely sorry. And which will delay his return."

Torres grinned with obvious delight.

Chakotay was smiling also. "Lying, Captain? That's certainly nonregulation."

"Tactical deception, Chakotay." She winked. "Let's get him." She turned to Tuvok and said, "Issue an invitation to Lord Kolias. Tell him I'd like to host him here for a private party."

The Vulcan nodded and reached for the comm link.

Janeway turned to B'Elanna. "Now, about that missing ligature—"

The chief of engineering held forth her hand. "Captain, I think I have a solution for you." In her palm was nestled a small matte black screen with a green and white display. "I rigged a molecular tracer set to the exact specifications of the missing part."

"Excellent. How soon can it be hooked up to the ship's main sensors?"

Torres's smile got a trifle broader. "I'm afraid it can't be used from orbit, Captain. There's too much interference in the atmosphere. It has to be operated on the planet itself."

"I wasn't hatched two minutes ago, B'Elanna. How do I know this isn't some elaborate ploy designed to enable you to make planetfall?"

"Captain, I'd like to think I'm more professional than that."

Janeway hesitated, pondering her choices. "Very well," she said after a moment. "You can go down to Vandorra to find the ligature. But you'll maintain constant contact with the ship, is that clear?"

"Aye, Captain." Torres's grin vanished. She was suddenly all business. "I'd also like to report that I've observed some odd readings on the warp-core shielding."

"Such as?"

"Fluctuations. I'm not sure what they indicate. My suspicion is that the shield is reacting to local radiation from the system's binaries."

"Is this a cause for concern?"

"It's too soon to tell. I'd like to do some tests while I'm on the planet to check the local radiation levels."

"Very well. The sooner you get going, B'Elanna, the sooner you'll be back with answers. Good luck."

"Captain," Tuvok said. "Bridge reports receiving a communication informing us that Lord Councillor Kolias would be pleased to accept your gracious invitation."

"Excellent. Perhaps we're going to clear up this confusion even sooner than we thought," Janeway said. She stood, rubbing her hands together with relish. "Any additional comments?"

Chakotay caught her eye and nodded. "Captain," he said. "What about Borizus?"

"Let's keep him under wraps just a little bit longer, Commander." She paused. "If there's no other discussion, you're all dismissed." Janeway strode toward the turbolift, eager to set her plans in motion. "Chakotay, you have the bridge. If you want me I'll be on the holodeck."

"Working through another chapter of your holo-novel?"

Janeway gave the first officer a cryptic smile. "Not this time. I'm going to prepare the reception for Lord Kolias."

"On the holodeck?"

"I can't think of a better place for the kind of surprise I'm planning." And before he could question her further, Janeway was out the door.

Night had overtaken the Micaszian vessel, and its occupants slept soundly in their cramped quarters, with the sole exception of Harry Kim.

Rocked in the cradle of the ship, surrounded by muffled snores and grunts, Kim was wide awake as the hours crawled by.

This was all Tom Paris's fault, he reflected. If only Tom had gone off into Vandorra on one of his own adventures, leaving him alone to pursue his own scientific interests. But then the little voice in his head, the one that argued for balance and maturity and sounded suspiciously like his mother asked him why he, Harry, had allowed himself to be dragged to that bar. Wasn't he an individual? Hadn't he had anything better to do with his time?

But Marima had seemed so alluring, so exotically beautiful, at first.

At first.

Kim's spirits sank even lower. On top of everything else, he felt stupid, too.

Paris lay beside him, snoring softly. It was maddening. How could the man sleep at a time like this?

Kim leaned over and nudged him, not gently, with his foot. "Tom! Tom, are you asleep?"

Paris mumbled something that sounded like *"Moi*

aussi, cherie," and curled into a ball with his back to his crewmate.

Kim's next nudge was considerably harder. "Tom!"

That brought a more gratifying response. Paris groaned, sat up, and said sleepily, "Why the hell are you kicking me?"

"How can you sleep?"

"I can think of better things to do, but I haven't exactly had the opportunity, have I? Sorry, Harry, you're just not my type."

Now Kim really wanted to kick him. "Is that the only thing on your mind?"

"What else would you suggest in the wee small hours?"

"Survival. Escape. Getting back to *Voyager.*"

Paris scratched his head and yawned. "The latter looks improbable, at least for the moment. As for the former, well, our kind rescuers haven't killed us yet."

"Yet."

"Harry, it's the middle of the night. They're not out sharpening their daggers. They're asleep. And when they're awake, they talk politics and boundary rights, not murder."

Kim desperately wanted to believe that Paris was right, but his nerves said just the opposite. "Don't be so sure. I think they're just biding their time, taking us someplace where they can dump our bodies in deep water."

"No wonder you can't sleep. So help me, Harry, if you kick me one more time I'm going to reverse my policy about never hitting a friend."

"Do you intend to just sit here and let them slaughter you like those *darra?"* He climbed out of his bunk and pulled on his clothing.

"No, of course not. But I don't have any weapons—neither do you—and there are more Micaszians than there are us."

"The Academy taught us to use surprise and the unexpected to deal with superior numbers."

"Well," Paris said. "Maybe I missed that class." Grumbling, he followed his friend out onto the deck.

A thick fog had began to seep up and around the boat. It was so chill and dense that soon Paris was only a blurred outline, and the rest of the ship had disappeared from Kim's view.

"Great," Kim said. "What next?"

"Actually, this gives me an idea."

Kim sensed rather than saw Paris creep away. "Where are you going?"

"Shh! Come on."

"Where? Tom, I can't see two feet in front of me."

"Yeah, and I'm betting that the Micazsians can't, either. This is the perfect opportunity."

"To do what?"

"Take over the boat."

"I thought you just said . . ." Kim scrambled along the deck, trying to follow his mercurial companion's dimly visible form.

The boat's control console was housed in the wheelhouse, a high-roofed cabin big enough to fit two Micaszians—or four Terrans. A greenish lamp burning at the doorway revealed one heavy-lidded guard slumped at the console, making a halfhearted attempt to keep watch.

Paris grabbed a coil of plaited wire. Standing to one side of the door, he smacked the rope against the wall of the cabin. It made a deep thundering noise.

The Micaszian started, peering about suspiciously.

Paris swung the rope again.

Thump!

"Who's there?"

For an answer Paris let go some strangled moans.

"Who's there? Assurna? Is someone hurt?" The Micaszian ventured farther out into the fog.

Paris hit him high and hung on, his legs dangling helplessly as he clung to the much taller Sardalian.

"C'mon, Harry, help me out here!"

Kim studied the situation, looking for a logical point of attack. In Starfleet Academy they taught you to tackle your antagonist just below the knee. But they had never specified which knee on multijointed species.

Kim tackled the Sardalian just under his lowest knee joints. The guard toppled over backward and struck the deck with a muffled thud.

"I think he might have hit his head," Kim said. He peered anxiously, but the fallen Micaszian was obscured from view. "Do you think he's all right? I can't hear him moving."

"I don't know what we can do about it if he isn't," said Paris. "Besides, weren't you the one who was worried about these folks trying to kill us? I wouldn't be so concerned about this guy's health if I were you." He ducked into the cabin, looked at the control console, and whistled sharply through his teeth. "Dials. Switches. A tachometer. Very cute. Maybe they've got a few flint knives tucked away somewhere around here, too."

Kim leaned around him, staring. "Do you have any idea how to steer this thing?"

"Maybe. Not that I'd have a clue as to where to take it even if I *could* steer it."

"What if you just disable the controls?"

"What good will that do?"

"They won't be able to take us someplace and kill us once they awaken and overpower us."

Paris looked over his shoulder. "I thought you were an optimist, Harry."

"I try to be," Kim said. "But the odds are against us, and we're not exactly in a defensible position here."

The windshield in front of the control console crazed suddenly, crisscrossed by orange lines.

"They're shooting at us," Paris cried. "Get down, Harry!"

Kim ducked, but Paris hung grimly over the chest-high console, pushing buttons and throwing switches. The shots continued.

"Tom, what are you doing? You'll get killed."

The engines were on now. The boat jerked sharply to port and listed slightly, churning the water as it began to describe a wide locked circle.

"That should make it harder for them to aim at us," Paris said. He sounded grimly satisfied. "C'mon, Harry. It's time to abandon ship."

"What about Marima?"

"She'd never last in the water. They won't kill her. They wouldn't dare."

Kim hoped that Paris was right. "Hey! Where are you going?"

He could just make out his crewmate swinging himself over the side of the boat, beckoning Kim to follow.

Kim froze.

"Harry, get a move on!"

Forcing himself to go forward, Kim peered over the railing and found Paris clinging to a long rope ladder that ran practically to water level.

A triumphant cry came from him. "Harry! Get down here and take a look at this!"

Squinting, Kim flung himself from rung to rung. The waves grew louder and his stomach began doing flip-flops. Just as it seemed that he would land in the soup, he saw what appeared to be a small craft cantilevered out of the main hull, hanging over the heaving waves. An escape vessel. Kim clambered into it, landing with a *thunk* that jolted him from stem to stern.

Paris sat at the prow of the small craft, grinning.

Kim glared at him, rubbing his rump. "Tell me something, Tom. Did you know there would be a lifeboat?"

"Harry, there's *always* a lifeboat if you look hard enough. Help me get this bucket launched. There's a hand crank right next to you."

Kim took a deep breath, and together they began to lower the lifeboat down its bucking cable toward the dark, turbulent sea.

CHAPTER

15

THE SINGING COLUMN OF LIGHT RELEASED B'ELANNA Torres in a street where elegant treelike plants rubbed long jade green limbs against one another. A mild breeze was blowing. Whispering seductively, the splayed orange tips of the branches exuded a fine mistlike pollen that gave off a sweet, subtle fragrance.

Torres took a deep breath. Wind, fresh air, and a city to explore! What more could anyone want? It felt good to have a solid planet beneath her feet again.

She fingered the molecular tracer at her wrist. She had calibrated it for the exact ID of the missing ligature's components. For security she had carried a phaser. She checked the medical tricorder that she had smuggled out of sickbay. It was working perfectly. *Good.*

Torres turned on the molecular tracer. A small green light flashed and a steady faint beep could be heard, growing stronger as she moved it to the left. The direction indicated was northwest.

She set off thinking, *Find the microrelay and then go find Harry.*

A ceremonial honor guard of Starfleet personnel awaited Lord Councillor Kolias in transporter room two, ready to escort him to the reception. An honor guard had meant full dress uniforms, which had led to a certain amount of grumbling on the part of several officers.

Nevertheless, at Janeway's command, at the appointed time they had assembled: Tuvok, Chakotay, Lieutenant Carey, freshly outfitted and resplendent, standing at attention as the transporter whine filled the air and molecules slowly coalesced into the elongated form of the lord councillor of Vandorra.

Lord Kolias stepped forward, nodding coolly. His golden eyes sparkled with his evident pleasure. "Captain, what a splendid company. Is this a special occasion?"

Janeway stepped forward. "Well, Lord Councillor, I like to think of this as a very significant ceremony. A ritual, so to speak."

"A ceremony? Of what sort?"

Her lips quirked, but she fought back the impulse to smile. "Innocence, you might say." *Or perhaps not.*

"Captain Janeway, you speak in fascinating riddles."

"I hope not to," Janeway said truthfully.

Kolias turned, looking to the left and then to the right in perplexity. "But where are my fellow councillors?"

Janeway turned to Chakotay. "Commander?"

"We're having a fluctuation in energy readings, Captain," said the first officer. "But they should subside soon. Your associates will no doubt be along shortly."

"Why don't we proceed to the reception?" said Janeway. "My crew will bring them along when they arrive."

"Very well." With great dignity Kolias allowed himself to be led to the holodeck.

It had been programmed for the occasion to serve as a vast theater, and the illusion was that of a fine old opera hall. Swags of deep red velvet festooned the box seats, while the central aisle was flanked by holographic ushers wearing red suits and top hats. A grand stage surmounted by a golden proscenium arch dominated the front of the room, its surface polished to mirrorlike perfection. The stage curtain was, of course, red.

Janeway gestured at an elevated high-backed vermilion seat in the center of the first row. "Please make yourself comfortable, Lord Councillor."

Kolias nodded his thanks and sank deeply into the tufted cushions, sighing with pleasure.

At a signal from Janeway, the senior officers of *Voyager* took seats alongside him.

The lights dimmed.

Music, soft and insinuating, began to play.

A lithe female figure, wraithlike, danced out of the shadows. All quicksilver movement and elongated limb, she made a series of graceful pirouettes, twirling across the floor, her lavender mane floating behind her. The stage reflected her every move, creating an illusion of twins dancing.

Janeway had programmed the holodeck music banks to play Delibes' *Coppelia*. She was certain that the choice would amuse no one but herself. However, she thought that Tuvok lifted an eyebrow and regarded her with the expression that he reserved for situations in which he understood that a human was engaged in humorous activity. He might not understand entirely, but his dark eyes showed a certain sympathy.

Bear with me, old friend. Just long enough for the trap to snap shut on our honored guest.

Again the girl twinkled past them, garments fluttering in the breeze that her own movement had generated.

Kolias was on his feet, mouth agape.

Janeway watched him closely.

His jaw worked as though he would speak, but no sound came forth. At least, none that Janeway could hear.

She made a quick gesture. The music died away.

The wraith approached, hovered before Kolias, and spoke in thin wavering tones. "Father? Father, are you there?"

"Marima," he said. His voice sounded half-caught in his throat. "But you were lost at sea. How is this possible?"

In an instant Janeway was at his side, bearing down on him. "Lost at sea? How do you know that, Kolias? Where is she? And where are my men? Were they with your daughter when they disappeared?"

The image of Marima turned hollow, fading on the dying breeze, and as the lights came up, winked out like a firefly at dawn.

"Marima!" Kolias reached for her. His hands closed on empty air. "Where has she gone? What have you done with her?"

"She was never here," said Janeway. "This was just an illusion projected by our holodeck."

Kolias looked thunderstruck.

"Spells and magic. Alien wizardry!"

"Nothing of the kind," Janeway said sharply. "This is merely a form of moving picture in three dimensions."

"Is this some cruel joke, Captain? Is this how you treat honored guests?"

Janeway felt a mild pang of conscience but she fought it down. "Kolias, you're not being honest with me. I need to know what happened to your daughter and my two missing crew members. *And* the missing linkage for our microrelay system."

Kolias turned to her. His face was lined with pain. "Captain, please believe me when I tell you that I don't know where any of them are, or your equipment. Don't you think that I would tell you if I knew? I have no reason to withhold this information from you. My daughter has been missing for several days, ever since she went on a sea outing with some friends. Whether or not your crew went with her, I have no way of knowing."

"This sea outing," Janeway said. "It wouldn't have involved the hunting of sea creatures, would it? Large sea creatures?"

Kolias gave her a startled look. "The *darra*, you mean? Of course not. I'm completely opposed to poaching them. My daughter would never indulge in such a thing."

"That's not what our reports show."

"Reports? Have you been spying upon me?" His nasal slits began to oscillate in distress.

"We've been monitoring all surface communications. And we've discovered that there have been transmissions made from your office and received by ships in what appear to be the territorial waters of another city-state."

"My office?" His nasal slits were mere blurs in the center of his face. "Messages sent from my office? You must be mistaken."

"I don't think so."

He reared back, head high. "Captain, is this an inquisition?"

"No." *Not quite.*

Kolias had recovered his self-possession and he used it at full force. "Where are my fellow councillors? Why haven't they arrived? I demand to be returned to Vandorra immediately."

"I'm afraid that's not possible. It appears that our transporters have malfunctioned."

He gave her a deeply suspicious look, but refrained from saying more.

Janeway avoided Tuvok's dark gaze. She knew what the Vulcan thought about lying—in fact, he was almost incapable of it. But he understood the exigencies of command. He would support her in her actions. And that was all that she required.

She had planned to bring in the doctor at the end of the show, to leave Kolias alone with him and observe. But instinct told her to wait.

Janeway selected her next words carefully. "Let us speak, then, of the gray plague."

There was a sharp intake of breath on the part of her guest. He fell back in his chair, staring at her. "Again, you bring this up. Where did you hear that term? What do you know about it?"

"We know there's some sort of devastating illness loose among your people," she said. "Please, I must know as much about it as you can tell me. In particular, I must know if it can be transmitted to my crew."

Still Kolias said nothing.

"Did the disease kill your daughter?" Janeway asked, eyes flashing. "Is that what happened? And do you wish us all to suffer the same fate as your daughter? My crew. One hundred fifty people, and each one of their deaths will be on your head!"

Harry Kim hung over the side of the tiny life raft and longed for the relative safety and stability of the ship from which he had just escaped.

The craft in which they sat was a strange device, half inflatable and half lightweight metal, and all of it bright purple.

There was nowhere to grab a handhold and Kim kept slipping down into the bottom of the raft—the last place he wanted to be. He could really feel the pitch of the waves there. But whenever he pushed himself up he found himself sliding steadily back down again. Finally he gave up and stayed put, aware of every twitch and jerk that the little vessel made.

A small engine of dubious power was attached to one end of the tiny craft. Tom Paris applied all of his attention to it, muttering darkly about primitive technology.

"I think that's the vent screw," he said. "Or is it the rewind starter? Or none of the above?"

Paris puttered and probed, cranking one handle then another. Suddenly the thing choked, sputtered, and came to life.

"Well, what do you know?"

With a loud gasp the motor conked out. Paris sighed and flipped up a hatch to fiddle with the engine's innards. Slapping the lid down, he worked the starter again.

It buzzed and coughed for a minute, then died once more.

"Come on, damn you!" Paris gave it a ferocious kick.

The engine coughed, buzzed, chuckled to itself, and caught. Slowly the life raft began to move away from the shadow of its parent ship.

"So," Kim said. "Did you learn that technique in Starfleet or with the Maquis?"

Paris smiled. "Just a little trick that B'Elanna taught me."

Again the engine wheezed, wheezed again, choked, and died. Paris stopped smiling. With a fierce oath he kicked the thing once more and it came back to life, purring.

"I guess you just have to know how to talk to these things," he said.

Kim started to smile, but a wave of nausea caught him and he closed his eyes, groaning.

"You going to survive over there?"

"I don't know," Kim said miserably. "And I'm not sure that I care, either."

"That's the spirit."

Kim felt a drop of moisture strike his head. He opened his eyes. Another drop struck him square on the nose. "Is it my imagination," he asked, "or is that fog getting thicker?" Even as he asked, thick droplets began pelting them, soaking through the rough cloth of their tunics.

"I wish it was your imagination, Harry. But I'd say it's doing more than getting thick out here, it's getting wet." Paris squinted up into the cloud cover. "Damned wet, in fact."

The wind rose sharply.

"I don't like this," Kim said.

"Think I do? But we've got no choice. I'm just steering away from the boat, trying to keep our bodies in one piece long enough to make landfall."

The wind increased, shrieking like a tormented soul. Paris had to work hard simply to keep the small craft upright in the cresting waves.

The raft pitched and fell, pitched and fell as the wind howled, plowing up bigger and bigger swells. Hillocks of water lifted and dropped it into troughs where it would sit for a few moments, becalmed, only to be lifted once more.

A wave the size of a mountain moved silently toward them, followed by another huge crest. The trough between them was as deep as a canyon.

"Hang on," Paris said grimly.

The raft took the first wave, dipped, and began the descent down the side of it. As the craft bounced in the water the wind caught the raft's edge and, before either of them knew what was happening, tossed the flimsy craft aside, turning it over.

Kim gasped for air. He got a mouthful of sour water instead. Choking, he spat it out and got another in return. Thrashing desperately in the dark, chill waters, he tried to keep his lungs clear, knowing that he was going to lose, that he was drowning.

A moment later he wasn't.

Something immense came up beneath him and pushed him up. Up, up, up, until he had broken the surface of the water. Gratefully Kim took in great aching lungfuls of cold air.

The life raft was there, upright and empty. Tom Paris was nowhere to be seen.

Kim scrambled back into the raft, slipping and

sliding on its wet rubbery surface. He turned to look behind him at whatever had saved him and saw the serrated fins of a *darra,* then another, and another.

The raft was surrounded.

Red eyes, rings of them, watched greedily. The air vibrated with the cries of the huge sea beasts. And, with a sinking feeling in his gut, Harry Kim remembered that the *darra* hadn't been fed recently.

CHAPTER

16

THE HOMING BEACON WAS A STEADY GREEN BLIP ON B'Elanna Torres's wristscreen, leading her toward the missing ligature. She strode briskly along the Vandorran street, ignoring the curious glances of the Sardalians she passed.

Had she noticed, she might have given them a smile of fierce good cheer. She was a warrior on the hunt and the elusive quarry was almost within her sight.

Following the beacon, Torres stalked through a neighborhood of residential nature, all high tidy facades and narrow well-swept walks. The foliage was a mixture of tall, silvery, leafless stalks and ground-hugging variegated stumps sprouting delicate sprays of pink berries. She moved on beyond the private homes into a gaudy mercantile district. Here each building was draped with banners loudly proclaiming the services and goods available within.

Primitive, Torres thought. But not awful. Almost civilized, really.

A few men and women sat at high outdoor tables,

dipping crimson snuff out of crystal decanters and sharing purple sweetmeats. They were an elegant group, chatting idly while a small band of musicians played for them. One of the women, a lissome lavender-haired beauty, rose, tossed back her hair, and began to execute a complicated, stately pirouette. Her seatmate, a purple-haired dandy, got up and glided into a languid box step. Soon the street was filled with dancers, their limbs undulating as they performed their exquisite slow-motion movements.

Enchanted, Torres lingered, watching.

"Come join us," cried an exuberant man, as he circled his tall partner. "You, stranger, yes, you! Come!"

Torres smiled. Perhaps if she had truly been on leave she might have gotten into more of a party mood. But she had things to do. She shook her head regretfully.

Then the lavender-haired dancer paused, faltered, and swooned to the pavement.

Not one of the others, not even the purple-haired swell who had been dancing beside her, paid any attention. They stepped over her, continuing their private dances as she lay beneath them, eyes closed, insensate.

This is one strange place, Torres thought. Shaking her head, she strode away from the dancers.

On the next corner she encountered a small bit of inadvertent street theater: two cadaverous merchants squabbling over a car for hire, one of them laden with many small parcels, the other balancing a huge roll of what might have been a patterned carpet on his topknot. If either man's hands had been free the scene might have devolved into a shoving match.

They stood, nose slit to nose slit, necks practically

buried between their shoulders, arguing furiously. As they debated who had a better claim to the car, a willowy woman with a single purple braid wound tightly around the top of her head walked up and stepped into the cab. It pulled away, bells jingling, as the two men turned and, back-to-back, began kicking each other in earnest. Again, no one intervened.

So much for Sardalian good manners. Passing through a small park, Torres saw a dozen Sardalians, most of them rather shabbily dressed, gathered in a small group near a high fountain whose jets of water formed a sparkling penumbra. They were singing a haunting lament whose main theme seemed to be about falling across centuries. Torres tried to make out all the words, but she could only catch the chorus:

> "On all sides we fell, and fell,
> And are falling, still."

The tune was haunting. She found herself pausing to listen. But another onlooker did more than listen. He held his multijointed arms at a strange angle, aimed at the singer, fists clenched.

"Fools," he cried. "While you spend your precious lives singing and blubbering, there are others who would remove the one source of deliverance that we have."

The singers continued bravely on.

His voice got louder, nearly drowning them out.

"Passive protest isn't the answer," he shouted. "Neither is singing. We've got to stop the government from killing us by inches. We need the *darra* blood *now*. On our terms, whenever we want it, not when someone else says we can have it."

His clear voice resonated with determination. He

wasn't particularly tall—for a Sardalian—but something about his confident stance, his glistening eyes, and his flared nose slits made people stop and listen.

The singers faltered and fell silent one by one.

A good-size crowd had gathered. The man played to them, saying, "Do you know what's happening right now? People are telling Lord Kolias to leave the *darra* alone. Yes, there are Sardalians who care more about a few fish than about all of the Sardalian brothers and sisters."

"No!" cried a voice.

"For shame!"

"Impossible. I can't believe it."

The Sardalian nodded gravely. "It's all too possible, friends. And it's happening right here in this city, right now." He pointed in the direction of the main plaza. "Come see the fool who would deny us our lives, and those of our children."

Like a general at the front of a small army, he led the singers and a few curious others down the street.

Torres followed.

A short walk brought them to a large plaza in which bushes topped by orange leaves rustled in sandpapery voices. A fountain bubbled and whispered. Near it stood a tall, thin woman holding a banner that read: "Save the *darra.*"

"Do you see what I mean?" the agitator shouted. "Are you going to stand for this?"

"No!"

"Do you see this traitor?"

"Yes!"

"You know what to do."

The singers attacked. Urged on by their leader, the army went after the lone protestor like wild animals, screaming insults at her.

"Traitor!"

"Suffer if you want to, but do it alone!"

They grabbed her, tearing her clothing and pulling her hair, screaming and kicking.

B'Elanna Torres felt her hackles rise. But prudence and training told her to stay out of it: It was a local problem. If nothing else, Starfleet's Prime Directive forbade direct involvement.

"If you don't want *darra* blood, give it to us!"

"Fish lover!"

A bruise appeared on the woman's forehead. Orange blood began leaking from the corner of her mouth. Nevertheless she seemed oddly passive, as though she had quickly realized that she was outnumbered and there was little use in fighting back.

Now just a minute. Torres didn't like that. Too often as a child she had been the lone target of those who hated and feared her mixed heritage. She had learned early on how to use her hybrid strength to deal with uneven odds.

Wading into the crowd, shoving Sardalians aside, Torres caught hold of the woman's arm and pulled her free of her tormenters. They fell back, all but the original agitator.

"Mind your own business, stranger!" he cried. He spread his arms to bar her way.

Torres straight-armed him in the throat. The man fell hard, coughing and gasping for air.

"Hold on to me," she told the woman. "I'll try to get you out of here." The woman didn't move. She seemed nearly catatonic, swaying on her feet.

"Come on," Torres cried, giving her a nudge. "Do you want to get killed?"

Practically carrying her, Torres strode across the street and around the corner. Peering down a narrow passage, she spied a small café tucked between two larger buildings. Sanctuary. She urged her charge into the alley and through the high doors of the café, looking back to make certain that they hadn't been pursued.

A waiter looked up lazily from a glittering orb he was studying. Torres pushed the woman into a tall, high-backed chair and turned toward the counter. "Something hot and strong," she snapped. "Now!"

The waiter let the orb drop. It rolled behind a pot, out of sight. "*Gaba* gruel okay?"

"Fine."

Quickly he ladled out a cup of steaming garnet broth from a huge bronzed pot. Torres handed the oversize bowl to the woman. "Here. This will make you feel better."

"You saved my life." The woman stared at her. "I was ready to die."

"Drink that." Torres stood over her and waited.

Bit by bit the soup disappeared. The woman nodded gratefully, her smile somewhat stronger. "Thank you."

Torres stared into the golden eyes. "Did you really want to die? Why?"

In reply, she got a glassy stare and a shrug. The woman's head seemed to recede slightly between her shoulders. "It might have been quicker than what awaits me."

"What do you mean?"

Now her nasal slits began to quiver in agitation. "I'm getting the illness. I can see it coming on, the first signs."

"The illness?"

"The gray plague. Everybody gets it sooner or later."

"I see. Go on."

The woman sighed. "As if things aren't bad enough, Borizus's schemes will finish us off for good."

"Borizus?" Torres said. "What's he got to do with it?"

"Borizus has gotten powerful, too powerful. Everybody knows that he covets the lord councillor's seat. And he'll get it. It's only a matter of time."

"What do you mean?"

"His operatives are working even now to discredit Kolias. People I know are in the pay of Borizus. Oh, he's clever and cold, and when he becomes lord councillor he intends to hunt all of the *darra*, harvest them, and give all the blood to us now. He thinks that will cure us."

"Will it?"

"No! Oh, it will stop the pain for many, for a time. But it will kill the only source we have for relief from the pain. And then the *darra* will be gone and we'll all suffer horribly."

"Kolias will stop him," Torres said.

"I don't think so. Kolias is weak. And now that his daughter is gone, he's half the man that he was." The woman paused and seemed to focus on Torres for the first time. "You're from the spaceship, aren't you?"

"That's right."

"Please be careful," the Sardalian said. "It's well known that Borizus wants your ship."

Torres smiled sourly. "Does he? Well, wanting and getting are two different things."

"He's dangerous."

"Maybe. We've faced worse." Torres's wristscreen beeped. She had to get moving. "Uh, look, can I get you anything?"

"I'll be all right. Thank you."

"Are you sure?" But Torres was already backing away, drawn by the steady compelling signal at her wrist. She waved once and went out the door.

The homing signal began beeping faster with a steady rhythmic urgency. The missing equipment's molecular signature flashed on Torres's wristscreen like an advertisement: *Near, very near. Hurry.*

Outdoors in the bracing air and back on the hunt, B'Elanna Torres quickened her pace.

On *Voyager*'s holodeck, Janeway held Lord Kolias in the unrelenting grip of her gaze. She wanted to shake him like a foolish child. "With your silence you've condemned your own daughter to death," she said. "And possibly us with her. Is that what you want? What sort of person are you? What sort of father?"

For a moment he met her eyes defiantly. Then something in the Lord Councillor broke. Slowly he fell back into his seat, his head sinking down between his shoulders. When he lifted his gaze to hers his eyes were flat, void of hope.

"It is a curse," he said quietly. "This disease, we can scarcely bear to talk of it. The name, the gray plague, is almost taboo among my people." His voice sounded thick, as though his tongue had gone numb. "Genetically transmitted among us. I cannot say that the gray plague is no threat to your people, but I doubt that it is. How could it be?

"The illness goes through a latency period that often lasts forty spans or more. But for the unlucky ones—and my beautiful Marima is unfortunately among them—the pain begins early, in young adulthood. It drives some of us mad. Others kill themselves to escape. The gray plague is not fatal until long past the prime of our lives. By then, of course, one scarcely cares.

"And no," he continued. "Of course I don't wish this fate upon anyone, anyone at all, much less your crew. But Captain, you have so many amazing machines, so much unheard-of technology. Help us, I beg you. I've seen your shipboard hospital. It's a wonder! You must see our plight. How can you remain unmoved?" He looked at her imploringly.

Janeway couldn't answer.

"Captain, please, I beg of you, help us."

She turned away. Janeway had been dreading this possible turn in the conversation. All of her instincts as a scientist told her to help the Sardalians. But she was, first and foremost, captain of the *Voyager,* a Starfleet officer—the ranking Starfleet officer in this quadrant. As such, her duty was clear, much though she might detest it.

The Prime Directive stated that no interference was allowed with developing civilizations. Even when it might result in saving lives. Janeway knew that the Prime Directive had caused many a captain and admiral sleepless nights, taxing their ingenuity—and their humanity.

Now, Janeway squirmed inside. But her face remained set and determined. "I'm sorry," she said, and the words felt like ashes in her mouth. She ignored Chakotay's stricken look. *He knows the rules, too.* "I'm terribly sorry," she repeated. "We sympathize with your plight, believe me. But we can't help you."

Kolias looked thunderstruck. "Can't? Why can't you do this? You'll save lives. Earn our eternal gratitude. We'll pay you any way that's within our power. We'll kneel before you . . ." He made a stiff attempt to get onto his knees before Janeway darted in front of him, forcing him back into his seat.

"Please," she said earnestly. "Try to understand. Even if our medical technology could solve this problem—and there's no guarantee that it could—we have specific orders not to interfere with the balance of power on another world."

"Interfere?" Kolias's voice rasped with indignation. "What sort of people would consider the merciful ending of suffering as interference?"

Janeway's throat swelled with self-hatred. The Sardalians seemed like fine people, cultivated, charming, with a promising civilization and a lovely world. But the laws of nature had taken an odd detour here and they were cursed, biologically cursed. And she, dedicated scientist and problem solver, was turning her back on them because of rules that had been set down seventy thousand light-years away. "I'm terribly sorry."

Kolias deflated like a spent balloon. He looked away, picking weakly at his cloak for a moment. Then, gathering the shreds of his dignity, he gave Janeway a defiant glare. "In that case, Captain, if your trickery is at an end, would you see if your transporter is fixed? I would like to return to my quarters and rest."

Feeling more than a stab of conscience, Janeway nodded her dismissal.

Tuvok and Chakotay stood. Without a word they escorted the Lord Councillor from the room.

Janeway watched them go with a heavy heart. She knew she would not sleep that night.

* * *

Another *darra* surfaced next to the life raft, trumpeted until Harry Kim's ears rang, and with a flick of its tail pitched Tom Paris into the boat.

Kim grabbed hold of his crewmate as the craft rocked violently, threatening to go over. With another triumphant, deafening clarion call, the *darra* submerged into the ruby depths.

"I'm not believing this," Paris muttered. "We're asleep, right? None of this is really happening. Tell me that I'm asleep, Harry. Please."

Kim nodded in fervent agreement. "Don't I wish it?"

A skin-tingling vibration filled the air, half purr, half growl. One *darra* trumpeted, then another, long bellowing notes ending in basso rumbles.

"Didn't the Micazsians tell us that the *darra* like to eat people?"

"They're not too fussy about what they eat," Kim said. "But I think they're having an argument. Listen to the way that first deep note fluctuates, rising to an almost interrogative tone as it slides up the scale."

Paris squinted and knocked water from his left ear by pounding on his right. "Maybe they're discussing whether to eat us now or later," he said.

"Very funny. I remind you that they saved us just now. Or weren't you paying attention?"

"Oh, I won't deny that they saved us. And I'd bet a month's rations that right now they're trying to figure out what to do with us."

The raft rose steadily upward until the smooth ocher hide of a *darra* could be seen beneath if one peered under the edge—a rash maneuver that Tom Paris performed once, and not a second time.

Supported on the back of the huge beast, the raft began to move through the turbulent water.

"I guess they've decided," Paris said.

"Where do you think we're going?" Kim said.

Paris rolled his eyes in exasperation. "Do I look like I speak *darra?* Besides, you're the animal expert here."

The fog had lifted just enough to show them the direction they were going in, and their destination. They were heading swiftly back to the Micaszian vessel from which they had escaped.

Within moments the ship's lower ladder was within reach.

"After you," Paris said.

With heavy hearts the two Starfleet officers pulled themselves hand over hand, up the ladder's length and back aboard their floating prison.

The deck was uninhabited.

"They must be in the wheelhouse," Paris whispered. "Let's see if we can surprise them," He made for the main cabin and Kim was right behind him.

The wheelhouse was empty. The door hung open, flapping in the stiff wind.

"Where is everybody?" Dropping his stealthy pose, Paris rapped hard against the wall. "Hello?" he called. "Anybody home? Can anybody hear me?"

There was no response.

"I'll go look belowdecks," Kim said.

Paris heard a low moaning sound and began moving from cabin to cabin. He found Marima alone, semiconscious, sprawled across a bunk. Settling her back under the covers, he wiped the sweat from her forehead and tucked her in.

Kim stuck his head in the door, frowning. "The small craft are all gone," he reported. "So are the refrigerated *darra* blood supplies. Looks like Assurna and everybody else abandoned ship not too long after we did."

"In that fog?"

"They know how to navigate around here," Kim said. *"We* don't. They probably thought they'd strand us to die of exposure."

"Those bastards. The great fish-loving Micaszians." Paris felt an urge to spit on the deck, but restrained himself. "I see that they took all the sea charts with them. But at least we've got a ship. Now if only I can figure out how to steer this bucket we can take it back to Vandorra."

Kim nodded sourly. "Great."

"Glad you think so. Got any idea which direction Vandorra is?"

The faces around the table of the ready room were somber. Chakotay looked as though he hadn't slept in a week and Tuvok was sunken into the Vulcan equivalent of gloom, while Lieutenant Carey, filling in for B'Elanna Torres, fairly simmered with ill-repressed temper.

So Kolias got to all of you, too. Janeway didn't allow herself to dwell on the thought. Briskly, she brought them to attention. "Suggestions? What shall we do about the Sardalians? About Kolias?"

"I think he's lying," Carey said. His ruddy face was pale with anger. "Playing on our sympathy to distract us. I say we ought to put the fear of several gods into him."

"You sound as if you should have been serving with the Maquis," said Chakotay, smiling tightly. "Myself, I'm much more sympathetic to the Sardalians. I don't think Kolias is responsible for the disappearance of

Paris or Kim." He shot Janeway a beseeching glance. "And I have to say that his plea for medical help certainly seemed sincere. Isn't there any way that we can help him? Help them?"

Janeway started to open her mouth and heard Tuvok say, "It is quite impossible, Commander. Starfleet regulations forbid—"

"Starfleet is thousands of light-years away," the first officer snapped.

"Gentlemen." Janeway silenced them both with a look. "I don't like it any better than you do, Chakotay, but Tuvok is right. The Prime Directive holds here. Besides, we don't really know if we *could* help them." She waited a beat then said, "Now, what about the microrelay ligature? Are we still convinced that Kolias is behind the disappearance of our property?"

Carey nodded. "I know I am."

"I'm less certain about his culpability there," Chakotay said. "But B'Elanna should return soon and clear up that part of the mystery."

"I remind you that ship's sensors pinpointed the ransom message as originating from Kolias's office," said Tuvok.

"Yet he just doesn't seem capable of planning this." Janeway shook her head in frustration.

"I'll grant you that," Chakotay chimed in. "He seems as bewildered as a child."

Lieutenant Carey looked from face to face, his eyes hard. "That's just an old politician's ploy. He's probably capable of masterminding anything that will advance his goals."

"I'm not so sure," said Janeway. "There may be others more capable, pulling the strings all around him while making him look like the puppetmaster."

"Borizus?" Chakotay said.

"Perhaps."

"But Borizus is locked up in our brig."

"Maybe there are others."

"Captain," Chakotay said. "Maybe we could arrange for Borizus to implicate himself."

"What do you mean?"

"For example, we could send Borizus back to his people, perhaps supplied with some disinformation regarding our technology, and see where that surfaces."

"Hmm. I think it may be too late for that," Janeway replied. "And I think that Borizus on ice is less of a nuisance than at large in Vandorra—even if Kolias has promised to slap his wrists. He's already managed to steal one piece of our equipment and beam it down. And I think he's the sort that carries a grudge."

"I second that observation," said Chakotay. "He may be alien but I know I've seen that type before. Ambitious. Cold. Unforgiving. He won't soon forget that we've apprehended and humiliated him."

"I think," Carey said slowly, "that we should give Borizus a taste of his own medicine."

All eyes were suddenly on him.

"Meaning?" Janeway prompted.

"If he's the real power behind the scenes in Vandorra, his people should be getting pretty restless."

Chakotay nodded. "He's been out of circulation. That's got to make them nervous. He'll want to reestablish his power right away, do something to make them all take notice."

"Let's make him think we believe his stories," Carey said. "Make him think we think that Kolias is behind everything he's done. Play to his weaknesses, his ambitions."

"What will that accomplish?" Tuvok asked.

"It'll make him overconfident."

"I see Mr. Carey's point," said Janeway. "Borizus will overstep himself. Especially if we encourage him, give him real impetus."

"We'll send him back with a full head of steam and he might lead us right to the missing equipment," said Carey.

Janeway turned to Chakotay. "Contact B'Elanna. If she hasn't found the microrelay ligature already, tell her to come back. We've got another plan."

"Captain." Tuvok's dark eyes gleamed. "Before we put any of this in motion I would like to talk to Borizus myself. Perhaps we should meet again at nineteen-hundred hours?"

"Fine." Janeway said. Her body was crying out for sleep but she ignored it. "Dismissed."

CHAPTER

17

HARRY KIM SPOONED STEAMING BROTH INTO MARIMA'S mouth and watched with frustration as half of it dribbled back out and down the girl's chin. He mopped at her face with part of his tunic and spooned up another mouthful of the soup.

Behind him, Paris tinkered with the ship controls, cursing quietly. He looked up, wiped his forehead, and asked, "Is she eating anything?"

"A bit."

"Not good enough."

"I'm not a nurse, Tom!"

"Down, boy. I wish Kes were here, too. Or even the doctor. But we have to do the best with what we've got. Which is you."

Marima moaned and opened her eyes.

"Swallow," Kim commanded.

Her lips closed around the spoon.

"Again."

She complied, then smiled weakly. "Good," she whispered. "What is it?"

"Some sort of soup."

"Is there any more?" She held out her hands. "I think I can manage to feed myself."

Gratefully Kim handed her the bowl and spoon.

When Marima had finished the soup, Paris put the engine in neutral and sidled over to sit down beside her, his back against a bulkhead.

"I want to ask you some questions, if you're strong enough," he said.

"Of course."

"I'm trying to steer this bucket back to Vandorra. Any idea what direction that might be?"

She nodded. "In the morning, aim toward the sun."

"Good enough. Do you know anything about steering a boat like this?"

"Nothing. Remember, I've led a pampered, privileged life—until recently." She managed a bitter, ironic smile. "How have we come to be alone on this vessel?"

"Our captors abandoned ship—and us."

"Strange."

"I don't think they expected us to survive. And to ensure that potential they removed the radio."

Marima frowned. "But they wanted to use us as hostages. Why did they abandon that effort?"

Kim met Paris's gaze and knew there was nothing for it but the truth. "Marima," he said. "The Micaszians told us that your father refused to negotiate for your release. Even upon pain of your death, he refused."

The girl's eyes widened. "I can't believe it. My father would never do that, never."

Kim wished he were somewhere, anywhere, else. "It's difficult for me to believe, too," he said gently. "But that appears to be what happened."

"So they abandoned us? Left us here to die?"

"Maybe something spooked them."

"No, no excuses for those cowards." There was fire in her eyes. "The Micaszians, such marvelous humanitarians. They care more about fish than people, the idiots. I refuse to believe that my father wouldn't ransom me. Those fools never reached him. That's the problem."

Squinting in surprise, Kim said, "What makes you draw that conclusion?"

Marima made a brief, disgusted gesture. "The resistance often jams communications in Vandorra. They must have intercepted the Micaszians' signals."

"The resistance?" Paris stared at her. "What resistance? Where? Who?"

Marima sighed as though the entire subject were really too tiresome to be pursued. "All those who are opposed to my father's rule. And foremost among them is that ingrate, Borizus. Oh, he pretends to grovel before my father, but he secretly resents him. He thinks that he, not Kolias, should be first councillor. His spies are woven into my father's administration. I'm sure that the Micaszians talked with Borizus's people, not my father. If they had reached my father we would be in Vandorra right now."

Paris nodded reluctantly. "I guess I see your point. But this resistance, what does it do to show its opposition?"

"Jam radio signals, protest, interrupt shipments: a thousand petty, annoying things. And there's no point to it, really. My father will be Lord Councillor until he dies."

Paris and Kim exchanged wary glances above the girl's head.

"And what's the history of assassination in your country?" Paris said lightly.

Marima's appalled stare made him wish that he had kept his mouth shut. "Assassination? It's unheard of. We're not savages, Tom."

"No, no, of course not."

Kim leaned over. "At least not when it comes to other Sardalians."

He saw Paris shoot him a warning glance. But it was too late, and he didn't really care.

"Are you implying that we treat the *darra* improperly?" Marima said.

Kim met her glare without flinching. "I think the Micaszians are right and you're wrong about the way to treat them."

"They've brainwashed you, haven't they?"

"Not at all. I'm just paying attention to the facts."

"You care more about fish than people!"

"Harry," Paris said. "Could I speak to you privately?"

Kim allowed Paris to steer him away from Marima.

"How could you say that?" Paris demanded. "Are you crazy, baiting a sick girl like that?"

"Oh, and I suppose it was better to bring up political assassination?" Kim said. "That was a subtle move."

"Okay, I grant you that it was a stupid thing to say." Paris threw his hands up. "But why are you picking a fight with her over those damned fish?"

"Because she's wrong, Tom. And if I can convince her about the intelligence of the *darra* then I'll have won an important ally for that species."

"And what about the Prime Directive?"

"Look," Kim said. "All I know is the *darra* saved our lives. The least I can do is return the favor."

"Harry, I've got to get back to the controls. For God's sake, give it a rest, all right?"

"For now."

Voyager's chief of security sat quietly watching the inmate Borizus pace his cell.

Vulcan composure betrayed no hint of what Tuvok was thinking. But the intensity of his gaze, never once straying from the viewscreen, was an indication of his concern.

Borizus was lying. Tuvok was convinced of that. He had not had time to observe Sardalians with the care that he had lavished upon humans. Neverthless, there were some similarities of temperament that were highly significant to the trained—and patient— observer.

Logic dictated that Borizus had not been operating alone. Therefore, it was important to discover who his comrades were. He claimed that Kolias controlled him. But nothing that Lord Kolias had said—or done—had supported Borizus's contention.

Tuvok grew weary of observing and decided to take more direct action.

He stood, nodded to the guard to have him stand down, and deactivated the forcefield keeping Borizus prisoner.

"Come out," Tuvok said. "I wish to talk with you."

The Sardalian looked no less fierce, no more accommodating than before. He seemed resigned to his fate—a bad sign.

Without preliminaries, Tuvok said, "You doubtless were aware that the daughter of the Lord Councillor was missing."

"Was?" The Sardalian peered at him uncertainly, head half-lifted from between his shoulders.

"She has been found alive and well and is even now speeding toward Vandorra to be reunited with her delighted father."

"Excuse me," Borizus said quickly. His nasal slits were beginning to flutter. "What did you say?"

Had Tuvok been human he would have felt a moment of sheer pleasure at the look of discomfiture on Borizus's stern features. As it was he noted a certain fleeting sense of satisfaction that the Sardalian had turned an undeniably vivid shade of purple.

"Kolias's daughter has been found."

Borizus stared, waiting.

"Alive," Tuvok said, giving extra weight to the word. "Safe."

"Alive?"

"We received notice of her rescue an hour ago."

"But she was terribly ill," said Borizus. His eyes looked wild. "Not expected to survive. Neither were your crew."

"Were they not?" Tuvok paused, watching the man's eyes widen as he realized the extent of his incriminating gaffe.

Borizus closed his eyes and pulled his neck down between his shoulders. "At least," he said lamely, "that was what I had heard, somewhere."

Tuvok didn't bother to reply. Instead, he tapped his commbadge. "Tuvok to Janeway. Captain, would you please join me in the brig? I believe that Borizus has something he would like to share with you."

The emergency medical interface peered one last time at his records screen and, face drawn in acerbic displeasure, activated the comm circuit. "Sickbay to bridge."

"Chakotay here. What can I do for you, Doctor?"

The interface sighed. He would much rather have dealt directly with Captain Janeway than with her enigmatic second in command. Janeway must be off doing something extremely important, he thought. No doubt getting in trouble and exposing herself to potential damage which he would then be called upon to repair. "Commander, I want to report that I'm missing the comprehensive medical records on Lieutenant Paris."

"I see." Chakotay sounded unimpressed. "Do you think that somebody took them? Deleted them?"

"That's unclear. But I only noticed the gap in my records a short time ago."

"Forgive me for asking, Doctor, but is this urgent?"

Stung, the doctor responded testily. "I'm merely logging this observation so that it will go on record as being the result of my unfortunate predecessor's sloppy record keeping rather than any shortcoming in my own programming."

"So noted. Chakotay out."

Not for the first time the doctor thought that Commander Chakotay sounded unusually tense and abrupt. He might be developing a stress-related condition, dangerous in a commanding officer. The doctor updated his short-term memoranda file to recommend that the first officer undergo a thorough checkup at the soonest possible opportunity.

B'Elanna Torres stood before a high, windowless wall and contemplated her options. The homing device told her that the microrelay components lay inside the building. Could she risk having *Voyager* beam parts of the building directly up to the ship until they found the missing ligature?

Too risky, although she had to admit that the

expression on the thieves' faces as they materialized unexpectedly in *Voyager*'s transporter room would almost be worth the bother. But no. She would simply have to find her way inside the building and get a better fix on the missing equipment.

Her commbadge chirped.

"Torres here."

"B'Elanna," said Chakotay. "We're recalling you. We're going to try another approach. Prepare for beam up."

"Dammit, Chakotay, I'm right on top of the micro-relay. Give me five more minutes, please!"

"You're sure?"

"I am. And you know what that means."

He chuckled. "Okay, five more minutes. Chakotay out."

Torres scanned the building with renewed urgency. Taking the stairs in long strides, she raced up to the massive door, nearly colliding with it headfirst, before she remembered that less-advanced cultures rarely had self-opening doors. She reached up and pushed against the door handle.

The door rattled but remained firmly in place. Locked.

She had anticipated something like this. Chuckling, she pulled out a laser pick of her own design and quickly made short work of the crude lock mechanism.

The door swung open. There was no light inside. Torres brought up the tricorder and scanned the upper stories of the building. Sardalian life-forms registered as blips on the tricorder screen.

Rather than attract attention by triggering the building's illumination system, she slapped on a pair of infrared goggles and stepped into the hallway.

To her left were two looming portals and what appeared to be a shallow curved niche sheltering a figure.

Torres felt battle madness surge through her body, giving her extra strength. Was that somebody hiding, waiting to attack her? They would regret it.

She got closer, close enough to see that the figure in the niche was a statue. The grayed-down vision of the infrared lenses didn't allow her to do more than make out the statue's ghostly outlines. It seemed to be a large toothy fish struggling with a humanoid. The elongated skeleton of the humanoid indicated that it was Sardalian. The fish looked to be winning.

Strange. Ugly, too. Why would anybody want to commemorate that?

Torres had no time to speculate. A stairway loomed and she made for it, walking soundlessly. The homing device had stopped emitting beeps and begun to give off a steady tone. The microrelay was here, upstairs.

Bounding up the high, steep stairs, Torres quickly made the second floor and its high, wide corridor. Still no light. Her wristscreen told her that the ligature wasn't here.

Up another flight into dazzling, painful light. She removed the goggles and saw that the light source that had almost blinded her was merely a wall lamp.

A door. An open room. A table.

She saw it. The ligature was there, sitting on a table. Surrounding the table were several guards.

CHAPTER

18

THE SUN WAS HIGH IN THE SKY, THE SEA WAS CALM, AND the boat seemed to be pointed in the right direction. Tom Paris let out a genuine sigh of relief as he locked in the crude autopilot—little more than tying down the steering—and prepared to take the first break he'd had in more than eighteen hours.

"Okay, Marima," he said. "It's time to come clean."

She gazed at him with her golden guileless eyes, and he had to remind himself that it was her fault that they were in this predicament to begin with.

Okay, so she's a beautiful girl, Thomas. You've seen beautiful girls before. And she recklessly endangered us without a moment's hesitation. Remember that. But she really is very attractive, isn't she?

"What do you mean, Tom?" Marima said. *"Come clean?* I'm afraid I don't understand the phrase."

"Sorry. It's an old-fashioned English figure of speech that means 'to be honest.' And I do want you to be honest with me, Marima. Tell me, what's the real story on these *darra?* Why are your people fighting so desperately over them? Don't they see that they're sentient?"

She waved a hand in languid dismissal. Paris was hard-pressed to see the sick woman in this lithe beauty. If the Sardalians' powers of recovery were this remarkable, why was there such an outcry over the gray plague?

"They're fish," Marima said. "Big stupid fish, that's all, with certain useful qualities in their blood. But in some quarters their lives are being valued more highly than ours."

To Paris's dismay, Harry Kim wandered over just in time to hear Marima's comments. "Just fish?" he said. "I'd say they're considerably more than that."

Marima shrugged. "People have romanticized them for years." Her exquisite lips curved into a pointed smile. "Especially in nursery rhymes."

Paris shot Kim a warning glance, but it was like trying to stop a tsunami with a butterfly net. Ensign Harry Kim was in the full flood of moral outrage. *Look out.*

"I don't consider our experience with the *darra* to have been particularly romantic," Kim said. "It was more practical. More like life saving."

"Just old fishermen's tales," Marima said. Her voice rose in mockery: *"Darra,* the singers of the deep, the nobles of the seas. I don't believe that for a moment. And neither should two seasoned travelers such as you."

"What I do know," Kim said slowly, "is that they saved us. They came up under me in the water and threw me back onto the boat. Intentionally."

Marima yawned with delicate, elaborate grace. Paris initially found the gesture amusing. But then he realized that it was a deliberate delaying tactic. If she was hoping that Kim would run out of steam, she could forget it.

Kim's face had gone bright red. "Listen to me, Marima! Stop ignoring the truth."

"How do you know what really happened?" she said. "You've already told me that it was the middle of the night, storming, and you were both half-drowned. Perhaps you were merely lucky. You could have hallucinated your entire experience with the *darra,* from start to finish."

Kim gave her a disgusted look. "How stubborn and flat-headed can you get?"

Paris put an avuncular arm around Kim. "Harry, she doesn't want to hear what you have to say."

"Tom, we didn't hallucinate the *darra.*"

"I sure as hell hope not. I mean, I'm usually not so good with animals. Who knows? Maybe I'm developing new talents."

"I'm serious!" Kim pulled away from him.

"Actually, I am, too." Paris's tone shifted and his expression became grave. Something in Marima's refusal to listen had nettled him. "That's why I'm convinced that we weren't dreaming. And that the *darra are* intelligent. What's more, Marima, I think you know they are, and you're terrified that if word spreads about this you'll lose the only source of relief that exists for your condition."

The girl stared at him, her face pale. "You don't understand," she said. "They're animals, all right? They have no special intelligence at all. Just animals. And they're our only hope of survival, because of the factor in their blood that we need. That. We. *need.*"

She turned away angrily.

Great, Tom thought. Now she's not talking to us. "I

think I'll check on the engines," he said, and beat a hasty retreat.

Back in the wheelhouse, he leaned hard against a flapping panel and tried to shove it back into place. To his dismay, it came loose, crashing to the floor.

Probably on a stupid spring-clasp mechanism.

Paris fumbled with the panel to no avail. Then in disgust, he set it aside. He looked up and his mouth opened.

Hanging in the narrow cabinet space, half-concealed, were pairs of pink, orange, and yellow wings. He had knocked the door off the closet.

Paris pulled out one set—bright apricot in hue—and hefted it. The wings felt like gossamer, but he saw that they were a form of thin-spun flexible polymer, more durable than they looked. The harnesses were stacked in a corner of the closet.

Probing his memory, Paris groped for a name.

What were these things called? Flappers? No. Cruisers? Gliders? Yeah, yeah, that was it. Hang gliders.

He paused, transfixed by a sudden vision of soaring high above the red waters that surrounded them. Floating on thermals, up, up, up, until he was high enough to signal *Voyager* by merely waving his arms.

Sure, Thomas. Dream on.

But he was already moving toward the cabin door, gesturing frantically to get Harry Kim's attention.

Kim saw him and came at a run. "What's up?"

"Look at this."

The young ensign stared in surprise. "Wings? Where'd you get them?"

"The wheelhouse."

"These look like the things I saw floating in the sky before the Micaszians picked us up on that beach."

"You think they were wearing them so that they could flit around and look for us?"

"Makes sense, doesn't it?"

"So if we used these we might be able to find land—maybe Vandorra?" Paris phrased it easily.

Despite his effort at seeming casual, Kim picked up the scent of danger. Staring at Paris in obvious dismay he backed away. "No. Absolutely not."

Paris reached out to him. "Come on, Harry. Be a sport. I'm navigating blind here. At least you'd give me more information. Critical information, maybe."

"Paris, I've never used these things."

"So you're telling me that these primitive Sardalians can master a skill that eludes a sophisticated scientific twenty-fourth-century galactic traveler like yourself?"

"Well, no. Wait, I mean yes."

Paris poured it on. "A seasoned space traveller like Harry Kim is afraid of flying? Wait until I tell B'Elanna Torres and all the other gals in engineering."

"Dammit, Paris!"

Ignoring Kim's protests, Paris held the wings up against the shorter man's back and said, "Perfect fit. Now if I can just figure out how to get this harness on you."

"Maybe I can help." Marima stood in the doorway, watching with a certain combination of amusement and horror.

Paris bowed in mock gallantry. "Please."

She held open a slim bag that looked like a cross between a segmented sleeping bag and a skirt. "First, step into the body sack."

Sighing in defeat, Kim did as he was told.

"Cinch it at the chest. Yes, like that. Lean toward

me, please." Marima hooked the bag to the harness, and that in turn to mounting pins between the wings, and looped it over Kim's arms, tightening it until he winced.

"Ow!"

"I'm sorry," she said. "But they must be tight to hold you in place. Stop wiggling. I've got to get them fitted just so in order for you to be able to steer."

She doubled a lace here, knotted another there. "That should do it."

"Take your time," Kim said. "Please. I'd rather that it be perfect. Less chance of my inadvertently repeating the Icarus scenario that way."

"Icarus?"

"Sorry. It's old Terran mythology, from my homeworld. A legend about a boy who flew too high on wax wings and was punished by the gods for his ambition. His wings melted and he fell into the sea and drowned."

"Sounds like a story intended to discourage ambition." Marima's look was faintly teasing. "A serious legend. Your people must love these tales."

Kim smiled. "I guess we do."

"Marima," Paris said. "I don't like to sweat the small stuff, but just how do we launch him?"

Smiling, she pointed to a complicated block-and-tackle device. "With that."

Paris stared at it in disbelief. "That? It looks like a catapult mechanism."

"Now wait just a minute." The color was draining out of Kim's face. "Just hold on now. You don't seriously think that I'm—"

Calculating rapidly, Paris nodded. "Okay, if we hook him to a towline like he's a kite and set him up on the platform, then so long as we're moving fast enough and we play out enough rope he should be pulled upward. The catapult can be the springboard that gives him that last little nudge."

"Paris!"

Paris gave him a look of mild contempt. "Look, do you or do you not want to get off this stinkin' ocean, Harry?"

"You really think that this will help?"

"Absolutely. You're gonna love this. Trust me. It'll give you a whole new perspective."

"That's what I'm afraid of."

B'Elanna Torres stared at the Sardalians guarding the microrelay, decided that they didn't look very intelligent, and chose to brazen it out with them.

"Hello, gentlemen," she said briskly. "I believe you have something that belongs to me."

The guards stared at Torres, openmouthed with surprise. Finally one of them found the presence of mind to speak.

"Did Borizus send you?"

Torres glowered at him. So Borizus was behind this, was he? Just wait until she got back to the ship.

Obviously taking her silence to mean no, the guard stood and shouted, "Seize her!"

They swarmed at Torres from every direction.

Not intelligent at all.

Grinning fiercely, Torres ducked a blow from the nearest guard, spun away from another, kicked her way between two other guards, swept up the microrelay in her arms, and, clutching it tightly, darted toward the door.

Another guard blocked her path.

She kicked.

He was quicker than the others and blocked the blow.

Torres feinted and turned, and as the guard came closer, bent to deliver a reverse kick, a quick slashing move that a Starfleet instructor had once shown her—and one she had since used to good advantage.

Her foot connected solidly with the Sardalian's ribcage. He was suddenly airborne, grunting with surprise, flying up and away to crash noisily against a fellow guard. The momentum propelled them both to hit hard against the far wall. The men remained standing, clutching each other for a moment before sliding slowly down to sprawl upon the floor, dazed.

Another guard grabbed her from behind.

Torres butted her head into his chin. His grip on her loosened as he sagged and went down.

A blow upon her left arm startled her. She took one step backward for balance and kicked her attacker in the jaw. He fell to the floor and stayed there.

Who would be next? She looked up, ready to grapple, scarcely winded. To her mild disappointment she saw that most of the guards were unconscious.

Then Torres heard the sound of running footsteps and knew that one of the guards had fled. That was no good. The alarm would be spread quickly and reinforcements would arrive.

Time to leave.

She smiled, the warrior blood throbbing in her veins. She always felt better after a good workout. It really was too bad that these Sardalians were built along such flimsy lines. They posed so little challenge.

She grinned in exhilaration. The shame, when it came, when her human half had regained control as it always did, and begun chiding her about her Klingon excesses, would force these thoughts—and others—deep into her subconscious. But for now she gloried in the moment, in her own sheer physical vigor and prowess. Holding the microrelay over her head, B'Elanna Torres gave a deep, triumphant Klingon war cry.

CHAPTER
19

Pulse subsiding, Torres clutched the precious microrelay ligature to her chest and thought eagerly of Chakotay's slow smile when he saw that she had it. If only he would smile at her—B'Elanna—and have it mean something other than "job well done."

It was not a thought she allowed herself very often.

Chakotay had been hurt, badly hurt, by Torres's friend, the traitor Seskia, his former lover. She knew he couldn't possibly return her feelings and might never again trust any woman when it came to his heart. Her foolish romantic desires had little chance of becoming reality, and therefore she shoved them out of sight with ruthless Klingon pride and determination. Nevertheless, her human side sighed, it would still be nice to see Chakotay smile, for whatever reason.

"Voyager, one to beam up."

As she assumed a rigid stance her tricorder began emitting a series of short, sharp beeps.

What had set that off?

Awkwardly balancing the microrelay ligature on one hip, Torres swiveled the tricorder around to stare at its screen.

A distant reading but distinct.

Harry Kim. And Paris with him, maybe.

"Voyager, cancel beam up." As she spoke she moved away quickly from where she'd been standing.

The beep from the tricorder showed her the direction she had to travel. But the damned microrelay ligature hampered every move that she made. What was she going to do with that?

She paused only for a moment then tapped her commbadge again and said, *"Voyager,* on my signal, beam up microrelay equipment half a meter south of my readings." She set it down and paced backward carefully. That, she thought, should do it.

"Energize."

Almost immediately a humming beam dematerialized the rescued components.

Torres nodded with intense satisfaction. Now she was free to hunt.

Quickly, back down the dark stairs, through the gloomy corridor and out onto the street. She raced through the crowd, turned a corner, skidded into an alley, and waited.

No pursuit. Good.

The tricorder was urging her toward the waterfront. Very well. She would investigate that area first.

Moving faster than a human—and possibly a Vulcan—Torres used her hybrid strength to cut through the crowds of Sardalians in her path.

Her commbadge chirped.

She ignored it.

"B'Elanna, report!"

She knew that if she stopped to respond, Chakotay

would find some premise for preventing her from finding Harry. And Harry had to be her first priority now.

The Sardalian waterfront was obviously thriving. One container ship after another was docked at the long piers, disgorging cargo via cranes and carts.

The tricorder readings intensified.

That ship, over there.

Were Harry and Tom Paris trapped somewhere aboard? But even as Torres strode toward the gangplank the reading shifted and faded out.

No! Don't do this to me.

Casting aside caution, Torres jolted up the gangplank and plowed into two startled Sardalian sailors, bowling them over like hoverball markers.

Ignoring their gasps of outrage, Torres began to shout. "Harry? Harry Kim? Can you hear me?"

Her voice echoed mockingly along the deck. She pulled the tricorder up and ran it along the boat.

The readings were even. Nothing there. Wait. A faint blip. But that seemed to be pointing off to starboard, toward open sea. Surely not. There was nothing out there but a few wispy clouds. Something must be wrong with the tricorder.

I'll just have to search the ship deck by deck.

"Ma'am? Excuse us, please. May we help you?" The voice was high and hesitant. The Sardalians were back, with their timid, ridiculous manners and protocols.

Torres grimaced fiercely at them. "I don't need any help, thanks."

The two sailors quickly withdrew, muttering and shaking their heads.

Torres clattered down a metal stairway to the second deck. "Harry? Tom? Can you hear me?"

She tried a door. Locked. The tricorder indicated that nothing alive lay behind it. Moving swiftly from door to door, she scanned the contents of each cabin.

Only one appeared to hold a living being. But the readings were Sardalian.

Down, down, down, deck by deck, stairway by stairway. She was below the waterline inside the primary hull now.

There are a lot of ships at dock. And I'll search each one, if necessary.

Briefly Torres regretted not bringing another tricorder with her. She could have used it in tandem with the other. Surely that would have bolstered the weak signal, narrowing her search. Even better would have been three tricorders, all cross-configured. Yes, three tricorders would have done the trick.

"B'Elanna." It was Chakotay. He sounded furious.

"Just give me five more minutes."

"Get back up here, now!"

She could feel the first tingling effects of the transporter as the air about her began to shimmer.

"No!" She flailed helplessly, rooted to the spot. And in that moment she felt comprehension dawn.

The tricorder reading off to starboard. Harry. He's out there, somewhere, on the open sea. That's what it meant. Oh, dammit to hell . . ."

The thought froze solid, suspended as the transporter whirled Torres up and away.

She materialized on the transporter platform to find Chakotay waiting for her, arms crossed in front of his broad chest. He wasn't smiling.

"Nice stunt." The first officer gestured angrily for her to step down. He tapped his commbadge. "Chakotay to Janeway."

"Go ahead."

"Both the microrelay ligature and B'Elanna have returned safely to *Voyager*."

"That's good news. I'm on my way to the brig to talk with Tuvok and Borizus. I'll debrief B'Elanna later. Tender my congratulations. Janeway out."

Chakotay turned to Torres and said, "What the hell did you think you were up to? This isn't the Maquis, B'Elanna."

"That's obvious."

He ignored the implied insult. "Look, get it through your head. You can't just go running off when the impulse strikes you."

"You're a fine one to talk," she said, remembering Chakotay's own occasionally impulsive actions.

"I've regretted my own foolishness, and apologized to Janeway for it. Listen to me, B'Elanna. This is *Voyager*, and we have protocols here that we rely on. The captain is furious."

Torres regretted that. She respected Kathryn Janeway and valued her reciprocal approval. "I'm sorry, Chakotay. I thought I could rescue the microrelay ligature *and* find Harry—"

"But you didn't."

"Will you just hold on a minute? I sure as hell did get the microrelay ligature and what's more—"

"There you go again. I'm not finished, B'Elanna. At least grant me the dignity of simple courtesy. I'm beginning to think you listened to me more when we were Maquis."

She said nothing, thinking: *Yes, but that was before I realized that I was falling for you. And you must never, never, never know it.*

Aloud, she said, a bit too loudly, "Don't be silly. We're all under a lot of stress here. I'm sorry if I've insulted you, Chakotay. But I think I've found a way to help locate Kim and Paris. And I've learned a few things about Borizus that might interest you."

"Oh." Now Chakotay did smile at her. "Tell me."

With Marima operating the release mechanism and Paris cranking the ship's engines for all they were worth, Harry Kim found himself propelled up, up, up into the lemon-colored sky.

For a terrifying moment he wondered if he would merely reverse his trajectory as gravity caught hold of him. Was he going to smash back down to break against the ship's hard deck? Or would he drown in the heaving red depths of the sea?

Then the wind caught him, he held out his arms, and—he was flying.

The boat receded beneath him, toylike in aspect. And Kim discovered another mighty truth.

He was airsick.

This never happens on Voyager.

Far beneath him was the tiny Micaszian vessel. Kim felt his stomach lurch and desperately wished that he were down there as well. He thought nostalgically of *Voyager's* gravitational compensators, ensuring a wonderfully smooth ride regardless of the ship's orientation and speed. To distract himself he looked up and out toward the curving horizon.

Massing clouds and a sudden splash that marked a flipper breaking the ocean's glassy surface were all that he saw.

The air currents lofted him and the rope attached to his harness played out, giving him room to soar. The wind pressed against him, a steady companion upon whose shoulders he could lean.

Hey, this isn't so bad.

Kim gave a hard tug to the right. He began slowly to turn, a graceful, almost balletic move that left him beaming.

Kind of fun, in fact.

He experimented with gliding along the columns of heated air, slipping from thermal to thermal in lazy swooping arcs. Emboldened, he pointed the nose of the glider up, catching the wind, allowing it to loft him even higher.

There. A dark mass on the edge of the horizon. A narrow slice of shoreline. Was it Vandorra? Craning his neck, Kim looked for—but didn't see—the city's gleaming towers.

Not Vandorra then. Was that Micaszia? Should we head for it? Kim couldn't help wondering about their chances if they landed there: Would they be saved or merely be stepping right into a hotter fire?

Straining against the air pressure, he moved his arms, bearing right and then back again, hard left. He scanned 360 degrees but found only the brown, unfamiliar shoreline.

Well, that's it.

As had been agreed, he moved his arms in a broad swimming motion, back and forth, back and forth, indicating that he should be reeled in.

The rope that tied him to the ship began tugging him lower. Marima or Paris had engaged the winch and cable that would wind him in like a flying fish on the line.

Lower and lower. The ship grew larger. Kim felt his stomach calming. In a moment he would be safely on deck.

With a sickening ping that might have been an Eflat, the rope broke. Harry's frenzied mind had a moment to fix the image of the white faces of Paris and Marima staring openmouthed beneath him before he went cartwheeling up and over the ship. For a time he rose, but then he spiraled down, down, down toward the wine-dark sea.

CHAPTER
20

KATHRYN JANEWAY SAT ACROSS FROM TUVOK IN HER ready room, her arms folded across her chest. She had just listened to what amounted to a partial confession from Borizus.

"Yes, Captain," he had said. "I *did* know that your missing men were at sea with Kolias's daughter. But now that she has been returned safely I assume that they, too, are safe."

The source of his information, he claimed, was talk he had overheard in Kolias's offices. Janeway doubted that very much. Borizus was a wily customer. She would just hold on to him for a little bit longer.

Once Borizus had been returned to his cell she pinned Tuvok with a penetrating stare. "I'm still curious as to how you elicited this confession, Lieutenant. It seems to me that you defied a primary Vulcan tenet and actually lied to achieve your goals."

He met her with a look of sincere concern and perhaps even wounded dignity. "Lied?" Tuvok said.

217

"Captain, you of all people should know that I am incapable of lying."

"Then what do you call it?"

Tuvok's eyes gleamed. "In your own words, Captain, I merely practiced tactical deception."

He sounded positively smug. Janeway couldn't restrain an indulgent smile. It was important to allow her officers their little triumphs. "All right, Tuvok, I give up. I won't play semantics with you. However you did it, I'm grateful to have gotten some information out of him. Let's review what we know."

Tuvok nodded. "Borizus obviously had some knowledge of the whereabouts of Kim and Paris. We have investigated what he told us, but the coordinates reveal empty sea. We are currently widening our scans, both above and beneath the water."

The implication in his words was an ugly possibility. Not for the first time did Janeway silently damn the Vulcan tendency to voice appalling possibilities in the calmest of tones. Paris and Kim drowned? To hell with logic: She wasn't willing to consider that alternative yet.

"That's—reasonable, Mr. Tuvok. But how did Borizus know where Paris and Kim had been? And Kolias's daughter?"

Here the Vulcan's face took on a perplexed cast. "If we are to believe Borizus, he overheard this information in Kolias's office. If, as we infer, he is truly behind the disappearance of our microrelay ligature and Paris, Kim, and Kolias's daughter as well, then we must assume that he is lying, and further, that he is part of an elaborate scheme to discredit—and unseat—Kolias."

Janeway leaned forward. "That's a bold projection."

"Not so much a projection, now that we have B'Elanna Torres's report to bolster our suspicions."

"And should we share those suspicions with Kolias? Warn him?"

Tuvok's dark countenance could have been carved from stone. "I remind you that we are prohibited from involvement by the Prime Directive."

"But Kolias might be deposed by Borizus."

"Our concerns lie elsewhere."

Not for the first time did Janeway feel her temper rising in the face of Vulcan implacability. "And I say it doesn't. If Kolias goes, then we'll have to deal with Borizus—definitely not in our best interests."

"I must point out, Captain, that our interests are secondary to the rights of Sardalia to evolve without interference. Kolias is still Lord Councillor of Vandorra, Borizus resides in our brig, and the balance of power on the surface of the planet is unlikely to change anytime soon."

Reluctantly, Janeway nodded. "You're right, Tuvok. I know you are. Still, I can't help asking—wondering—if there's anything we should do."

"As do I."

She gazed at him in amazement. "You?"

"Captain, as I have said before, do not interpret my composure for ease—or even acceptance. I merely know what the regulations state, and therefore what is required of me. I may not like it. But I will adhere to Starfleet's regulations."

Janeway reached out to pat his hand, then caught herself, remembering the Vulcan dislike of bodily contact. She settled for a sympathetic smile. "So will I, old friend, so will I."

* * *

Harry Kim hit the water hard. It felt as though he had been slammed against a bulkhead. A dim, blurry sense told him that he was drowning. He didn't really care.

I'll just float here and take a nap.

Try as he might to fall asleep, something wouldn't release him. It nagged. It worried. It kept at him the way his mother had when as a child, he had been late for a clarinet lesson.

Okay, Ma, I'll do it. I'll get up, I promise.

Kim opened his eyes. But instead of his mother's loving face he saw a ring of reddish eyes surrounding a broad, domed, transparent membrane through which a large orange brain could be seen, pulsating slowly.

He saw an open mouth with parallel rows of double-tipped triangular teeth.

"The cutting teeth and crushing teeth can do real damage if you grab them the wrong way."

Bronzy ocher skin, spiny and mottled with iridescent spots.

It's a *darra,* Kim thought dimly. It's going to eat me this time, I know it. They're not very fussy, especially when they're hungry.

But the cavernous mouth veered off into the blood-red depths.

Bye.

Kim found himself suddenly rising up, up, up toward a gelatinous light that wavered and shifted enticingly. A blue-green mass dotted with iridescent spots had come up beneath him and was supporting him as it gently nosed him upward. The *darra* wouldn't let him sink.

Breaking the surface, Kim remembered suddenly

that it felt good to breath, and took a huge lungful of air just to confirm it.

The ship was a hundred yards away, getting closer. Kim could see Marima's ashen face as she threw a life preserver toward him. And then he was grasping the float, flailing and pushing himself toward the boat.

As he neared, he heard Marima's voice crying, "Harry!"

He reached and she grabbed his outstretched arm. For a moment as they balanced precariously it seemed that she would topple into the water herself. But then Marima gained her balance and pulled him, coughing and choking, onto the ship. Gently she patted his back while he got his breath.

"The *darra*. It saved you."

He looked up to see her staring at him with wide wonder-struck eyes. Her nose slits vibrated rapidly.

Kim nodded wearily. "Now do you believe me?"

Chakotay leaned back in his chair and mused over what B'Elanna Torres had told him. He had shared her information on Borizus with the captain. But he had kept her suggestion regarding tricorder cross-configurations to himself until he decided if it was worth pursuing.

The visual scan of Vandorra played across the bridge screen. Tall buildings, lacy bridges, graceful people: It had already become familiar. The main plaza and its fountain, the leafy grand promenade, and the massive Great Hall.

He thought that B'Elanna's suggestion to cross-configure tricorder readings and run a multiple scan using the coordinates that she had picked up had merit. But it would be an awkward, time-consuming procedure. And what if her readings had been wrong?

A group of people stood outside the Great Hall, near its vast portal, gesturing furiously.

Caught by the image, Chakotay leaned forward and said, "Computer, freeze that."

His eyes flickered over the crowd. There was something odd about these people. The usual Sardalian mask of serenity seemed to have been discarded. In its place was anger, fear, and a certain kind of hysteria that Chakotay had seen on people's faces in large groups too many times before. A riot was in the making, he was sure of it.

"Continue."

The first officer disliked violence, but he was familiar with many of its early markers. He watched in horrified fascination as the crowd of Sardalians continued to grow in size and outcry until the shouts of the protestors were clearly audible.

"We're dying by inches!"

"Stop rationing the drug or we'll take matters into our own hands."

"We'll hire our own fleets to harvest the *darra.*"

"Kolias! Kolias!"

"Help us or abdicate."

"Stop rationing the drug."

Chakotay pursed his lips in disapproval. Why didn't these people look for the natural sources of their problems instead of demanding artificial cures for their ills?

He thought briefly of the doctor's complaints and contemplated the astounding self-absorption of certain programs. His beliefs included respect for the integrity of all living things—but how would his spirit guide regard the hologrammic doctor? Living? Dead?

He shelved the question for later exploration.

Something was nagging hard at the periphery of his awareness, something large and important.

What was it that the medical interface had told him?

Lieutenant Paris's medical records are missing.

Tom Paris.

Chakotay felt the usual tingle of mistrust at the thought of his former Maquis comrade. Tom Paris had briefly sold his services to the Maquis before being apprehended by Federation agents. Not that Paris had been much good as a mercenary—or as a revolutionary. Then his heart had belonged to no cause, to no one.

The first officer was suddenly struck by a fugitive memory of Paris wrestling a heavy supply barrel into the bowels of a battered Maquis ship.

Tom's shirt had gotten caught in the barrel's clasp and ripped halfway up his chest, exposing a good section of scrawny ribcage, most of which was bisected by a livid red scar. When Chakotay had questioned him about it, Paris had laughed it off as just another souvenir of his days on the Marseilles waterfront, collected one booze-soaked night when he had propositioned the right woman at the wrong time.

Only later had Chakotay learned that Paris had lied about the scar. He had received it as a student at Starfleet Academy when he rescued a fellow cadet during a survival training course that had gone wrong on the hellish world of Altemos IV.

Chakotay understood then that Tom Paris was a misfit who pretended to glory in his outcast status, hiding his strengths behind a foolish mask of hell-raising recklessness.

His irreverent manner grated hard against

Chakotay's meditative and spiritual nature. In his opinion, Paris was a spoiled admiral's son who had thrown away every advantage that he'd been given. By Chakotay's lights he was unreliable. As temperamental as a high-strung colt . . . and a damned fine pilot, the best that Chakotay had ever seen.

He may be reckless but he came after me and saved my life on Ocampa. And that was after I spit in his eye. He may be a convicted traitor to Starfleet, but by that measure so am I. All the former Maquis are.

I owe Paris, whether I like it or not, whether I like him or not. If I don't manage to save his life in return for what he did for me, I'll be haunted by his wiseass spirit forever.

The image of Paris's scar cut across his sight once again, a strange river vividly bisecting the image of Sardalia rotating slowly on the viewscreen.

Chakotay felt the same mystical clarity that he occasionally experienced during his waking-dream journeys with his spirit guide. Instantly he knew that this was a sign: The way to Tom Paris was through this image.

He pressed his commbadge. "Chakotay to sickbay."

"Yes?"

"Doctor, I'm coming down to have a chat with you. It concerns Mr. Paris."

CHAPTER

21

"HEY," PARIS CALLED. "LOOK AT WHAT I FOUND IN Assurna's cabin. What do you think of this?" He held up a brightly colored object. It appeared to be a row of crudely modeled images, painted in garish tones.

"Look like toy *darra*, don't they?"

Kim had to grant him that. The figures looked very much like badly rendered *darra*—or big eggs with fins, rings of eyes, and brain cases. He fingered the piece, wondering. "Is this for decoration? And why did they leave it behind?"

"Maybe they were in too much of a hurry."

Marima drew her head down between her shoulders in a show of contempt. "Years ago, the Micaszians worshiped the *darra*. But it was an old cult. I thought it had died out before I was born."

"Worship? They worshiped the *darra?*" Paris stared at her in disbelief.

"They were fools to worship fish," Marima said. Her voice shook with vehemence.

Paris assumed a mock-religious stance and intoned: "The *darra* giveth and the *darra* taketh away."

"Seriously," Kim said. "Isn't the reverence the Micazsians feel for the *darra* a form of worship?"

"I suppose." Marima suddenly seemed very interested in organizing and arranging her hair.

"And," Kim added, "the Vandorrans have an opposing belief."

Marima stopped fiddling with her hair to stare at him. "It's not a belief."

"Call it whatever you wish," Kim countered. "Say that your health is your religion. And in order to maintain it, you've got to slay the god of their religion."

Nasal slits vibrating, Marima said, "You're getting carried away, Harry."

"Am I? You saw the *darra* rescue me. That's twice. They could have eaten me. They should have. They were hungry enough, I'm sure. But they didn't."

"What does that prove, aside from the fact that you're attractive to large fish?"

Kim slapped his palms against the deck in disgust. "Prove? It proves that they're intelligent. Even *you* can't deny that, Marima. And yet you'd kill them all, despite the cost to you eventually. Despite the fact that it would earn the hatred of your neighbors and trading partners."

She flounced her purple hair. "Is there a point to this harangue?

"Simply this," Kim said tightly. "As your disagreements with the Micazsians intensify—and I see no reason why they won't—what you're headed for is nothing less than a major religious and civil war. It'll start over the gray plague. And it'll only end when you're all dead."

"Are you certain, Doctor?" Chakotay stared at the emergency medical interface and wished again that he had been programmed with a slightly less astringent personality.

"As I've said *before*, Commander, my files on Lieutenant Paris are incomplete. I now believe that they were destroyed along with others by the secondary power surge that occurred in sickbay—killing Dr. Fitzgerald and Nurse T'Prena—when the Caretaker drew *Voyager* across the galaxy. All I have in here is the treatment record for Paris's burn."

Chakotay persisted, leaning over the diagnostics table. "I need information on his ribcage—specifically the skin and a scar on the left side."

"A scar? Hmm, let me see."

"Doctor," Kes said. "Tom does have a scar. I remember your remarking upon it."

The holograph stared at Kes for a moment. Then a light seemed to come on behind his eyes. "Yes, I seem to recall seeing that scar. I believe that I offered to remove it. And Mr. Paris certainly had a strange reaction."

"What do you mean, Doctor?" Chakotay said.

"Well, he blushed and said that he had a very sentimental attachment to it." The doctor shook his head. "Humans and their peculiar emotions."

"Mr. Tuvok might agree with you," said Kes, dimpling.

"Doctor," Chakotay said. "I want to scan for Paris using the scar as a specific tissue marker."

"Well, why didn't you say so, Commander? I don't

have specific tissue samples of that part of his anatomy, but I suppose I could extrapolate the components given his blood type. Allow me a few moments."

The moments stretched as the doctor blipped from his central diagnostic station to peripheral locations in sickbay, jumping back and forth in a disconcerting matter as he compiled data. His perpetual frown seemed to deepen as his fingers flew over a keyboard. Finally he glanced up, nodded, and held out a data chip. "That's the best I can do, Commander."

Chakotay grabbed the chip. "Thanks," he called over his shoulder as he hurried out of sickbay.

CHAPTER 22

THE SKY WAS A SICK METALLIC COLOR, RAPIDLY FILLING with dark, massive clouds. An eerie shrieking wind whipped loose ropes across the deck of the Micaszian ship. Harry Kim nearly tripped over them as he made his way toward the wheelhouse.

"Tom, shouldn't we have been in Vandorra by now?"

Paris, leaning across the console, looked up and stared daggers at him. "Would you like to try and pilot this thing? Please, be my guest."

"Sorry. I think we've got a really bad storm brewing."

"Nothing we can do about it but ride it out, buddy. Get a life preserver on, and make sure Marima has one, too." Paris stepped outside to sniff the wind, and Kim followed.

A sudden gust of wind grabbed hold of Kim and tried to throw him overboard. "Hey!"

Paris caught him at the last moment, and the

combined weight of the two men sent them crashing onto the deck.

Kim sat up rubbing his head. "Give me the calmer tides of space, anytime."

"Amen," Paris said. "I wish I'd studied seismography. Or maybe mining. Nice dark, safe, underground work. Anything that would have kept me off the water and out of the wind."

A bucket, wrenched loose from its moorings, came half-rolling, half-flying across the gangway.

Paris yanked Kim out of the way just in time. "Look," he said. "Why don't you come join me in the wheelhouse? At least that way you won't be a target for every stray feed bucket that comes along."

"Fine by me."

"Where's Marima?"

"In her bunk. Tied in, probably."

Paris frowned. "That might not be such a good idea."

"Why? You think this storm is going to be dangerous? Could we capsize?"

"Let's just say that if we have to move quickly Marima'll be in big trouble if she's tied down. Get her up here. I want us to ride this thing out together."

"Aye, Captain."

"Please." Paris gave him a deeply weary look. "Just do it, Harry."

Chakotay's face was bathed in the reddish light of the sensor console. He peered into its depths, as intent as any hunter of his people upon his prey.

The particular characteristics of Tom Paris's epidermis and scar tissue had been fed into the ship's scan parameters. Now the sensors ticked patiently over the surface of the planet, a kilometer at a time.

It was slow, careful work, maddeningly painstaking, to look for just one person—with one special scar—on a planet's curving surface.

B'Elanna Torres's suggestions had helped a bit and Chakotay was grateful yet again for her inspiration. He vowed to stick with the search even if he had to scrutinize every single person on Sardalia, beginning with Kolias.

The storm struck with howling ferocity. The mirror-smooth sea erupted, heaving and churning. Lightning crackled, cutting sizzling green zigzags across the sky.

Sea bats battled the howling winds, teeth showing while they struggled to stay aloft. Many lost the struggle and met their fates in the seething red waters.

Caught by each towering wave, the Micaszian boat shook and rang with the force of the gale, shuddering as it plummeted from trough to trough.

White-faced, Paris, Kim, and Marima clung together in a sodden clump that nearly filled the tiny pilot's cabin. Paris had long ago given up any pretense of steering. Now he was just praying that they would make it safely through the storm.

The door to the wheelhouse swung open. Paris could see bits of debris swirling through the air. Was it part of their boat or stormswept debris from some other hapless mariner?

We're still intact. We've made it this far.

A sea bat, shrieking loudly, was blown across the deck and over the side.

Paris closed his eyes. Just now he found himself seriously regretting that few twenty-fourth-century humans found anything of value in organized religion. *If I survive this, maybe I'll give it another try.*

The scan screen blinked, dilated, then narrowed its focus, triangulating a target. On-screen a tiny circle marked the spot, pulsing like a heart's steady tom-tom: here, here, here, alive. Alive.

Chakotay gripped the edge of the console and felt his own pulse begin to pound. Hours of steady painstaking searching had finally paid off. Eagerly he fed the coordinates into the transporter grid and commanded that the transporter chief lock on to them.

"Energize, Chief."

On the run, he made it to the transporter room in time to hear the last fading whine of the beam die away to silence.

The doors slid open.

On the platform stood an elderly bone-thin Sardalian, his pink scalp peeking through between thin strands of feathery purple hair. All along the length of his spidery frame, his red wrinkled skin bore the mark of precise, elaborate scars.

He blinked, peered myopically at the *Voyager* officers, and said, "Pardon?"

The transporter chief looked at Chakotay in obvious confusion. "Orders, sir?"

"Reverse coordinates and energize," Chakotay said. The taste of disappointment was sharp in his mouth.

A white column of light whisked the old man back to his starting point.

"Sir," said the transporter chief. "What was that?"

"A mistake." Chakotay gave him a brief frustrated glance and made his way back to the bridge, lecturing himself.

Don't be so anxious. They'll survive the extra seconds it takes you to confirm their identity.

But seconds were exactly what Paris, Kim, and Marima didn't have. A monstrous wave had swept the ship up its slick orange side and was about to release it to the forces of gravity and almost certain destruction.

"Paris, it's been really nice knowing you," Kim said. "I mean that."

Paris forced himself to form a jaunty grin. "Please, don't get noble on me, Harry."

"We're going to die!" Marima cried. "The ship is coming apart. We'll drown."

The mast crashed down as she spoke, nearly wrecking their hiding place. The shattered window gave, and gallons of rain and seawater poured in.

Coughing, Paris pulled the other two to their feet. "Get ready to swim for it!"

The three of them staggered to the deck railing.

Far below, a familiar ovoid shape broke the surface, and then another, and another. They bobbed in the wild surf, reddish eyes winking, orange brains pulsating.

"The *darra!*" Kim cried.

Marima stared in horror. "They've come to finish us," she said. "They'll eat us."

"No," Kim said. "No, that's not it at all. I think they're trying to save us."

The dying ship teetered, spun, and began its descent.

"Jump!" Paris cried. "Jump while you can!"

Chakotay listened to the sensors chitter and beep. *Fool me twice, shame on me.*

The coordinates it showed didn't make sense to him. Twelve miles off the shore of Vandorra.

There was a terrible storm in that location. Who but a fool would be out in it?

The sensor was relentless. Chakotay watched it a moment longer. Now he was convinced.

Got you, Poocuh. Aloud, he said, "Transporter, two to beam up on my signal."

The computer's flat voice cut in. "Impossible to get lock on targets. Surface is shifting."

"Approximate the area with margin for error," Chakotay said. "And beam them directly into sick-bay."

CHAPTER

23

TOM PARIS HAD BEEN CERTAIN THAT THE SURGE OF WHITE light he had seen was a lightning bolt about to kill him. He had heard the old wives' tales that people never saw the lightning bolts that hit them, but he was prepared to discount them as compared with direct experience.

Then he woke up in *Voyager*'s sickbay.

Harry Kim was in the next bed over, and Marima one down from him.

"If I'm dreaming," he said, "don't wake me."

A dour face stared down at him. Paris could have kissed it. It was that wonderful sourpuss, the ship's emergency medical interface. Never, never had he been so happy to see anybody—or thing.

"Doctor," Paris said. "Good morning! Or afternoon. Or whatever." He grinned helplessly.

The doctor frowned. "Are you feeling all right, Mr. Paris? You've evidently been quite shaken. No pain in any of your extremities? Not feverish? Not delusional? Good. Then I'll assume that your babbling is merely a symptom of your extreme relief at returning safely to the ship."

"Uh, right." Paris blinked, trying hard to think. "Doc, does anybody else know we're back yet?"

"I should think that the word is traveling fairly swiftly throughout the ship."

"Who saved us?"

"Why, I believe it was Commander Chakotay who found you. Of course, he was helped immeasurably by information that I provided." The doctor sounded quite pleased with himself.

"Hey, thanks. I mean it." Paris struggled to hold on to consciousness, but the edges of his vision dimmed and he found that his arms and legs were growing rubbery and unreliable. "What's happening?"

"I gave you a mild tranquilizer to relax you. You're getting agitated. Now rest. That's an order."

Paris tried to nod. It was too much effort. His tongue felt heavy in his mouth. Dreams came and lured him away.

"Janeway to sickbay."

"Yes, Captain?" the doctor replied.

"How are they?"

"Paris and Kim, I'm happy to report, are no worse for their adventure beyond a bit of wear and tear due to exposure. However, their lady friend was not so lucky."

"Lady friend?"

The doctor raised his voice slightly. "Yes, Captain, the Sardalian woman who transported up with them." There was no response from the bridge. "I thought you knew."

Janeway let out a sigh. "The captain is always the last to know," she said.

The doctor detected a note of amused displeasure in her voice and assigned the adjective *mordant* to it.

"I'll have Mr. Tuvok join you to debrief Harry, Tom, and their friend. Janeway out."

Tuvok. Good. The doctor nodded with satisfaction. Out of the entire crew, he had found the Vulcan Tuvok to be the least foolish. Lieutenant Tuvok, at least, could be relied upon for logic, calm, and efficiency.

Lieutenant Tuvok entered sickbay and took in the situation in a glance.

Paris and Kim were sleeping peacefully in their beds.

The Sardalian woman seemed to be sleeping as well, but her rest was not so tranquil. She thrashed her head from side to side, tensed her shoulders, and, if not for her restraints, would surely have propelled herself out of the bed and onto the floor. Her strained breath came in grunts from between clenched teeth.

Kes stood on tiptoe, leaning over the woman as she took a tricorder reading. "Doctor, her peripherals are weaker than before. Her blood gases still aren't in balance."

"I believe I know who she is." Tuvok said.

Kes glanced up at him. "Who?"

"A friend of Paris and Kim."

Tuvok studied the woman's agitation. "Is she convulsing?"

"Not exactly."

The doctor appeared suddenly. "She's suffering what appear to be small seizures. Look at these hormonal ratings. The ratios are appalling. If I can't stop these seizures she may suffer considerable brain damage." He held up a slim silvery hypo, checking its contents.

Tuvok nodded stiffly. "Please inform Captain Janeway if there is any change in her condition." Not waiting for a reply, he turned and walked out of sickbay.

Staring at the unconscious Sardalian woman, the doctor faced the incontrovertible truth: she was dying and he couldn't save her. He had already investigated 1,329 separate decision tracks in an attempt to solve the enigma of her disease. But time was finite. Defeat looked imminent. He would have to do what he could to save the crew.

"Kes," he said. "Please notify the captain that I'll be instituting a full quarantine of the ship's crew, effective immediately."

"Quarantine!" Kes looked thunderstruck. "Why?"

"Until I can identify the components of this disease—and whether or not it poses any threat to any member of the crew—I want to limit the number of interactions—and opportunity for infection—taking place."

"They won't like it."

"They don't have to like it. They just have to do it." The doctor nodded firmly. Why were humans and humanoids so irrational? Constantly working against their own best interests. "Oh, we'll have to close the mess halls, of course."

"What about meals?"

"Emergency rations will have to suffice. And, with all due respect to Neelix's culinary efforts, I've heard enough complaints about the food on this ship—and its aftereffects—to suspect that not a few members of the crew will welcome the sudden change in cuisine."

"There's no need to be rude."

The doctor's frown deepened. "I'm not programmed to be rude, merely truthful. Oh, and nonessential personnel should remain in their quarters until further notice, don't you think?"

"If this doesn't cause a mutiny," Kes muttered, "nothing will. Have you forgotten anything?"

"Not forgotten," said the doctor. "I never forget anything. My program won't allow for that. I merely haven't mentioned yet that I want you to get samples of Mr. Tuvok's blood, and that of your own, Mr. Paris, Mr. Kim, and anybody else who has been in the presence of this Sardalian woman."

"Right away, Doctor. Just as soon as I've told the captain."

A loud yawn caught the attention of both doctor and nurse.

Tom Paris sat up in bed, stretching his arms. "Hey, Doc. Kes." He winked.

"You're awake, Lieutenant?" the doctor said. "Good. Quickly, what do you know about this disease that the girl's suffering from?"

Paris glanced at the unconscious woman. Winced. "It's called the gray plague, I think. It's congenital, debilitating, fatal over the long run."

"Congenital? You're sure of that?"

"Yes. Absolutely."

"Kes, cancel the quarantine order." The doctor turned away before he could see her relieved smile. "Go on, Lieutenant. How do they treat it?"

"The blood of the *darra* seems to have an enzyme that controls it."

"A what? Darry?"

"Darra. A sort of big fish."

"How big?"

"About the size of that wall console—maybe larger."

"Big," the doctor muttered. "Is it rare? Easy to catch? How can I get one? I need a sample of its blood and flesh right away."

"While you're at it, might as well wish for a quadrant full of pleasure planets," Paris said. "These are fish the size of elephants, Doc. They live in deep water, miles from land. They're fighters, with razor-sharp fins and double sets of teeth."

"Nevertheless—"

"Doc, you just don't understand. These are huge ferocious animals and they'll fight to the death to avoid capture. Besides, they're a protected species. Sort of."

The doctor glared at him. "Are you saying I can't get a sample of these *darra?"*

"Looks that way."

Kes smiled sweetly. "Would you all excuse me?" She was out the door before anyone thought to ask her where she was going.

Neelix was bent over a chopping block, hacking away at something moist, orange, and gluey as Kes walked into the galley.

"Neelix?"

The Talaxian smiled broadly in a distracted manner. "Hello, my darling. Hush for a moment. I'm in the midst of gastronomic invention, and as you know, genius—especially in the kitchen—must never be disturbed."

"But Neelix, I just need to ask—"

"In a minute, my sweet, in a minute."

"Neelix, I don't have a minute!" Before she could say more, he rushed over, hands behind his back, and popped a cool morsel into her mouth.

"Have you ever tasted anything more sublime?" he said grinning. "Don't answer. Chew."

"Mmmph." Kes swallowed quickly. "Neelix, have you got any *darra* flesh?"

"Darra?" Neelix avoided her gaze and began shifting from foot to foot. "You mean those big, ugly, ovoid things with all the teeth?"

"Yes."

"Nasty sharp fins?"

Kes sighed. *"Yes."*

"What would I be doing with their flesh?"

She took a step toward him. "I know that look, Neelix. You're nervous. You feel guilty about something, don't you? Now answer me, yes or no, do you have any *darra* or not?"

Neelix began backing toward his cutting board.

"What's that? What have you got there?"

It was covered with a towel.

Kes reached for it but Neelix blocked her way. "That's a surprise! Leave it alone."

Scurrying around behind him, Kes whipped the towel away to reveal glistening orange slices of an unfamiliar meat.

"Neelix! Is that *darra?*"

"I need it. I've got a great recipe in mind."

"Neelix!"

"I know," he said, hanging his head. "Kes, before you say anything, I know. I shouldn't have brought it onboard after the captain's fit over those *gaba*. But I couldn't resist. It was such a bargain. Wait until you taste this, smoked and spiced."

Kes grabbed the fleshy fragments. Neelix grabbed

hold of them as well. "Let go," Kes said. "You've got to let go. This is a medical emergency!"

Neelix released the meat. With a wounded look he said softly, "If you don't like my cooking, just tell me. You don't have to insult me."

Kes wheeled, blew him a kiss, and hurried out of the room.

CHAPTER

24

THE DOCTOR STARED AT THE MASS OF ORANGE MEAT THAT Kes had placed—with great ceremony—on the medical scanner.

"Is this supposed to be some sort of joke, Kes? You know that I'm not programmed for jokes."

"It's *darra* flesh, Doctor."

"Where did you get it?"

"Does it matter?"

"Well, I need to know if some other researcher has been using this."

"Neelix was using it, Doctor."

"That's fairly harmless, I should think." The doctor decided that a shrug was in order. He ran a tricorder over the meat. "Hmmm. Some interesting components here. I'll have to do a battery of tests, of course. Prepare the plasm spectra analyzer, the dentronal scanner, and the microreplicator."

Paris threw aside his blankets and got out of bed. "Hey, that looks like the real thing, Kes. Where did Neelix find it?"

"Get back in bed, Mr. Paris."

"But I feel all right."

"Mr. Paris, if you don't get back in bed I'll experiment on you with this flesh before I work on the girl, and I'll expect Mr. Kim to stay put as well."

Without a word, Paris hurried back under the covers.

The turbolift doors slid open and Tuvok stalked out onto the bridge. "Captain, could I have a word with you?"

"In a moment, Mr. Tuvok."

"Captain," Chakotay said. "We're receiving a message from the planet—it's difficult to decipher because of solar flare interference."

"Can you put it on audio, Commander?"

Chakotay pressed his earpiece, listening hard. "I don't think it will be coherent. Too much static. But what I'm getting is that Micaszia is threatening to cut off the supply of *darra* blood to Vandorra—citing recent attacks on breeding grounds and the theft of their own ships. The announcement is causing riots."

Janeway shook her head. Whatever she might have said was overridden by the beep of her commbadge.

"Sickbay to Captain Janeway."

Janeway cast her gaze up to the ceiling in silent entreaty to whatever gods might be napping there. "Yes, Doctor?"

"Captain, this is Kes. I'm calling on the doctor's behalf. He'd like blood samples from everybody who has been on the surface of the planet, or exposed to anyone from the planet."

"What for?"

"To determine if there are any risks of infection from the disease the Sardalian woman has."

"Understood. Well, I'll take all of that under advisement, Kes. Janeway out."

Tuvok was looming to her side, looking a bit impatient.

"It's your turn, Tuvok."

"Captain, we must return the Sardalian woman to Vandorra immediately or I fear we will be in direct violation of the Prime Directive."

"I see." The captain rubbed her hands together and peered combatively around the bridge. "Anybody else have any good news for me?"

They were all silent.

"Fine," Janeway snapped. "All senior officers to the ready room. On the double."

"Now let me get this straight," Janeway said slowly. "Chakotay, you say that you've intercepted a message that Vandorra's rival city-state, Micaszia, has threatened to cut off the supply of *darra* blood. Word of this has gotten out and now the Sardalians are truly rioting. Kolias's rule has been severely threatened."

"Yes," replied the first officer. "I don't know how long he can hang on as Lord Councillor."

"That could cause problems for us," Janeway said. She swung around to face B'Elanna Torres. "How far along are you on finalizing helm repairs?"

"Thanks to Borizus we're considerably behind."

"Can you give me any estimate on completion?"

"If nothing else goes wrong? I should have the majority of the helm controls up and running in fifteen hours. Twenty, if we're unlucky."

"I'd say we're just about due for some good luck," Chakotay drawled.

Tuvok lifted a disdainful eyebrow. "Luck is not logical. One cannot be due it."

Chakotay rounded on him. "Are you saying that luck doesn't exist?"

"I'm merely saying that there are other more precise ways in which to interpret the variability of chance events."

"Gentlemen." Janeway's tone was a warning.

Both men fell silent.

"Anything else, B'Elanna?"

Torres nodded. "I could use at least one more pair of hands. Lieutenant Carey's running the engineering department while I've been working on repairs fulltime."

Janeway lifted her head decisively. "B'Elanna, pull any personnel you may need to assist you. I want hourly reports. I'd like to be out of orbit and on our way before the government of Vandorra falls. Chakotay, do we have any idea who that unconscious woman is in sickbay?"

"Yes, Captain." The first officer looked suddenly uncomfortable. "I thought you already knew. She's Marima, Lord Kolias's daughter."

There was stunned silence in the room.

A slow smile curved along Janeway's lips. "Of course. I should have suspected as much. And what's her condition?"

"Critical. The doctor seems unable to stabilize her."

"Captain," Tuvok said. "I propose—strongly—that we return her to the care of her own people."

"In her current condition? Dying?" Janeway stared in surprise at her chief of security. "That's not the way I like to do things, Tuvok."

"Understood, Captain. Nevertheless, I think it is for the best if we do not attempt to treat her ourselves.

We are in breach of Starfleet regulations if we treat her."

"I'm sorry. I disagree." Janeway stared at the Vulcan. Was that a flash of displeasure in his eyes? No, certainly not from Tuvok. She told herself that the light had played tricks on her. "How, in good conscience, can we abandon a dying girl? No, Tuvok. I'd at least like to see the doctor stabilize her. But inform her father immediately that she's with us."

"And if she dies in our care?" Tuvok's dark gaze burned into her. "What then?"

Janeway's mouth formed a straight, grim line. "I see your point. I don't like it but I see it. All right. We won't notify Kolias just yet." She shook her head. Sometimes, she thought, command decisions led her into swamps of moral ambiguity. It was one aspect of her job that she particularly didn't relish. A worried father deserved to be told that his daughter had been found. But what father would want to hear that his daughter was dying and that her rescuers might just allow that to happen?

CHAPTER
25

THE DOORS TO SICKBAY FLEW OPEN AND AN AGITATED
B'Elanna Torres marched into the room. She made
straight for Harry Kim's bedside. Staring down at
him she said, "Stop malingering, Starfleet. I need
you."

"B'Elanna?" Kim stared at her in surprise. "What's
wrong?"

"Now don't argue with me, Harry. Just come
along."

"I'm not arguing. Will you give me a chance to get
free from this bed?"

Tom Paris sat up in the next bed and said mordantly, "Nice to see you too, B'Elanna."

The doctor appeared from out of thin air. When he
saw Torres he frowned. "What's this? What's the
meaning of this disruptive intrusion in my sickbay,
Lieutenant? I'm conducting delicate tests."

"Forgive me, Doctor, but I need Harry Kim's help
right away. You'll have to discharge him."

"I'm afraid that's impossible," he said. "These men have been through prolonged traumatic exposure to hostile elements. They need rest in order to completely recuperate."

Torres crossed her arms in front of her chest. "Doctor, if you have a problem with this, check with the captain." She grabbed Kim by the arm. "C'mon."

Kim shrugged helplessly, waved at Paris, and stumbled after Torres saying, "I'm coming, I'm coming, all right? You can let go now."

Torres glared over her shoulder at Paris. "You could make yourself helpful."

Paris winked and said "I've heard better lines from androids."

Her look might have frozen a lesser man's blood. "Stuff it, Paris. When you're done lounging around here you might actually report to the bridge, where you could relay information to me about the helm control reactions."

Paris got to his feet. "For you, anything."

She gave him a half-snarl as she towed Harry Kim across the room and out the door.

"Well," Kes said brightly. "That's two fewer patients for us to worry about."

The doctor gave her an unreadable look and said curtly, "How are the readings on the girl?"

Quickly, Kes stared at the diagnostic readout above the still figure. "No change." She turned to find that the doctor had vanished. He had a disconcerting habit of doing that when her back was turned.

"Hello? Doctor, are you there?"

"Over here." The voice came from the corner of sickbay that functioned as a laboratory.

The doctor was busy testing the *darra* flesh, puttering, probing, muttering to himself. Kes knew better than to disturb him.

Suddenly he reappeared with a vial of thin brownish fluid. "Here," he said. "This is all the enzyme I was able to produce. Inject it."

"Is it enough?"

"It will have to be. As I understand it, this should act as a palliative, easing the condition. Monitor her life signs and alert me if anything changes." He vanished before Kes could respond.

Kes pressed the hypospray to the girl's arm.

Live! Come on, you've got to live!

Slowly the vital signs moved upward. The blips on the tricorder were encouraging. But as Kes watched, they began to change direction once again.

"Doctor! She's sinking."

The doctor was there instantly, a small beaker of pale apricot fluid in his hand.

"Vital signs down to thirty percent," Kes reported.

Moving so swiftly that he was almost a blur, the doctor attached the vial to a hypo, held it to the girl's arm, and pressed the trigger.

A spasm passed over Marima's face. Her mouth grimaced and nasal slits fluttered, and her eyes flew open.

"Young lady," the doctor called. "Can you hear me?"

Her eyes closed and the girl groaned. Her limbs thrashed wildly.

"Better restrain her, Kes."

The groans became gasps.

"Doctor, what's happening? Is she dying?"

"I don't know."

The gasps died away. Marima stopped thrashing

and lay still. Her lavender hair scattered in a wild tangle over the pillow.

"Vital signs are still fluctuating," Kes said.

A minute passed, and then another.

The doctor sighed. "I knew that I should have tested it more fully." He turned away.

The girl twitched.

"Doctor!" Kes cried. "Look!"

Marima's eyelids fluttered. She gasped and took a deep breath, and then another.

"Respiration is up," Kes said. "General improvement in all autonomic functions. Life signs are strengthening. Doctor, I think she's awakening."

The girl's eyes opened. She peered up at them weakly, her eyes glinting pale gold. "Where am I?"

Harry Kim watched B'Elanna Torres's fingers fly over the diagnostics control board and marveled at her skill. The blips danced across the diagnostic screen.

Torres nodded in grim satisfaction. "We've got two thirds of the new parts in place. Harry, you take the impulse engine controls and start connecting the microrelays."

She leaned over, made a few adjustments on the remote helm console, and tapped her commbadge. "Paris?"

"Yes, B'Elanna."

"I'm going to transfer Helm control from engineering to the Conn. Let's do a thruster check for ten seconds. What I want from you is to know how quickly the helm responds, any sluggishness, and so forth. Monitor it for any glitches on your end. After that, when Harry's finished here, we'll check control of the impulse engines."

"Right."

"Transferring control to you . . . now!"

There was a pause and then the gentle roar of the maneuvering thrusters echoed through the main bay of engineering.

Kim counted down the burn. "Four, three, two, one."

The thrusters cut off.

"Torres to Paris. How'd we do?"

"Not so well. Maneuverability was only forty percent."

"Damn." Torres's brow grew more furrowed.

"Don't shoot the messenger."

"Okay, we're going to try again. Hold on while I adjust something. Right. Okay, now."

The thrusters roared again.

"That was better," Paris said. "Seventy-eight percent. Nearly there."

The doctor looked up from the analysis of Marima's blood sample and nodded. "Well, that's encouraging."

The Sardalian girl was sitting up in bed, smiling wanly.

"Thank you for helping me," she said. "I hope my next attack won't come soon."

"It won't come at all, ever."

Her eyes narrowed. "What do you mean?"

"You're cured."

"Doctor, please don't joke with me."

"Young lady, I'm not programmed for levity. You are, quite simply, cured. The serum I synthesized and injected you with has enabled you to battle the disease."

Marima's eyes welled with tears. She reached toward the doctor, faltered, and turned away speechless.

Kes stared at the doctor in surprise. "Synthesized the enzyme? But what about the *darra* meat I brought you from Neelix?"

He gave her a smug smile. "It was too decomposed to be of much use. You might want to have a word with your paramour concerning the freshness of his foodstuffs before he gives the entire crew food poisoning."

"And the serum you gave me? I thought—"

"You thought incorrectly. It was of my own manufacture. I analyzed the meat and improvised using the genetronic replicator. A benefit of the new serum is that it completely cures the gray plague syndrome, something the *darra* blood never could do. Of course, I had to approximate the proper dosage—there was no time to determine it exactly."

Marima turned swiftly. "Is it really true?"

"Is what true?"

"That you've cured me?"

"For the third time, yes."

"And that this serum doesn't require the *darra*'s blood?"

"Didn't I just say that? I'm not programmed to lie, either."

She held out her hands once again in joy and supplication. "Doctor, this is wonderful, miraculous. My people need this treatment, all of them. You'll come, won't you?"

"I'm afraid that's impossible."

Her smile grew rigid and died. "Why?"

"I can't leave the ship."

"Not even for something as important as this?"

"I'm sorry."

"You have to," she said.

"Impossible."

"Is it?" Marima said. She leaned over and grabbed an exoscalpel from the bed tray. Somehow she managed to trigger it and a vibrating laser scalpel emerged. Grasping the base with both hands, she aimed the blade at the doctor's chest.

"And *I'm* sorry, Doctor. I dislike using force or violence, but you have to come with me to save my people. I'll do whatever's necessary to help them."

"May I point out that killing your physician wouldn't be very helpful? Not that you could, actually."

The girl gave him a wild look. "You think I don't have the courage?"

The doctor sighed. "Courage has nothing to do with it. Don't you understand? It's impossible for you to harm me for the same reasons that it's impossible— *physically* impossible—for me to travel to your planet, even if I wanted to."

"You're talking nonsense."

"No. In fact, I may be the only one making sense on this entire ship—a suspicion I often entertain."

"You're a coward."

"No, I don't think so. The plain fact is that I'm an emergency medical holographic program."

"A what?"

"A holographic doctor."

Marima stared at him, uncomprehending.

The doctor spoke slowly and loudly, as though the girl might be hard of hearing. "I'm what you might call a shaped-field, converted-matter beam and program."

She shook her head. "I still don't understand. What

are you trying to say?" The point of the exoscalpel wavered for a moment, then came back to the airspace near the doctor's chest.

"Just how primitive is your culture?" he demanded. "All right, think of it this way: I'm a solid three-dimensional projection with independent programming. Let me illustrate. If you'll watch the movements of my hands closely—"

While the doctor drew diagrams in the air, Kes was moving swiftly toward the side of the room, a hypospray cupped out of sight in her hand. She drifted back and away from the bed, got behind the girl, and pressed the hypospray to her exposed arm.

There was a quick hiss and the sedative spray set about its work.

Marima's eyes rolled up in her head. Her grip on the exoscalpel loosened and she began to fall backward. Pulling the exoscalpel from her hand, the doctor eased her onto the bunk. He returned the scalpel to storage.

Then, giving Kes an outraged look, he said crisply, "Why is the predilection for violence so widespread across the galaxy? I'll never understand living species."

CHAPTER
26

KATHRYN JANEWAY LEANED ACROSS THE ARMREST OF HER command chair to face her first officer. "Chakotay, please contact sickbay and ask Mr. Paris and Mr. Kim to meet me in the ready room."

"Sickbay reports that Mr. Paris and Mr. Kim have been discharged under Lieutenant Torres's authority, Captain."

"They have?" Janeway was both surprised and chagrined. "B'Elanna should know better than to do something like that without checking with me first. And where are they?"

The turbolift doors whooshed open and Tom Paris walked onto the bridge, looking a bit thinner and somewhat pensive.

"Mr. Paris," Janeway said. "Good to have you back with us."

"You have no idea just how good it is to be back, Captain." He sounded subdued and sincere.

Chakotay favored him with a smile. "Had sufficient shore leave, *Poocuh*?"

Paris nodded wearily. "More than enough."

"Chakotay," Janeway said. "Have Mr. Kim meet us in the ready room. I want to begin the debriefing."

Paris shifted with obvious discomfort. "Captain?"

"Yes, Mr. Paris."

"Lieutenant Torres wants to test the new helm controls and asked me to monitor them—now—so that she can speed repairs, with Harry's help." He stared at Janeway, obviously torn between his captain's request and what seemed to make better sense for the ship.

Janeway's lips quirked. How often had she squirmed and sighed at meetings that senior officers had needlessly called, when she knew that what was really needed was going and doing? She sympathized with Tom Paris's dilemma.

"I see. Well, Mr. Paris. I think it's reasonable that you honor the request of the chief of engineering. I'll meet with my senior officers at fourteen-thirty. I want Neelix and Kes there as well. That should give you enough time to see if you can actually control this ship."

At 1430, Kathryn Janeway sat in her ready room and gazed at the assembled staff: Chakotay, Tuvok, Torres, Paris, Kim, Neelix, and Kes.

"Mr. Kim, Mr. Paris," she said. "Welcome. I'd like to hear your impressions of this planet and how you came to be taken prisoner. What I want to know is whether military response is indicated here."

Both Paris and Kim looked horrified. "No!" Kim said. "That's the last thing they need."

"Captain, he's right. We can't punish the Sardalians for what a few thickheaded people did."

Harry Kim leaned forward eagerly. "And I want to

talk about the *darra!* That's what I think we need to concentrate on. There's a problem here."

"Gentlemen?" The note in the captain's voice caught the attention of everyone in the room.

"Now I appreciate your . . . enthusiasm, Mr. Kim. But I want coherent—and rational—explanations for what happened down there."

Paris cleared his throat. "Yes, Captain. We were invited by Kolias's daughter, Marima, to participate in a social activity she referred to as a harvest. Only belatedly did we realize that what she meant was a raid upon sea farms of *darra.*"

"Darra?"

"The huge sea creatures whose blood supplies an enzyme that relieves the pain of a widespread disease and forces it back into remission."

"The gray plague, you mean?" Janeway said.

"Correct. It seems there are rival factions, city-states. Micaszia looks after the *darra* and parcels out their blood. Vandorra wants more blood. Micaszia says no can do. I guess some folks in Vandorra are getting a bit impatient."

"To put it mildly," said Janeway. "Apparently, Micaszia is threatening to withhold the blood entirely and the Vandorrans are rioting."

"I'm not surprised, Captain. We were attacked by Micaszians while we were at sea. The ship was destroyed. And we were cast away onto a deserted shore."

"I thought it was the Micaszians who rescued you."

"That came later. And they only picked us up to hold Marima for ransom. They wanted to use her as a bargaining chip with Kolias."

"Over the *darra* blood?"

"Over the illegal poaching of the animals."

Janeway nodded. "I see. So you were attacked and kidnaped by Micaszians after invading their territorial waters. What were you doing invading anything on that planet?"

"Captain, believe me, we had no idea what we were getting into. All we knew was that we were going harvesting. It sounded like it was some kind of party."

"A good reason to do more research on an activity before you accept invitations from strangers, Mr. Paris."

"Yes, ma'am." He shot her a contrite look. "Of course we didn't realize that it was a raid on the sea farms."

"Captain," Kim said urgently. "We're getting away from the main point. The *darra* are intelligent creatures. I'm certain that they're capable of sentience. They saved our lives."

"Will you corroborate that, Tom?"

Paris nodded. "They saved us, yes."

"And," Kim said, "they're being wiped out because of this disease and the desperation of the people on the planet "

"I still say that they're only fish," said Paris.

Kes leaned forward excitedly. "No, Harry's right! Those empathic flashes I'd been feeling. They were so alien, so unfamiliar that I didn't think about it at the time. But they must have been coming from the *darra*. It was emotion interwoven with thought. Perhaps some of it was buried within the actual tissue fiber of the animals. A sort of subverbal communication. Captain, those creatures *are* sentient, I'm sure of it." Her eyes glistened.

The officers turned expectant faces to Janeway.

Her heart sank. Choosing her words carefully, she said, "I'm sorry, Kes, this is still purely subjective judgment. Mr. Kim, I'm sure the data you've collected on the *darra* will provide an interesting addition to our xenobiology data bank. Perhaps you can furnish us with a full report later."

The young ensign's face turned to stone. "Yes, Captain."

"I'm sorry, Harry. I can't save every species in the quadrant, much as I'd like to. The Prime Directive prevents us from getting involved."

"But Starfleet is very far away," he said.

Janeway's eyes flashed. "No, it's not. It's right here, on this ship."

"Yes, ma'am."

"Captain?" Kes said. "I'd just like to say one more thing."

"Go ahead."

"We have a cure for the gray plague. Or think we do, anyway. The doctor just developed it."

"What?" It was Janeway's turn to be thunderstruck.

"Isn't it wonderful?" Kes beamed. "He did it to save the life of Kolias's daughter."

The captain leaned across the table, staring into Kes's guileless blue eyes. "She's cured? He's certain of that?"

"Yes, and what's more, his cure doesn't involve the *darra* blood at all."

Paris gave a low whistle.

Janeway shook her head. "This can change everything if it's true. Get the doctor on-screen."

Kes nodded. "I'll have to return to sickbay, Captain. Someone must watch Marima."

"Can't she be released?"

"Well, no, there was a problem. We had to sedate her."

"What? Why?"

"She tried to attack the doctor."

"I see," Janeway said, not seeing at all. "Was this before or after he cured her?"

"After."

Tuvok spoke up, asking, "And is this how Sardalians show gratitude?"

"Oh, no, Lieutenant. She was very grateful. But she got agitated when the doctor refused to go down to Sardalia with her and cure everybody."

"I think I understand." Tuvok's eyes met Janeway's across the room.

"I think we have a problem," Janeway said slowly.

"Captain," Chakotay said. "We've got to give them the formula. We can't withhold it. Lives are at stake."

"Not to give them the cure would be cruel," Paris said. "Unbelievably cruel."

"Cruelty is not the issue here," Tuvok shot back. "The Prime Directive is clear."

"Isn't anyone here concerned about the sanctity of life?" Chakotay thundered. "We have an entire civilization—a world—at risk! And an entire species, the *darra,* about to be sacrificed. Isn't that more important than the Prime Directive?"

"Commander," Tuvok said. "Calm yourself."

"If Starfleet won't help them, *I* will. I'll resign my commission, Captain. I was Maquis before—"

Janeway shook her head sadly. "That won't help, Chakotay. Believe me."

The first officer gave her a black look and subsided.

"What if I resign instead?" Paris said quickly. "Chakotay can pilot *Voyager.* I could take the formula down and give it to Marima's people. If you saw how she had suffered . . ." He shook his head.

Chakotay leaned close and said, *sotto voce,* "Trying to expiate your past sins?"

The tips of Paris's ears turned bright red, but he continued bravely on. "Maybe. But mostly I'm trying to do what I think is right. Those people need this formula. If Starfleet won't let you give it to them, then I'll resign, give it to them, and get you all off the hook."

Janeway gave him an approving glance. The boy was shaping up, even if what he said was foolish. "Your impulsive heroism is misplaced, Tom. Even if I were to allow you to make good on your offer to resign, you'd be guilty of stealing Starfleet property if you took the formula down to Sardalia. I'd be forced to apprehend you."

Paris swore softly.

Janeway chose to ignore it. "That goes for you too, Chakotay," she continued. "Tom, you're the best pilot I've got. I can't afford to lose you—and I don't want to. And Commander, you're absolutely indispensable on the bridge. Everybody, every single member of this crew, is precious. Is that clear?"

Despite his disappointment Paris seemed to sit a bit straighter after that.

"Captain?" It was Kes. "What if I were to go down to the surface and try to help with their medical needs? I don't really know anything about the Prime Directive. But if my empathic flashes are truly from the *darra*, then I know that those animals are in terrible distress from the harvesting. I can't bear to think that we won't help them, or the people, when we can."

Janeway softened as she faced the Ocampa. She was very young, and she knew very little about Starfleet. Gently, she said, "Kes, your offer is very kind. But you've joined this crew and therefore you're bound by our rules and regulations."

"But the *darra* . . . " The girl's soft voice trailed off in wordless regret.

"I know." Janeway forced the steel back into her voice. "Mr. Neelix, any recommendations?"

The Talaxian scratched his elaborately pigmented head. "I don't know these Sardalian people very well, Captain. Nor do I know much about Starfleet and its regulation book. But I do know that trade and compromise are always preferable to cruelty and violence, at least in *my* book."

"I'll try to remember that the next time we engage in trade, Mr. Neelix." Janeway shook her head. "Meanwhile, I'm afraid that we have no choice but to return Marima to her people and go."

"But what about the serum?" Kes said.

"And the *darra?*" Kim echoed. "Captain, if we leave now we're condemning the *darra* to extinction and the Sardalians to civil war over them."

"That's really not our responsibility," Janeway said unhappily. She glanced at Chakotay, hoping to draw comfort and determination from her first officer's solid, unflappable presence.

His features were drawn into a tight, disapproving mask. "The *darra* have rights, too, Captain. As I said before, I believe in the sanctity of all life."

No comfort there. And no need for even a sidelong glance at Tuvok: She already knew what the Vulcan thought.

Janeway's glance slipped down to her deskscreen and the portrait of her dog, Molly Malone. Sweet Molly. Her puppies must be nearly weaned. And suddenly she thought of that funny lavender *mogwik* she had encountered in Vandorra's great hall, Marima's beloved pet, Dai.

Bless the beasts, she thought. And a fragment of a

sacred text, half-remembered, unscrolled across her memory:

". . . This great and wide sea,
Wherein are things creeping innumerable,
Both small and great beasts.
There is that leviathan,
Whom thou has made to play therein.
There go the ships:
They mount up to the heavens,
They go down again to the depths . . ."

Was it the I Ching? Proverbs? Psalms? She couldn't recall. Once, long ago, she had been a small and serious girl researching great words of Earth's past. Now she was light-years distant from that place, that young girl and her studies, and yet certain memories and phrases had sunk their grapples into the bedrock of her soul.

Bless the beasts. There must be a way. I've dedicated my life to finding solutions. And I may be at the far end of a great and wide sea, but that's no reason to trade on an old habit.

Janeway hesitated, struck by inspiration.

Trade.

She turned to her senior officers, lips curving slightly. "What if we were to follow Neelix's suggestion?" she said.

"Captain?" It was Tuvok, frowning slightly.

"I said, what if we were to merely trade a commodity with the Sardalians?"

Chakotay shook his head. "Trade? I don't understand."

The other officers looked similarly mystified, all but Tom Paris. He had been watching Janeway carefully, and when her eye caught his he broke into a joyous smile, obviously on her wavelength.

Buoyed up by that, she smiled back. "Yes, trade. Say that, in return for goods they have provided us, the Sardalians receive a commodity. A quantity of serum, let's say."

Eyes and smiles lit up all around the table.

"An inspired solution, Captain," Tuvok said. "We can provide the serum without trading them technology *or* the formula. A mission of mercy. And if the Sardalians manage to analyze and produce the serum, that is not our responsibility. Surely Starfleet would approve."

"And if not," Chakotay said, "well, we just won't tell them."

"Thereby saving the *darra*." Harry Kim smiled radiantly. Beside him, Kes clapped her hands in joy.

"Thank you," Janeway said. "That leaves one last little piece of business." She held up a restraining hand as mischief played through her mind. For a moment she hesitated. But only for a moment. "Borizus. I think it's finally time to return him to Vandorra—with one vital piece of misinformation."

Again the officers of *Voyager* seemed quietly taken aback.

"Mr. Kim," Janeway said. "I'll need your help."

CHAPTER
27

KATHRYN JANEWAY SAT IN HER COMMAND CHAIR AT THE heart of *Voyager's* bridge, waiting.

The bridge buzzed around her, relays clicking, lights blinking, people busy at their consoles. Chakotay studied a diagnostic screen. Behind him, Tuvok was intent upon his own security systems check.

Marima stood next to the captain, watching the activity swirl around her with obvious fascination. Kes was close by, running a tricorder over her for last-minute results and relaying them to the doctor.

At his operations station, Harry Kim stared into his screen, made a series of fine adjustments, rethought them, and recalibrated. Finally, he nodded and said, "Ready, Captain. I've got the projection and channel open to Kolias."

"Very good, ensign," said the captain. "Put it on-screen."

A moment later, the Lord Councillor stared out at the bridge crew. His eyes widened as he saw Marima, but when he spoke his words were directed at Kathryn Janeway.

"More trickery, Captain?"

Janeway met his stare, although she felt a pang of conscience for the trick she'd played on him earlier. "Lord Kolias, I assure you, this time it's the real article. Your daughter is safe with us."

"How did she come to be aboard your ship?"

"It's a long story. I'll let her tell it to you when you're reunited."

Now Kolias addressed his daughter directly. "My dearest girl," he said, wiping away a tear. "To see you safe is the answer to my prayers."

Marima leaned forward, her face aglow. "Even better than safe, Father. I'm cured. *Voyager*'s doctor has cured my case of the gray plague. And he'll cure everybody else on Sardalia. Captain Janeway has promised."

Kolias stared, mouth working. "Can this be true?" His eyes sought Janeway. "What is she saying, Captain?"

Janeway felt her spirits soar. "It's true, Kolias. Marima was so ill when she came aboard that we had no choice but to try to save her. In the process we found a cure for the gray plague. And we're willing to trade you enough serum to innoculate every person on Sardalia."

"Trade? But what could we give you in return for this precious, marvelous cure?"

"You've already provided it: the materials with which we repaired our ship."

"Captain, your names and that of your ship will go down in our history as the most blessed of benefactors."

Janeway reflected briefly that it would be a nice

change to leave somebody in the Delta Quadrant happier because of their inadvertent presence. "We'll begin transporting the serum as soon as we've manufactured sufficient quantities. In the meantime, I'll send your daughter back. I know that she has a great deal to tell you."

The image on-screen faded. Janeway turned to Marima. "I'll say good-bye now. Convey my best wishes to your father. Mr. Tuvok and I have some unfinished business to which we must attend." She stood. Behind her, Tuvok was already moving toward the turbolift. "Mr. Paris, please escort Marima to transporter room two."

Marima stood on the platform of transporter room two, poised for the quick journey back to her planet.

The doors opened and Tom Paris entered.

"Tom!"

"I couldn't let you leave without an appropriate farewell," he said. From behind his back he brought forth a bouquet of yellow daisies. It had cost him a week's worth of replicator rations, and meant a week's endurance of Neelix's cooking. But it was worth it to see Marima's delight.

"How beautiful and strange!" Marima beamed, cradling the bouquet. "I've never seen flowers this color before."

"They're from my homeworld, Earth. I've had them irradiated so they won't degrade. They'll be something to remember us by."

"Tom, how could I ever forget all that you've done?"

"I hope you forgive us for being so hesitant to provide the cure for the gray plague."

"Of course. I understand that your culture has its

own prohibitions. The trade of the serum makes perfect sense. Besides, my people have always been merchants at heart."

"What about that bastard Borizus, and his intrigues?"

There was a sudden flinty look to her as she spoke. "The people will rally to my father once they have the cure. And I'll make certain they find out all about Borizus's plots. He'll be deposed, I'm sure of it. And who knows? Perhaps I'll campaign for the post of second councillor myself." Her eyes gleamed with newfound ambition. "Most certainly I'll explain to my father that his beloved rituals and ceremonies have perhaps become a bit too baroque for efficiency's sake."

"Efficiency?" Tom Paris couldn't believe what he was hearing. The pampered young girl he had met had been annealed by her odyssey into a tough-minded woman.

"Yes," she shot back. "Efficiency. I've seen how your Captain Janeway manages things. Very impressive."

"Marima, whatever happened to the carefree party girl I met on shore leave?"

Marima squared her slender shoulders and threw back her head. "Perhaps she's grown tired of the party. I have responsibilities. With the gray plague cured—and your doctor tells me that the immunity will be transmitted to future generations—there's much work to be done to heal the breach between the Vandorrans and Micaszians. And one of the first places to start is with the *darra,* protecting them for the future." A sly smile lit her face. "Please tell Harry that he was right."

Paris grinned. "He'll be glad to hear it. But I confess I'm amazed."

"Oh, Tom, let's get real," she said, and her eyes twinkled. "You, too, were correct: Sometimes being direct is the best policy." She blew him a kiss and then the transporter whisked her away.

Borizus sat beside Janeway and Tuvok in the darkened viewing room. He seemed unusually restive—even nervous.

Onscreen, a remarkable series of images was unfolding, especially remarkable if the viewer was aware of the original appearance of the taped record.

Crowds of angry Sardalians surged around the doorway of the Great Hall in Vandorra. They milled like mad things, circling the plaza, rebounding off one another, screaming and rending their clothing.

"End the rationing."

"We want the *darra* and we want them now!"

"Stop killing us by inches!"

"War with Micaszia. War!"

Screaming out their demands, they overpowered the two sentries and rushed inside the building.

Moments later they emerged, dragging Kolias behind them.

He was trying to reason with them. "Friends," he cried. "Friends, listen to me."

It was a vain gesture. They shook him until he crumpled to the ground, a broken man.

The tape faded to black.

"Lights," Janeway said.

Borizus sat in his chair, scarcely breathing. "What was that? What happened?"

"There's been a coup," said Tuvok. "Kolias has

been deposed and Vandorra awaits its new ruler. But there's more. Watch."

Again the lights dimmed and the screen came to life.

A crowd was gathered in the main plaza, but it was no longer angry. Now its message was a pulse of joy and anticipation. Above the welter of crowd noise, one name could be heard, an invocation to a new order, a new way.

"Borizus! We want Borizus!"

Tuvok turned to the stunned Sardalian. "They seem to be calling for you."

Slowly, as though dazed, Borizus nodded. "I'm the second councillor. I rule if the Lord Councillor is deemed unfit."

"It seems that the people have deemed Kolias unfit. I'm afraid that we must send you back," Janeway said. "Under the circumstances it would be unseemly to hold you in custody."

Borizus nodded. "I must go immediately. The people need me." He threw back his shoulders. "Vandorra needs me."

Gravely, Janeway and Tuvok escorted Borizus to the transporter chamber and watched him dematerialize in a blaze of white singing light.

Janeway tapped her commbadge. "Chakotay, notify Lord Kolias that we are remanding Borizus to his custody. Warn him that the man appears delusional."

"Aye, Captain."

Janeway gave Tuvok a mischievous look. "C'mon, let's go to my ready room and watch the fun."

Once settled at the conference table in the ready room, Janeway and Tuvok paid careful attention to the screen.

Borizus appeared and approached the lord councillor's apartments. The Sardalian walked with a new confidence. If he had been arrogant before he was downright contemptuous now, issuing orders, berating the guards. They ignored him.

Kolias emerged from a nearby doorway.

Borizus fell back as if struck. "But you've been deposed," he managed.

Kolias stared at him but said nothing.

"I'm in charge here," Borizus said. "You need a doctor's care immediately."

More in sorrow than anger, Kolias replied, "It is you who need the medical care, Borizus." He nodded to the guards, and they swept forward to seize Borizus.

He struggled and cried out. "No! Wait, you don't understand. The people want me! Me! No. No, let me go!"

"Don't worry," Kolias said. "I'll see to it that you have a nice, safe, quiet place to stay. You'll be decently cared for, for the rest of your life—in Micaszia."

He gestured to the guards. "Take him away."

The last that the crew of the *Voyager* saw of Second Councillor Borizus was the back of his purple head as Kolias's guards dragged him away across the grand plaza.

Back on the bridge, Tom settled happily into his seat at the newly reconfigured helm. What a joy to have all this power under his fingertips! B'Elanna had surpassed herself, and in record time. The helm was fully operational once again. He turned happily to Harry Kim.

"Marima wanted you to know that she's changed her mind about the *darra.*"

Kim's smile could have powered a small impulse engine. "Great."

"So, tell me, Harry, did you manage to remember that song you wanted to copy?"

"Yeah. I had to transpose it from voice to clarinet but I've got most of it."

"Will you let me hear it?"

"Sure, as long as you promise to do me a favor."

"For you? Anything."

"Don't take me along on any future shore leaves. Ever."

Kathryn Janeway smiled indulgently. Things were back to normal. They could resume their journey homeward. The black velvet of deep space was beckoning.

"Mr. Paris, plot the most direct course from here toward the Alpha Quadrant and engage when ready."

"Yes, Captain."

Sardalia receded rapidly on the main bridge screen, just another small light in the endless night.

"Torres to Janeway."

"Go ahead, B'Elanna."

"Captain, I've got some good news."

"I'm listening."

"The Sardalian alloys: You remember all the trouble I had refining them? Well, I was so busy recasting the helm controls, I didn't bother to analyze the waste elements. But I've just discovered an element in the alloy's waste will allow me to compensate for the problem with the theta-matric compositing system, increasing the speed of the dilithium recrystallization."

"That is good news, B'Elanna." Janeway smiled. The girl was pure gold. "Thank you. Janeway out."

She gazed around the bridge with satisfaction. This was the best crew she had ever worked with. Precious, every single one of them. However, it wouldn't do to relax bridge discipline and encourage sloppiness. They were still in unfamiliar territory. "Okay, folks, let's get back to work."

The doctor was still on the viewscreen brimming with obvious impatience.

"Is there any further need for me here, Captain?"

"Not at the moment."

"Then, with your permission, I'll turn myself off."

The doctor vanished. And Kathryn Janeway, practical empiricist though she was, nevertheless would have sworn that the very last part of him to fade away was his frown.

A complete year-by-year history of the
STAR TREK universe including
almost 500 photos!

STAR TREK®
CHRONOLOGY

THE HISTORY
OF THE FUTURE

A completely revised edition of the bestselling
official illustrated time line of the incredible
and ever-expanding Star Trek universe—
presented for the first time in full color.

From the founding of the Federation, to Zefram Cochrane's
invention of warp drive, to James T. Kirk's early days in
Starfleet Academy®, to the voyages of the *Starship
Enterprise*™ under Captain Jean-Luc Picard, to the newest
adventures of the *U.S.S. Voyager*™, this book provides a
comprehensive look at *Star Trek*'s incredible history. The
STAR TREK CHRONOLOGY documents every important
event from every *Star Trek* episode and film, and
includes both stardates and Earth calendar dates.

by **MICHAEL OKUDA** and **DENISE OKUDA**

POCKET
BOOKS

**Available in trade paperback
from Pocket Books**

718-01